STRONG FOR POTATOES

STRONG FOR POTATOES

Cynthia Thayer

St. Martin's Press
New York

Design by Ellen R. Sasahara

Library of Congress Cataloging-in-Publication Data

Thayer, Cynthia A.
Strong for potatoes / Cynthia Thayer.—1st ed.
p.   cm.
ISBN 0-312-18187-6
1. Indians of North America—Maine—Fiction.   2. Passamaquoddy
Indians—Fiction.   I. Title.
PS3570.H344S77   1998
813'.54—dc21   97-31883
CIP

First Edition: January 1998

10 9 8 7 6 5 4 3 2 1

To the beautiful and strong memory
of our sweet Melissa

ACKNOWLEDGMENTS

Many thanks to many people:

First, to the members of the Peninsula Writing Group; Joyce Varney, Peggy Bryant, Thelma White, John McIntosh, Mick Mickelson, Carrie Ciciotte, David Fickett, Dan Harper, Beppie Noyes, David Chapais, Tim Littlefield, and Bettina Dudley who told me what worked and what didn't.

To my patient, loving, and sagacious husband, Bill Thayer, who read when I asked him to and told the truth, as he always does.

To Sheila Unvala Saad, Susan Hand Shetterly, Wendy Gignoux, Geri Valentine, Ann Vidor, Marnie Crowell, Ian Underwood, Diane Benedict, and Hester Lyons who did the same.

To my granddaughter Leila Saad, who galloped to my lap when I needed a break.

To the Wednesday Spinners who encouraged, listened, and celebrated.

To Passamaquoddies Vera Francis and Debbie Brooks, who were kind enough to spend time talking to me, assisting me with the language and customs, inviting me into their homes.

To Passamaquoddy Allen Socabasin, whose songs and singing inspired me and whose computer-generated, phonetically spelled Passamaquoddy words are used in this book.

Acknowledgments

To Professor Joseph DeRocco, who, years ago, taught me to strive for perfection, and Professor Tom Watson, who, years ago, helped me experience the human condition through the Southern writers.

To my marvelous agent, Sandy Choron, whose faith, passion, and savvy worked together on our behalf.

To my editors, Lauren Sarat, for her intuition, enthusiasm, and insightful suggestions, and Kelley Ragland, for stepping in without missing a beat and knowing instinctively what was good for the book.

PROLOGUE

Twenty-seven photograph albums, all different colors, all engraved, line the shelves. I hold one that says, "The Willoughby Family, Book IV," in raised gold letters on the blue leatherette cover. My father's legacy, there in the photographs, our lives, our loves, our experiences, neatly packaged for posterity. Brian and I sit on the couch, no longer the children we were when we first met, both of us taller, more mature, older. My beloved Brian. He watches me as we look through the pictures, his eyes magnified behind his thick lenses. I take his hand and tell him that it's OK, that I want to look at these pictures, that there are so many good memories. I play with the red tufts of hair on his knuckles. We once did so much for each other, we had so much history. It's all here in the albums.

We try to avoid the desecrated pictures, automatically fill in the cut-out parts. Other events are all here: me as a star on the set; first day of school; on the reservation with Grandpa; playing with Brian; high-school graduation; off to college; Marten; but intertwined are the telling photos, the juxtaposition of my family's relationships, all organized and pasted, ready for us to look through. Each photograph has a caption under it, written in Daddy's handwriting. Poor Daddy.

I move a little closer to Brian. He flips the page. The day we went to the frog pond. I can tell because I had mud all over my shoes. I was twelve. "Remember this?" I say.

He remembers.

Blue riding her new bike. June 25, 1991
First pictures with my new tripod.

CHAPTER 1

✇

"*Hey, you got* an eyedropper?" Brian asked.

"You mean one of those things in the bottles, those long glass things?"

"Yeah, you know, you squeeze the rubber thing at the top and the stuff drips out."

The linen closet where the medicines were kept was dark and full of boxes and bottles. I rummaged through old towels, Halloween makeup, blond hair dye Mama used once when she found a gray hair, and finally found a bottle of antibiotic that I used when my eye socket got infected. I unscrewed the top and left the bottle in the closet, intending to replace the top later.

"Here, you mean this." I held up the dropper as if it were a trophy.

"Man, you are great. You can come up with anything. Now how about some booze."

"For us? For our picnic?" We were way too young to drink. I'd tried it a couple of times but never really took to it.

"No stupid, I'll tell you when we get to the pond. It's a surprise. We'll need some booze and a razor blade. Now this isn't

2

dangerous or anything like that." Even though he looked at me through those thick glasses and his eyeballs seemed to be swimming around behind the lenses, I could see his eyes sparkle with excitement.

I went back to the linen closet. Daddy had a scraggly beard and Mama hadn't ever shaved anything. Said she never would as long as she was of sound mind. But I remember some blades being there from Grandpa when he stayed overnight at Christmas. Grandpa only had a few facial hairs, being Passamaquoddy Indian and all, but what hairs he had, he shaved. The razor blades were under the hot-water bottle. I grabbed the package, Gillette Blue, in a steel safety case, and stuck it in my pocket. I wanted to insist that Brian tell me what we were going to do, but I liked the idea of a surprise so much I didn't.

The liquor was in the old sideboard at the end of the big room. Mostly gin. That was what Daddy drank. I guessed it would do. There were two large bottles with a foreign sounding name and "gin" underneath. Behind them was a brand-new pint bottle of Fleischmann's that I grabbed and stuck in my jacket pocket. So far I had only stolen small amounts of change from my parents, never anything as serious as liquor. But they were both out and probably wouldn't notice anyway. I thought about calling Berry for advice, but Brian didn't even know about her, and it would be too complicated to explain her to him. I never called Berry to come when anyone else was around because people wouldn't understand. They would think that I didn't know that she died years ago. They would think that I was delusional.

Brian was in the kitchen finishing our lunches. One sprouts and one peanut butter sandwich for each of us. It was kind of a joke, but we never changed the menu. "Hey, Blue, made you a sandwich."

"I got 'em. The blades. In my pocket. Let's go."

Brian grabbed the bucket he brought from home and the bag of sandwiches, and we headed down the dirt driveway on our bikes toward the pond.

We chose the shorter way through the woods rather than take the scenic road near the shore. The wild strawberry plants along the side of the road had blossomed overnight, promising luscious berries in a few weeks.

The pond was beautiful that day, wildflowers everywhere, little violets, daffodils that the Ladies of the Pond had planted. It had just rained, and that smell that tells you it is going to rain or that it has just rained was strong. We pedaled our way through the mud around the pond and settled into our spot under the willow tree. We had just finished the seventh grade and had been coming here for years. No one else ever sat at our willow tree. But today there were two used rubbers in our spot. Looked pretty fresh, too. I knew what they were, saw them in the church parking lot one time and Daddy said that at least they could have taken the evidence with them. Mama said not to touch them. She said we didn't know whose they were. I wonder if that would have made a difference.

Brian picked the condoms up with a leaf and threw them into the rosebushes. He raked the grass with his feet like an animal might, to make a predator think that a large and strong animal had been there. He brushed his hands together and turned to face me.

"Ready to catch frogs?" Brian asked, raising his eyebrows, which made his eyes look even bigger.

"Does this have something to do with all the stuff we brought?"

"You'll see. Let's leave everything here 'til we get back with the frogs."

Brian put the lunch by the base of a large willow, and we headed for the swamp. Brian always waited for me to catch

4

up. I ran with my right eye leading, and I still limped a bit from the accident. As we ran through the wild rosebushes, I grabbed at his sweatshirt. I hated that I couldn't keep up.

"Hey, Brian," I shouted. "Wait up. What are we doing?"

He kept running, the bucket swinging and banging on his leg. We often caught frogs and tried to have races to see whose frog was faster, but they always got away, and we couldn't keep up with them to decide the winner. I ran on behind, a little like Superman, my fist stuck out ahead to push away the bushes and occasionally grab Brian, my head cocked to the side to see where I was going. We both slid down the bank by the swampy little pond and took off our shoes and socks. My shoes took forever to unlace; they were black and high and ugly and I hated them. I let Brian help me. The doctor said soon I could have sneakers like the other kids, and Mama said I could have any kind I wanted. But I didn't have them yet.

We didn't have to confer on the frog-catching plan. Slowly and quietly we crept along the edge of the pond, the mud squishing up between our toes the only sound except for the croaking of the frogs. They sat at the edge of the pond, in the grass, or on a rock close to shore. Sometimes they sat on a lily pad, waiting for something good to pass by. Frogs can't leap backwards, so the trick was to be ready with one of your hands to head off the frog's leap to freedom.

"Got one."

"Yup, me too. Here." I held out my frog and Brian held out his bucket.

We worked the edge of the pond about half-way around, taking turns carrying the bucket, which grew heavy. Our feet made sucking sounds when we pulled them out of the mud, turning the water around us a murky brown.

"We must have enough by now. Here, you carry it back."

"Fair enough," Brian said as he reached for the handle.

The way back to the willow tree was slower. We had put our muddy feet right into our socks and shoes, so walking was soggy, and our feet squished as we walked. Gone was my Superman image. Every once in a while a frog would jump out of the bucket.

"Escapee!" I shouted.

I knew there were lots of frogs in that bucket, and it didn't matter if we lost one or two, but the excitement of catching the ones who tried to get away was irresistible.

"There's another." I grabbed for the frog as it made frantic jumps toward the pond. "Got it." I looked back at Brian to see if he was watching. I held my pose, one leg in the air with the very large frog wriggling in my hand, until I was sure he had a good look.

"I can get one that big." He looked through the grass frantically, with his face close to the muddy bank.

"That's enough. Don't we have enough?" I started back, knowing that he would follow.

Back at the willow tree we took our places at the bucket. We usually chose what we thought to be the strongest and most agile frogs for the race.

"Get the eye-dropper out, and the liquor," Brian said. His voice sounded louder than usual, as if he was making a speech. I pulled the bottle and glass tube out from the big pockets of my lumberjack shirt and presented them over the frog bucket.

"But what about the razor blades?"

"Not yet," Brian said as he drew some of the gin up into the dropper. "First we're going to get these babies drunk. Now, get a frog, a big one, and hold it good and tight." His freckled hand shook a little as he held the rubber tube at the top of the dropper.

I knew then that whatever we were going to do to the frog, I would not want done to me. I also knew that I was going to go along with just about anything Brian suggested. The worst part of it all was that I felt that I was going to enjoy every minute of it.

I picked the biggest, most well developed, oldest-looking frog in the bucket and held it out to Brian, mouth facing him. Brian opened the frog's mouth with one hand while he squirted the gin in with the other. The frog kicked its back legs against the air and its front legs against my hand. I had to slip the fingers from my other hand around the frog's head like scissors to keep his head still. Again Brian filled the dropper and squirted more gin into the frog. They told us in school that too many drinks of alcohol could kill a person. I wondered at that moment how many drinks it would take to kill a frog, and if it really mattered. It occurred to me that frogs might not be embarrassed about being so exposed. I certainly would be.

We waited for a minute to see if the frog would pass out.

"Brian, I think it needs a bit more."

He squeezed the bulb at the top of the dropper and more gin filled the glass tube. "OK, but this oughta do it."

He squeezed very slowly this time, watching me, watching the frog. I felt the frog change in my hand, relax sort of, legs moving a bit in slow motion, jaw opening and closing. I sensed that we were in control. That the frog had lost everything.

"That's it, he's crocked," I said with all the confidence I could muster.

"Gimme the frog." Brian gently transferred the frog into his own hands. "Let's put him down over here." There was a flat piece of ledge near the willow tree where he placed the frog, belly up. Its underside was so white, smooth.

We crouched around the heaving thing. It looked like rubber, like the rubber frogs you can find in a dime store. But it wasn't rubber.

"Now the razor blades." Brian looked at me sternly and held

7

out his hand. "Now, not tomorrow." I knew we were going to cut that frog somewhere. I looked at the belly moving up and down on the rock. "Jeeze, do ya want to be part of this or are you a baby?"

My hand went to my pocket. The blades were still there, in that little blue steel package. I took the package out and looked at it. I was trying to hurry but seemed to be operating in slow motion. My thumb pushed at the opening in the package, pushed on the blade, and it eased its way out of the slot on the end. Brian pulled the blade away before it was all the way out and nicked my thumb.

"Ohh." I made some kind of noise, and stuck my thumb in my mouth to lick the salty blood off. I didn't want him to think I was a wimp just because I was a girl.

Brian started the cut, started at the neck, right where the frog would wear a necklace if it were a princess. We had done this to the formaldehyde frogs in science lab but never to a live one. Its arm made a little fluttering movement and then fell back onto the rock. "Jeeze, Blue, you do some now. I can't do everything just because I'm the boy." As I reached for the blade I could see his hand still shaking a little. I tried hard to hold my own hand still. I knew I could do this.

"I'll do the next cut." I continued with the blade from the neck to where the hind legs joined the body. The cut was so straight. It didn't need to be deep. Just deep enough to cut through the packaging. My hand seemed to act on its own as I watched. The blade ran across its chest and pelvis, like one of those little variety packs of cereal where you cut the box, lift the flaps, and eat right out of the container. Brian sat there on the grass watching as I peeled back the white covering of skin. The arm no longer moved, but things were still moving inside.

"Wow, look at that." I looked up at Brian. He swallowed. For the first time I noticed his Adam's apple bobbing up and down.

The frog's heart, thump, thump, and the rest of the stuff, all working, moving. I could tell the organs from science lab, and they were all doing something, except that the whole frog wasn't working together, just its individual parts. I leaned closer to see the breathing and we sat, watching the frog slowly die. It took a long time. Exposed, open for us to see, spread out. No privacy here. I remembered how frantically they had tried to get away. The heart slowed way down, the breathing became light, the other organs stopped one at a time. Poop came out, the same frog poop that we always threatened to wipe on each other. Now it just dripped down the ledge. Not a threat to anyone. I wondered if people pooped when they died. I thought that if Daddy was here, he would take a picture of the opened frog as Brian and I leaned over it, watching the results of our handiwork. Perhaps he would write, *Blue and Brian carve up a live frog, June 25, 1990,* underneath the picture.

"Look at that." Brian's voice shook. The frog body gave a small shudder and then flattened itself to the rock. The organs had quit. "Oh shit, the frog is dead." His voice didn't sound familiar, and that scared me. "Oh shit, what did I do?"

As if some early training took over, I slipped the used blade into the disposal slot in the blue steel package and put it back in my pocket, all the while watching Brian out of the corner of my eye. His hand stayed where it had been as if still holding the blade and his face screwed up like that crybaby girl in the class below us. I had never seen a boy cry; my dad a few times, but never a boy in class, never Brian, and certainly never with a screwed-up face and big sobs coming out like this. "Ahhhh. I killed the stupid frog. Ahhhhh," he cried out of his very open mouth. I glanced at the frog. Its mouth was very open, too, but no noise came out.

I reached for Brian's hand, the one that had been holding the blade, and brought it close to me. When I was little, Mama always held me if I cried, and Daddy would carry me to his chair and tell me stories. I held Brian's hand as he sobbed. That's all, but it was enough. He cried for a long time, and I held on tight with both hands. I didn't watch him. Instead I watched the frog. The flies came and buzzed loudly in the guts, and more green stuff dripped down the rocks. It was alright, everything, it would be alright.

Brian stopped after a while and pulled his hand back. I gave it to him, but I kissed it first. He didn't seem to mind. He took his glasses off and sniffed and wiped his nose and eyes on his shirt without saying anything. After he put his glasses back on, he got up quietly and headed toward the bikes. I stood up and dumped the bucket of frogs near the little lily pond. We never ate our lunch.

"But the lunch," I said.

It wasn't important, so the lunch and the frog body were left by the willow tree. I pedaled behind him. Usually Brian waited for me to catch up, but he didn't wait, and I didn't push myself. He needed some time alone. I'd known Brian a long time, since my first day at school.

Daddy had been taking pictures that day. Click, click. "Blue dear, turn to the right, smile at Daddy, now, oh great, what a shot," he would say. Daddy with his new tripod, trying to get my good side. The side with the eye, not the eye patch. There was another father there taking pictures of his little boy, no tripod, just a little Instamatic. "Smile, Brian," and the little boy stuck his thumbs in his ears and wiggled his fingers at the camera. I looked wistfully at his feet. Sneakers.

I stayed just behind him as we biked along the ocean road. I think he was embarrassed about the frog. I wondered if we would stay the same kind of friends as we'd always been. His head was down as he pedaled along, and it almost made me want to cry.

Brian liked me in school. That first year he was about the only one who did. After the accident I couldn't talk right. Words that I thought in my head came out all wrong. That first week he gave me a cookie from his snack. I tried to say thank you but it came out "piss on it." He seemed to understand what I meant and said, "You're welcome." He was very polite.

"Gee, Blue, what's that stuff in your sandwich?" Brian said that day at lunch. I looked at Brian, waiting for Berry to tell me what to say but knowing she wouldn't. "Looks like little worms to me." Brian always sat with me at lunch. No one wanted to be seen with him either. He wore thick glasses. "Well, what is that stuff?" Brian put down his lunch and looked at my eye through his lenses.

"Poop cookies."

"How come everything is poop?" He poked at the sprouts sticking out between the cheese slices and mustard. "Doesn't look like poop to me, worms more like it." I wanted peanut butter sandwiches like his mother made him. Since then, that's why we always took one of each.

Berry just lay in my mind that first day of school, drooling, her both eyes open, her mouth open, too. I knew it wasn't really Berry who told me what to say, I knew she was just in my mind, that the real Berry, my dead, brainless twin, must be in some coffin in some cemetery somewhere.

As we biked back along the ocean road, I glanced at the headstones in the little cemetery. Brian was still just ahead of me, his head down, as if he might still be crying. The stones were spread out under all the trees and around a little pond. I had stopped there many times. Looked at the stones. No Berry Willoughby. But she could be in there. There were a lot of stones and a lot of names. "Brian, want to stop for a minute?" No response. Just slow, steady pedaling. I stopped for a second, looked around, then started up again.

Mama and Daddy hardly ever talked about Berry, but I picked up bits and pieces. They found out about us just before we were born. Two babies. Twins. I was born first, so they named me Blue, and my twin, Berry. Almost born in a blueberry field, everyone said. For months they had been thinking, "Baby." The Baby will sleep here, one high chair, one crib, one stroller. As it turned out, one of each was enough because Berry never made it out of the hospital alive. Something was very wrong inside that couldn't be fixed. There was no brain. There we were, lying side by side on Mama's hospital bed, identical, except Berry didn't have a brain, and I did. She knew nothing, absolutely nothing. Then she died. As I grew, she grew, too, in my mind, lying there, unresponsive, blank faced. And no one else knew about her.

Brian stopped suddenly. I pulled up to his bike. "Blue, I would've finished the cutting. I just never did anything like that before. But I could do it. Next time, I'll do it." His eyebrows raised, as if questioning himself, and I could see the apprehension in his eyes.

"OK," I said. "I know you could. Just as good as me." I didn't want to say anything more.

We never talked about that incident until many years later. The summer was full of biking, swimming, lazing around, having picnics in the cemetery, ostensibly because I liked the scenery. The first day of school came again. Brian and I were still close friends. He was the best.

Blue's new haircut.
November 1991

CHAPTER 2

My grandpa looked like a TV Indian. His hair was still black, no gray, just black, shiny, straight. Indian hair, Maria would have said. I begged him to grow it long so I could braid it and he would look like an Indian in the movies, but he had a regular short haircut. Said he didn't want to look like no TV Indian. His limbs were thick. Not fat. Arms, legs, fingers, thick and strong. His thick legs filled his blue jeans, and he kept pulling at them. His pant legs wouldn't slide down by themselves, and he couldn't find anything wider. And his neck. Brown and wide. Never had his shirts buttoned, guess he couldn't button them.

"That's it." Daddy came away from his camera, scratching his head under his hat. He always wore it in the house unless Mama made him take it off. "Think I got some great shots. Especially of you, my Beautiful Blue." Daddy winked at me. Daddy always called me Beautiful Blue, even after the accident.

It was the year I turned five that it happened, in October. I remember our old gray Buick idling at the mailbox while Daddy grabbed the contents. "Here it is." He had held it up to the light of the sky as if he were trying to read someone else's mail. "The letter from New York, from the movie people." Daddy thought I was so beautiful he signed me up for a career in the movies, sent my picture around to all the studios, and when he heard there was a movie going to be made in Belfast, right here in Maine, he took me down to audition. Mama had taught me to sing, to dance, to be cuddly, flirtatious, irresistible, and I was better than all the others. They picked me and paid Daddy and Mama a lot of money. Once I heard Mama tell Aunt Marcia that she had wasted all her hard-earned money on getting me that part. She said she could have had a great dancing career if her parents had given her lessons. She danced in *West Side Story* when she was in high school, one of the lead parts. Every-one said she was the best.

"Dear Mr. and Mrs. Willoughby," Daddy read after he tore open the letter, "Your daughter, Blue Willoughby, has been se-lected from a group of over two hundred original applicants to play the part of Sally Sutherland in the movie, *Farewell to Sum-mer. . . .*" Mama screeched, Daddy hugged me hard, all be-cause I was beautiful. The original letter is in one of the photo albums, nestled between pictures of me on the set. "Before" pictures. They had taken me to four auditions in order to get the part, and I was adorable. I was to be the daughter of an ex-otic dancer in a mystery love story, not really an integral part of the movie, but an important prop nonetheless. Everything Mama had taught me finally paid off. But now, well, it was wasted, all those lessons.

Grandpa didn't care if I was beautiful. "Come on, Miss Brown," said Grandpa. "Let's you and me go find some deer." I knew that meant going for a walk in the woods. Grandpa knew all the animal tracks and scats and how to tell who was eating whom. He came to visit for the weekend whenever he could. He still called me Miss Brown, because my one eye was brown and I had very very dark hair. Indian hair just like his. Only I wore mine in braids.

Daddy wanted me to wear my hair down and curly, but my hair wasn't curly. "Blue, please, for Daddy, put some curl in your hair," he would say. "It's so beautiful, but straight. Shows up in the photos better with just a little curl." Mama and Daddy both had curly hair. It must have surprised them for mine to be so straight. I think he would have liked it better if it were golden, like Mama's. I could see from the way he looked at Grandpa, especially when Grandpa wasn't watching, that Daddy loved him a lot, loved his straight black hair because it was Grandpa's, but not because it was Indian hair. Just the sad way his face was, like he wanted to touch him, maybe talk about Grandma, but afraid of getting into that Passamaquoddy talk about the reservation and baskets and poverty. Daddy knew Grandpa and I talked about the church on the reservation and the ash trees dying off and wild plants, and sometimes I got the feeling that he wanted to be included. But he never joined us, just listened from a distance, and urged me to put a little curl in my hair. Once when I curled it, just to make him happy, he called me "Curly." "Hey, Curly, your breakfast is ready," he had said.

Mama said there was a lot of talk about my name when I was a little baby and the relatives came to see me. "Blue, that's her name? Aren't you going to give her a real name?"

"What if that other twin was normal, Blue and Berry? Isn't that kind of odd? Just because Mattie went into labor in the blueberry field?"

"The kids will make fun of her, mark my words."

Daddy thought Blue was a pretty name but would have rather called me Sarah or Jessica or Melanie. In fact my name was just Blue, not Blue Ann or Blue Margaret, or Angela Blue. No middle name, just Blue, Blue Willoughby. Grandpa said it sounded like a china plate. That I should be called "Brown," for at least that would match my eyes and hair. Apparently, hardly anyone mentioned Berry, who at that time was still alive in the hospital. I guess they just left her there, my twin, my brainless twin. I guess she just faded away until she died. Grandpa said that ever since that day he called me Miss Brown. Mama really didn't like it, but she didn't say anything to him. Just said "Blue" in conversation more often when he was with us.

Mama looked up from the new sweater she was knitting for Daddy. Her hair blended with the wool, and I wondered if she ever got mixed up. "I don't want you talking to Blue about hunting. She's too young, and I want her to appreciate live animals, not dead ones." I thought of the frog. Lying there on the granite, spread open. It had been five months since the frog, and we had not been back there. Probably some crow had pecked all the meat off the rock by now.

"Don't worry, Mattie, we're just going tracking." Grandpa kissed Mama's cheek. "Be back before dark. And if you finish that one, I could use a new sweater for winter." Mama knit one sweater a year, and this year was Daddy's. Mama tucked a little bag of sunflower seeds and dried blueberries into my pocket as she patted my shoulder. She smelled of patchouli and balsam, and her hands were rough as she held my chin. "Pay attention to what you are doing and listen to your grandpa. He knows the ways of the woods." She gave Daddy that "isn't she cute" look.

"Come on, Grandpa." I pulled on his arm. I hated when Mama intruded on my life. I couldn't seem to have anything to myself. Of course Grandpa knew the ways of the woods. Daddy looked up from his camera as we went out the door. I looked back at the two of them. Daddy, his watch cap on his head, his hair and beard sticking out everywhere; she so fair, delicate, healthy, her hair the color of caramel, standing close together like an ad in COUNTRY CRAFTS MAGAZINE.

Our house was near the woods, and we often saw deer and rabbits and an occasional fox from the big window in the living area, but going tracking with Grandpa was much better than that. We felt them around us, understood their ways, were almost a part of them. We walked down the dirt road away from the ocean to a place where Grandpa and I had cut a path through the dense underbrush of raspberry canes into the deeper woods. I switched sides, so I could see him through my good eye, and took his hand.

"Well, good mornin' Miss Brown, well, how do you do?" he sang as we walked down the road, "Good mornin' Miss Brown, well, how do you do, I'm just fine now, and how 'bout you?" He always sang that old blues song to me on our walks, softly and slowly, so as not to disturb anything in the woods. Grandpa had a sense about things. He knew when to be quiet, when to slow down so I could comfortably keep up with him, and when to stop.

Soon the path became too narrow to hold hands, so he dropped mine, and I fell in behind him. Even though it was November and there were brittle leaves on the ground, there was no sound from Grandpa's feet. I walked as softly and carefully as I could, but often there was the crack of a dry stick or a thump as I tripped over an exposed root. Grandpa had been watching a doe for several weeks and on one of our walks I caught a glimpse of her just before I stumbled in a hole and scared her away. Grandpa said that deer don't see very well, and unless they smell you or hear you, they will go about their business. He had seen her running with the buck, Otuhk, the day before. The title was entirely too grand a name for a buck, but I pretended I was Koluskap, the great warrior god of the People, and Grandpa was Marten, Glue-skub's helper. They might have named the buck such a fancy name. Grandpa called him Otuhk because that was the People's word for deer. Grandpa said that he knew the doe's mother and hers before that, but I wasn't sure that was really true.

We passed a large tree that had been rubbed by the buck's antlers, the bark torn off in shreds. Grandpa didn't point it out, just slowed almost imperceptibly. Off to the left of the path was a spot under a small sapling that had been pawed bare of leaves and debris. Otuhk had left his sign that he was closing in on his mate. I tugged at Grandpa to look. He nodded. He had seen it, too. We walked without speaking, without touching.

Grandpa's hand went out to the side to signal me. I slowed, knowing that he sensed a presence. "El" he called her, from the language of the People. He bent his knees, and I followed, like a shadow, mimicking his body, watching. His hand turned back toward me and rested on my knee for a moment, not moving. He sniffed. His head nodded down then up and I looked where he was looking. I think I saw him first. Otuhk. He was standing in the clearing with his neck extended and his upper lip curled close to his nose, which meant the doe, El, was close. There was no sound except for my own heart beating and my own breathing. No matter how I tried to breathe quietly, it sounded to me like elephant breath. I listened for Grandpa's breathing but could not hear it beyond my own. We crouched, my hand on Grandpa's back to steady myself. My leg started to shake, so I shifted my position slightly. I felt Grandpa's back muscles tense, but he didn't move. Then I saw her, in the thicket, her tail up and off to the side, standing, ready. We were very close to them, and I was surprised the buck couldn't hear me breathing, but if he did, he paid no attention. His head was held low, lip still curled, as he approached her. I knew then that

I was going to witness something very private, very important, something only Grandpa and I would see.

The doe stood still, only her tail moving, as Otuhk approached. We could see her squat, and a few drops of liquid squeezed out. That's how close we were. Otuhk trotted up to her and sniffed at the drops. His lip curled as if checking to see if he liked the smell. For a few moments there was no movement. The two deer stood like small trees. Then the buck mounted. It was very quick. His front hooves grabbed her flanks and he pumped three times and threw his head in the air. It was over. He was off her and walking away. El began to browse the bracken in front of her, and I had a funny feeling between my legs. I knew then that I didn't want that. I wanted more than that. There had to be more to sex than what they did. The doe ambled away, Otuhk following closely, with his head down and lip curled. Again, I became aware of my body noises. When the deer disappeared, Grandpa turned and said, "There will be fawns in the spring."

As we got up and stretched from the long watch, I wanted to ask questions. I wanted to know about people and was it the same with them. But Grandpa was silent. It was not the time for asking questions. The fluttering feeling continued, and my stomach lurched every so often. My leg was sore from crouching so long and I had a hard time following without tripping. For the first time, I wished I had worn my high leather boots instead of my new sneakers.

The path again became too narrow to walk together, so Grandpa stopped and bent down so that our faces were close. "Miss Brown, where should we go now?" Grandpa had always chosen the way and now, for the first time, he was acquiescing.

I held my head upright, facing straight, but kept a close watch on the ground and to the sides, like Grandpa taught me.

We walked slower this time, and I could feel Grandpa off to the side and slightly behind me. He made no sound, but something told me just where he was. Exposed roots and small sticks jutted out from the forest floor as we moved silently along the path. I stopped and put my hand out to the side. I felt Grandpa stop and we both stood like one of Daddy's still shots as a small, mangy red fox trotted across the path without even glancing our way. After a time, Grandpa patted my shoulder gently and we moved on.

His presence around me was intense. I couldn't hear anything, but I knew where he was every second. Suddenly, I felt the loneliness. His mostly, but mine, too. He missed Grandma, and I missed Maria, Berry, and something else I couldn't define. We crept over the brush and under branches without making a sound or disturbing a twig. It was as if there was no one else in the woods, only me alone, and him, alone beside me, connected but so terribly isolated.

Mama would ruin the day when we got home. She would ask what we saw on our walk without waiting for an answer. Make it seem silly and unimportant.

The path widened, signaling the nearness of the road. I would no longer be connected and no longer be alone. As we came out of the woods onto the road, Grandpa put his hands on my shoulders, turned me around, tugged on my braids. "Miss Brown, you are my life." I knew he was crying a little. I could feel it. I didn't want him to know I was upset about the deer, confused, curious. He didn't want me to know he had tears in his eyes.

"You miss her, don't you," I said, a little afraid of intruding.

"Yes," was all he said.

I didn't know what was missing inside me, but I knew I would find it. Grandpa turned away from me but stood silently, watching the woods, waiting until he was ready to continue.

Maybe he didn't want to face Mama either. The walk home was longer because we came out of the woods at a spot farther down the road. The sun was just beginning to go down behind the hills, and the light reflected off the mountains on Mount Desert. "The Bubbles," as we called them, because they looked like soap bubbles sitting on the water, had snow on top already and caught the setting sun's resonance.

Mama and Daddy had hot chocolate waiting for us when we got home. They sat together at the table, on the same side, watching us, Daddy with his hat still on, ready for the interview. The camera was put away, and there were chocolate chip cookies in a basket on the table.

"Well, how was the walk? Any deer?" Mama asked. "Here, sit down. I'll get you some hot chocolate. What do you call them? El and some Indian word? Blue, go and wash your hands." She never waited for an answer. It was as if the question stood on its own. "Let me get your hot chocolate," she said as she left Daddy to get the steaming pitcher from the woodstove.

"We saw a fox, old and mangy, but it trotted by right in front of us, didn't even see us," Grandpa said to Mama as he pulled up a chair. "Blue is getting to be an intuitive tracker," I heard as I walked past them to the bathroom.

"Blue, are you alright?" she called after me. "Don't be too long. The hot chocolate will cool down."

"Yes, fine." I felt as if I were spitting the words out, that they might land on her and stain her overalls.

I locked the door with the hook and eye that Aunt Marcia had insisted Daddy put on when she was here. She said that folks needed a private space to take care of private matters. I never really understood about the lock until that moment.

I caught a glimpse of my self in the mirror and stopped. Braids. Children wore braids, children and old Indians. I was neither. I dropped my jacket on the floor. My stomach lurched and resumed its quiet ache. I didn't feel like a woman. Too old to sit on Grandpa's lap. But not a woman.

I grabbed one of my braids. Braids. I was changed. Older. Different. The scissors were there on the little table next to the sink. Mama used them to trim a chin hair that grew and grew. I looked into the mirror at myself. Two eyes. It was hard to tell which one was glass, especially in poor light. And my black Indian hair. Maria, the wardrobe woman on the movie set called it that. That day of the accident Maria took the rags out of my hair that Mama had put in. Mama had given me a bubble bath and curled my hair the night before. I remember the smell of the curl-set lotion and the coldness of it as it dripped onto my bare shoulders. She cordoned off one small section of hair at a time for the treatment, dipped her fingers into the lotion and smeared it onto the tips. Then she placed the torn sheet onto the tip of my straight Indian hair and rolled, all the way up, until she could go no farther, until it pinched, until those few hairs that had been too tight in the beginning caught and pulled out.

Maria unrolled the rags one at a time as she murmured, "I will miss you, my bambino." She was so gentle. Maria let me watch in the mirror as she made ringlets out of my ordinarily straight hair. She said I had Indian hair as she stroked the side of my face. She wrapped that Indian hair around her index finger and let go with a flourish, causing the ringlet to bounce like a wire spring. Then she kissed the top of my head and sent me out to do my scene. She must have been watching when the golf cart smashed into me. She must have seen the blood.

That was the day they filmed my "kitten" line. I remember Daddy was taking pictures off to the side. They told him he could come on the set if he stayed out of the way. I was to walk down a sidewalk, stop by a large apple tree which hadn't been there the day before, with a kitten in my arms, and say to a suspicious-looking character, "Hey, Mister, is this your kitten?" The first time I said, "Hey, kitten, is this your mister?" After that I got the line right every time, but there was always something else wrong. The kitten was meowing, I looked into the camera, and once I tripped on the sidewalk crack and had to go back to makeup to cover the scratch on my knee. That last time before the accident when I said my line, "Hey, Mister, is this your kitten?" I got the line right but my expression wasn't quite right. "Cut, look, Blue darling, look into his eyes. Great how you say the line. But look into those big brown eyes and melt. Blue, you do a good job this time and . . . any sundae you want. You want nuts? You want cherries? Think about it. Now, again. One more time. And keep that guy with the camera out of my way." The director pointed at Daddy, who was standing behind his tripod, a little too close. "He's distracting me. He's going to cause an accident."

Mama had motioned for Daddy to step back, but I don't think he moved. The kitten was orange and black. I remember that. Very fluffy. I called her "Fluffy," even though her name was Amanda. I had to walk about twenty-five feet holding Amanda, skipping part of the way, and look up at the stranger who wasn't really a stranger, and say my line. At the fourth crack in the sidewalk, Amanda's claws dug into my shoulder. I don't remember anything after that until I woke up in the hospital and all my beautiful black curly hair had been shaved off.

I held my right braid out to the side. Her scissors. I was too old for ringlets and braids. Snip. Well, it wasn't really a snip. I wanted it to snip, but it was more like a sawing motion. My fingers got sore. Five times before it would come off. I wanted it to be quick, final. I held the braid out, now detached from my head. I would save them. Then the other. Four times with the scissors for that one.

"Maaaaaama. Maaaaaama." I called for what seemed a long time.

"Blue, unlock the hook," Mama called as she rattled the door.

"Maaaaama," I continued.

"Blue. Stop it. Now. Open the door." Mama had never sounded so firm.

I stood holding the braids.

"Robert, Nicholas, come help me with the door. Blue's got herself locked in the bathroom."

I turned toward the door and watched. The men, my father, his father, were there on the other side of the door, pulling at it. The eye of the lock was beginning to loosen. I had stopped calling for Mama by this time and was just waiting for the door to open, unable put the braids down.

As the door burst open, they came in, the three of them. All lined up in a row. It seemed like a long time that we stood looking at each other. Grandpa grabbed my father's arm.

"Come on, Robert, this is for Mattie."

I thought for a moment that Daddy had gone to get the camera, but he didn't return. Mama seemed frozen in her spot, watched me stand there, a braid in each hand. I smiled over my hysteria. I'm not sure why. She pulled the door shut, and I wondered if she, too, expected Daddy to come back with the camera.

"I cut my hair."

"Oh baby," crooned Mama as she rushed forward and put her arms around my body, holding me. I stood, straight, unmoving, wishing she were someone else, wishing she would say something, wishing the lock on the bathroom door had been stronger. She held my rigid body at arm's length. "Oh, you look so much older. A young woman."

I didn't feel like a woman. I knew that she said what all

mothers say. What she felt she was supposed to say. I was cold and wet and still held the braids. I wanted her to put them back on my head, glue them back. I didn't really know what I felt. My arms hung at my sides, holding a braid in each hand. I needed my mother. I needed someone. Berry, Brian, Maria. Maria's fingers putting on my makeup, stroking my face and neck over and over. She would hum softly as her fingers found the crevices in my ears and beside my nose and at the corners of my lips while I lay with my eyes closed, wishing she would never stop. She always kissed me when she was finished, sometimes on the eyelids, once on my earlobe, and that last morning, before the golf cart ran out of control, before the cat scratched me, before the accident, on the corner of my mouth.

Mama held me, doing the best she could. I never saw Maria again after the accident but sometimes in the night I pretended she was holding me. I pretended she was holding me that day in the bathroom.

Simon, Blue, and Mattie in front of the
"Bubbles" painting. New lens.
June 1992

C H A P T E R 3

That winter, I sent five letters to Maria at the address she wrote on her picture but they all came back with, "Forwarding Time Expired," typed on them. I guess that meant that she had moved. She had sent the picture to the hospital and Mama saved it for me. "To my dearest Blue, love, Maria." That was all. Then her address underneath. In the picture, she was holding me on her lap, her hands wrapped around me. My ringlets hid some of her face.

That spring, when the fruit trees were in bloom, the smell made me think of Maria. The apple tree by our back door snowed blossom petals for a week, and I would stand in them and breathe and think of her. Sometimes I would stroke my own face and make believe it was Maria.

That following summer, Simon, the artist, came to our house. Daddy took pictures of him outside painting the woods. Taking pictures of someone painting was even more removed than Daddy usually was. Maybe that's why he took so many. There were pictures of Simon with me and Simon with

Grandpa and even Simon with Mama. Most of the pictures were taken from behind Simon, looking at the painting of our house or the tree line off to the side. One of them is of Mama with her hand on Simon's shoulder as he painted. Daddy enlarged it and hung it in a gold frame on the living-room wall. She had changed out of her overalls. Her thin dress was blowing in the breeze, and her honey hair matched the amber necklace she always wore. She looked like a movie star.

Simon arrived on my last day of school before summer vacation. I had managed to deal with the trauma of getting my period and finished the eighth grade near the top of my class. I was almost home before I saw the old powder blue van parked behind Dad's truck. They were outside, the two men, talking and gesturing toward the "view." Daddy studied that view for a year before he decided to build the house there. He wanted it to be the perfect spot, and it was. So perfect that we had tourists driving up into the driveway asking if they could get out and take pictures of the "view." The mountains rose up out of the sea as if they had been pushed by creatures in the underworld and were happy to oblige. We were surrounded by woods, our woods, but through the cleft in the trees, we could see the ocean and those mountains, those bubbles sitting on the water.

Daddy designed and built our house to look like it belonged in the woods, that it had been there for centuries. The timbers for the frame had been milled from the trees he had to cut to make room for the foundation. Every room had a view into a different part of the Maine wilderness. From the living room, the window framed the mountains as if it were a large three-dimensional mural. The kitchen looked out over the blueberry fields ringed by a row of birches and maples with a few apple trees interspersed here and there. Mama and Daddy's room looked out over the forest where the deer lived. The window in my room looked down the driveway and beyond to the ocean in the distance. Even though we weren't far from some other houses, it seemed as if we were in the middle of a vast wilderness.

Daddy beckoned to me. I hated meeting new people. They always wondered why I limped and why I carried my body to one side a little, and what was funny about my eyes. But they seldom asked. Perhaps Daddy had told him already. Sometimes I would tell people that one eye was glass and ask them to try to guess which one it was. It always made them uncomfortable. They stammered and looked off to the side, and said, "Oh, I never would have known."

I pretended not to notice Daddy's gesture. "Blue, come on over here. I want you to meet someone," he called. Of course he had his camera.

"Be right there. Gotta get rid of my stuff." I set my books and a school year's worth of accumulated junk on the stone wall by the driveway and walked over to the two men. They were watching me, Daddy adjusting his invisible hat, the real one gone for the summer. That's how we knew summer had come. Daddy's hat went into the closet until September.

"Blue, this is Simon. Simon, my Beautiful Blue."

Simon looked right at me. His hand shot forward and shook mine. "Blue, what a wonderful name. I'm going to paint here for a while. Hope you don't mind. Your Dad said it was OK. It has the best view in town. Thought I'd set my easel up right here."

"He just happened upon our house while looking for the best vantage point to paint The Bubbles," Daddy said. He was so proud of our view. He pointed over to the mountains as if we were seeing them for the first time.

Simon's hand still held mine, and I couldn't pull it away. His other hand joined the clasped shake for a moment. His face. Its skin was thin, stretched across his nose and his right cheek. The other side was smooth and beautiful. But his right side.

Thin with lines streaking through it. From his nose right over to his hairline. He was smiling on one side, but the stretched side stayed where it was.

"I was burned. Working on my car. The gas. Well. How about you? Accident? Car?"

I stood with my hand still outstretched. My mouth probably hung open. Another deformed being. And he wanted to know what happened to me. He continued to look directly at me.

"I was in a movie. I only had two lines. A golf cart ran into me. Which one? Which one is glass?" I heard myself asking. "Can you guess? My eye. Which one is glass?" It seemed at the time that I was talking too fast.

Simon bent down a little so he was at my height and took my chin in his hand. His gaze went from one eye to the other eye and back and forth. "Wow. You must have a good eyeball maker. They look the same."

"You have to guess," I heard myself saying.

"The left," he said as he stood up and released my chin. "Did I guess right?"

"You did." I wanted to hold him. To thank him. To touch his scar. To feel how thick his hair was. "Most people can't tell the difference."

My father stood off to the side. I knew he wanted to take a picture, but his camera just hung there, around his neck. He always felt uncomfortable when I talked about the accident. He kept saying, "I'm sorry, I'm so sorry. I didn't mean to get in the way." I remember Daddy sitting at the edge of my bed in the hospital saying over and over that he was sorry and that it was his fault.

"It was hard to tell. It was really a guess," Simon said.

"Oh, oh, my eye. Oh, sorry, I was thinking about something."

"I'll be here every day for a while. I'm painting a group of pictures of the mountains." His speech was a little slurred. One side of his mouth didn't move as well as the other.

"Sure, see ya around." I turned from him and walked over to my books and things. I thought he might be watching, but I heard him talking to Daddy. I walked slowly, so I wouldn't seem to be running away. The books made me walk even slower, and my room seemed so far.

Simon came again the next day. Mama had not yet met him. Daddy was in between carpentry jobs and Mama's real-estate business was slow that second day he came, so we were all working in the garden. Weeding. I sat on the earth, my legs spread out, feet bare. I had on a long cotton wraparound skirt that hid the scars on my leg. The earth was warming up, and I sat between the rows of beans, pulling the little lamb's-quarters and dandelions. I made piles for eating and piles for the compost. Mama made salads with lamb's-quarters and dandelions, but only the tender young ones.

I heard the van. I kept weeding. Daddy and I had told Mama all about the painter, Simon, and his scarred face and dense black curls. The van pulled off to the side of the driveway and he got out. I could see him without looking up from the earth in front of me. Simon opened the side door of his van and pulled out a lawn chair and a bulky easel. He set them up at the spot he had discussed with Daddy. After a few minutes of rooting around in the back of the van he pulled out a box of paints and a canvas bag overflowing with tubes and bottles and canvas. He shut the van with a thud and walked to his spot. After he set up everything, he came down to the garden. Mama stopped weeding, and Daddy leaned his hoe on the side of the toolshed.

I sat still in the garden, my hands moving over the tiny weeds, saving the good ones in the colander, piling the bad varieties and bigger weeds in a heap to the side. I used my bare heels to pull myself forward in the path. My skirt dragged in back of me, and the dirt drove itself into my underwear. My back was to them and I was getting farther and farther away. I wondered if Simon would notice me. He didn't.

But he noticed Mama. Daddy went out to the hardware store to get some supplies for the next day's job, and I stayed in the garden. I loved to sit in the soil with my bare legs sticking out in front of me. Sometimes I would lie down with my ear on the ground to listen, pressing my body into it as hard as I could. Mama was gone. I could feel it. I turned to see. She was not in the garden. She was with Simon. Sitting down on the grass, legs spread out in front of her. Watching. Simon was painting a little and then looking at her. They were talking. I lay down on my belly in the row, facing them. In the next row was Berry, lying on her belly. She usually was on her back, so I could see her better. But today she was on her belly, with her head facing me. Her eyes and mouth were open, and her breathing was loud and heavy.

"Berry," I whispered. "Berry, give me a sign. If you can hear me, blink twice."

Nothing.

They were still talking. "Something's not right. Don't even know what it is," I said as I looked over at Berry. She was gone.

I got up quickly, brushed myself off, and headed toward Simon and Mama.

"Ah, it's Beautiful Blue. Would you like to see what I'm doing?"

The painting was very colorful. Splotches of red and blue and purple. No mountains, no ocean, just splotches.

"Where are the mountains?"

"Well, they're my ideas of the mountains. It's impressionistic." Suddenly I was sorry I asked. I knew about the impressionists from school. They're supposed to give you the feeling of something. But I didn't get it. The feeling of the mountains.

"Did you get the greens for supper?" Mama interrupted. "Why don't you bring them in and rinse them. I'll be in soon."

That was it. Dismissed. I stayed away after that. But I watched them. From my room I could see them clearly, but they couldn't see me. It was always the same. Mama let him paint for a few hours while she worked on her real estate, then she left the house and sat outside on the grass beside him. Daddy was on his new house job so he wasn't home during the day much. I was going to Grandpa's house soon for a week, so I was just lounging, packing, listening to tapes, waiting to go, watching. I couldn't tell what they were saying. Their mouths moved, their bodies were still, too still.

Several weeks after the dismissal, I watched from my bedroom window as Simon and Mama were talking, looking at each other. His right side faced Mama. His bad side. Mama touched his face with her hand. She held it there for a long time. She traced his scar. I could tell even from the distance. He stayed still, allowed her to touch him there. His black curls fell over her fingers and she played with his hair. Simon reached out and cupped the back of her head. I couldn't watch anymore. I went downstairs and called Brian. I didn't say anything about them, we just talked about school and music and what we were doing for the summer.

The next day I came down very late for breakfast. Daddy was gone, Mama had been at her desk and was getting ready to go out to the garden. Simon's van was there, parked off to the side.

"I'm going to Brian's today. I'll bike over. Be back for supper." I grabbed a piece of toast and left Mama there holding my juice.

I rode my bike around the little roads, crisscrossing the main

routes. The air was still and damp. Even though the sun was
out, the air hung, warm and oppressive. I felt the dampness
on my chest, under my arms, between my legs. Everything
was sticky. I rode along a path by the ocean and looked at
the mountains. I didn't see red-and-purple splotches. I saw big
mountains with rock on top, growing out of the still, blue
ocean. I wondered if Mama saw the splotches. My bike tires
bounced a bit on the stones at the edge of the macadam. I
pulled to the side and dropped my bike. Raspberry bushes full
of berries. I stuck my arm into the center and pulled some
raspberries into my hand and wished I had brought a container.
I sat near the bush and ate the raspberries. At my feet were low
blueberry bushes covered with little green berries. Soon, I
thought, they will be ready.

I didn't really want to see Brian. Eventually I found myself
on the road home. I felt apprehension, as if something were not
quite right. I got off my bike and walked it slowly up the road
toward the house. The van was there. But the chair and easel
were empty. The painting with the splotches lay on the easel
near the box of paints and the canvas bag.

The walk to the house was longer than usual. I tried to be
very quiet and move slowly. A part of me wanted to call out,
"Hello, where are you?" The other part wanted to see. I wasn't
sure exactly what I would see, but I knew it wasn't good. I wondered if they would be in Mama's and Daddy's bedroom. Or
maybe they were in my room, but what would they be doing in
my room?

Just as I approached the walkway, I heard a noise off by the
line of trees at the edge of the field. I thought that maybe it was
the dog, but he was lying on the front stoop. I could have gone
up to my room, but I turned away from the house and walked
toward the trees. There were blueberry bushes and sweet fern
along the way, and I tried to avoid stepping on any twigs. I re-

membered Grandpa's advice. I walked so softly that I could not even hear myself. I heard the noise again. It was Mama, talking low, like she did to me when I was sick or sad. Again I thought of calling out, but I got down on my hands and knees and crawled toward the sound. Behind the safety of a line of old rosebushes full of blooms, I tried to call Berry. I knew she wouldn't come. I remembered what Grandpa had said about being quiet and peered around the bushes. They were there, on the ground, lying next to each other by the old russet apple tree, the one with my tree house in it.

Mama was lying on her back. Simon's hand was in Mama's tee shirt, pulling it up and exposing her breasts. I had seen her naked many times, but they looked different. Bigger. He put his mouth on one of the nipples. I didn't think of calling out again. Mama was making groaning noises, and Simon started kissing her everywhere. I could see her hand in his hair as he rolled over on top of her.

"Mattie, yes," he finally said as he looked down at her. I was so close I could hear the whisper. Mama's shirt was up around her neck and Simon opened his shirt, too, so that their bare chests touched together after he pulled off her tee shirt. Mama played with his hair while Simon began to pull down her shorts. I thought that maybe she was trying to push him away, but then I could see she was helping him with her foot. It took a very long time to get her shorts down to her ankles. They giggled. Like we did in school. She unsnapped his pants and I heard his zipper coming down. I knew what they were going to do. I had seen the deer, and I had seen pictures in books. My beautiful Mama. Under Simon. Moving with him. Mama was naked except for the amber beads which hung over her breast. Simon fumbled at his pants and Mama opened her legs for him and they started moving together. He didn't even take his pants off. She groaned, and I thought for a moment that she was hurt, but I didn't want to stay and find out. I turned from the bushes and crawled away toward the house. I was not so quiet this time. My bare knees hit rocks and roots and hurt so much it made me cry. My bangs hung in front of my face, so I couldn't see the next rock or stump. I began to hear the cries before I could reach the safety of the house. Before I could turn on the water tap and the TV, before I could take a shower. Both of them, then one, then the other, and last, Mama, alone, a high wail that went on and on and on.

I sat in the corner of my room with my hands over my ears, blocking out the noise, humming to myself. Maria used to hum to me. Spanish songs. And then in words I couldn't understand, songs about babies, and lovers, and sadness, and love. I tried to sing them to myself, but I only remembered a few of the words. She would know what to do. Maria would hold me and sing those songs and drown out the sound of the wailing.

Blue going off to visit her grandpa at Indian Beach.
First roll with the new camera.
August 1, 1992

CHAPTER 4

The rest of that day was a blur. They came back to the house about an hour later. First I noticed from my bedroom window that Simon was out by his truck putting his art supplies away. I ran into Mama and Daddy's room to look over to the apple tree. She was almost past the rosebushes when she stopped and bent to pick a branch of white roses. She brought a rose to her face. Her walk was light—almost as if she were walking across the tops of the bushes, her hair flying out behind her, catching the sun. The sound of Simon's truck permeated the stillness and she stopped and smiled. Although I couldn't really tell at that distance. After waiting a few minutes, I went into the kitchen just as she came through the door. "Just got back. Brian was busy," I said.

"Oh, I went out to pick some roses for the table. See? They're white ones. Aren't they pretty?" The vases were kept on the top shelf of the cupboard, and she had to reach to get the small vase down. We had a garden full of beautiful flowers. She had never before picked any of the scrub roses in the field.

They were small and covered with thorns. Mama and I ate supper. I did the dishes. Mama was real quiet and kept looking at me funny. I knew she was wondering if I'd seen something.

The next morning I was to leave for Grandpa's. I woke up with a big lump under me. I felt around and pulled out two of my old dolls.

I was kind of old for dolls. One was an Indian kewpie doll named Hiawatha that I made Grandpa buy me at the Blue Hill fair the year I turned eight. The other was a cloth doll that Daddy gave me when I had the accident. I called her Ugli. She was dirty and her clothes had long since been taken off and misplaced, but she had one eye and I loved her. Once I dreamed that Maria came to my house and slept in my bed with Berry and me. She wanted her own doll, so I gave her Ugli. She caressed Ugli's face and sang something very quietly to her in Spanish.

It was just light enough for me to see around my room. It was set up like a queen's court. The canopy bed was in the middle of the far wall, facing the door and shelves full of dolls; dolls that went around and played music, porcelain dolls with costumes from different countries, baby dolls. They all watched me there in bed. The canopy was pink, like the icing on a cake, pink ruffles all over. On the opposite wall there was a poster print of me before the accident. It took up most of the wall. It was the eyes that were the worst. Two beautiful eyes gazing out from the most perfect face framed by black Indian hair in ringlets. Daddy had a hundred of them made up and passed them out to customers and relatives. He even gave one to Brian's parents. Grandpa put his out in the big closet in the garage. Said it didn't really look like me and he liked the real "me." Daddy said that I was still beautiful, and Mama said there are reasons for everything. Even accidents.

37

Mama said that the director was distracted by Daddy and his camera but that it wasn't really his fault. Daddy kept saying "I'm sorry," and brought me presents. My favorite was Ugli, the doll that had two eyes when I got her but I pulled one out. I never got the sundae from the director and never again saw the suspicious-looking character. The golf-cart driver was thrown on the cart's impact with me and was released from the hospital that very day. But I was not so lucky. I was changed. A different person. No longer cute, adorable, beautiful, Blue. My face, my beautiful movie-star face was cut so badly that they needed pictures of me so they could try to piece me together in some recognizable form. The scars healed well, but if you looked closely, you can see them. The nerves on the side of my face never healed exactly right, so when I'm tired, my mouth sags on one side. Daddy took pictures of everything. Mama said he couldn't bear to watch me with his own eyes, that the view from the camera lens might make the sight easier to take. Shots of me wrapped in gauze, comatose. Shots of the bandages being removed. My hospital memories flow between Daddy's pictures and images of the nurses hovering around me. But I do remember coming home.

I walked carefully, not wanting to fall. I looked down at my feet. Oxfords, heavy black oxfords. And me not even six. The crack in the sidewalk in front of the hospital made me stop. "The cat shit on," I said. I knew it wasn't right but it was all I could get out. I didn't want to walk on the crack. "The cat shit on."

"Jesus, Blue, don't say that," Daddy had said.

"It's alright honey, Mama knows. You don't want to step on the crack," Mama said as she lifted me over it.

The car ride home was quiet. I sat in the back, with Aunt Marcia holding my hand. Our house looked different when we pulled up the driveway, but I couldn't figure out what it was. I remembered the feeling of something being out of place.

The dog, Maggie, ran out to meet us, tail wagging, waiting to see if I still knew her. "Micky, Micky," I screeched in delight. I clapped my hands. "Bitch, bitch." I was telling Maggie to come. I had taught her that, as well as sit and fetch, but the words came out wrong. They seemed alright to me. I understood them, but I knew they were wrong.

There had been cake on the table. Pale pink, with a ballet dancer in arabesque pose on the top. Written in Mama's hand around the dancer were the words, "Welcome home, Blue." Daddy took a picture of it. My guess was that I would never be a ballet dancer. I clunked over to the table in my black oxford shoes to look more closely. She had tiny legs with perfectly pointed toes and a pink tutu. I picked up the dancer and stuck her foot in my mouth. The frosting was so sweet, all pink and gooey. I sucked all the pink frosting off her toes and when it was gone, I brought her toe down into the cake, I think to get more frosting, again and again and again, each time harder than the first, until the cake was in pieces, scattered about on the table and floor. I could hear Mama crying softly and Daddy repeating, "Jesus, Jesus, I'm sorry, I'm so sorry." Finally the pink dancer fell onto the floor and was quickly scooped up by Maggie. "More cake for Jesus," I said, "More cake for Jesus." That night I held Ugli and called to Berry to help me with the words, the right words for things.

After the accident, I heard Mama tell Daddy that she wanted another baby. She couldn't. Something happened inside when she had us. I heard them talking.

The morning I left for Grandpa's I knew that Ugli and Hiawatha wouldn't want to be out there with those other dolls, so I kept them under the covers. I pulled the covers up over my head and made a tent inside. There we were, Blue, Ugli, and Hiawatha. I knew Berry would come if I wanted her to, but I didn't, not just yet. I wasn't sure what to say to her. I wanted to work it out myself first.

I couldn't see the dolls very well under those covers, but I held them while I cried without noise. If they heard me, my parents would be at the side of the bed, saying, "What's the matter, dear?" Pulling the covers down, patting me on the head, telling me to come down for a good breakfast, just what you need, they would say. My insides were hot and sore, and the shaking of the sobs made me feel a little better. I put Ugli's head in my mouth to keep the sound in. Her whole head fit but made me gag a little. I felt like I was going to throw up, so I pulled her out and jerked the covers off my face. I looked at Ugli. Her face was all wet. Like mine.

The scene kept coming back, the noise from the bushes, Simon pulling at himself, Mama pulling at his zipper. I stuck my index finger in my mouth and bit down hard. I couldn't get that finger to bleed. I kept biting on it, making dents in it. But no blood. There they were. She was smiling at him, laughing, turning toward him. I grabbed the dolls and stuck them under the pillow. I had to pee.

I grabbed the shorts and tee shirt from the floor and got into them quickly. I wasn't about to go down to the bathroom in my underwear, not today. They were having breakfast. I could see them there at the table as I came out of the bathroom, Daddy and Mama. Having breakfast. They were talking, smiling at each other. He didn't know. What a stupid idiot. And she said she went out to pick roses.

"Blue," Daddy called. "You're late this morning. Come. Have breakfast. I saved you some bacon. And look, Mama picked some roses out in the blueberry field."

That he could talk about bacon and roses at a time like this amazed me. He poured me some juice. He always served my breakfast. He served Mama hers, too. Probably did that very morning, before I got up.

"Grandpa's coming at 11:30. Are you packed?" I looked at Mama to see if she was really asking me this question.

"Am I packed? You're asking if I'm packed?" I knew I was raising my voice. I didn't care.

"You look tired, dear. Did you have a bad dream?"

God, why didn't she just shut up.

"Here's your English muffin." Daddy placed it on the plate in front of me, buttered, with orange marmalade on it, just the way I liked it, right next to the bacon. "We'll miss you around here. It'll be awful quiet."

I looked up at him. Pleading with him to get it. To not be so stupid. But he was just Daddy. He wasn't going to get it, and I wasn't going to tell him. I ate my breakfast slowly and quietly. Mama fussed, and Daddy insisted I have another muffin, which I couldn't finish.

"I'm going to Brian's. We're going for a bike ride. I'll be back in time to pack."

"Didn't you do that yesterday? Well, be back soon." I heard her call as I raced down the steps to grab my bike. I was thirteen and going into the eighth grade, and I still had only one friend. And Berry, of course, but only one real live friend. Brian had only one friend, too.

I rode fast to his house. The bike jarred at the potholes in the road. I pedaled along the same roads as yesterday. The mountains looked gray and distant and not at all purple and red and blue. I never noticed the raspberry bushes that day. My loose hair flew back out of my face. It had grown out some but still not long enough to tie back or braid. My leg hurt a little with each pedal.

"Brian," I yelled through the screen door. "Brian, come on,

get your bike, it's my last day." I opened the door and walked in. "Brian, come on. I'm going to Grandpa's. I won't see you for a week."

Brian slunk down the stairs dressed in rumpled clothes and yawning. "OK, give me a minute," he said, heading for the kitchen. He grabbed a piece of bread and took a swig of juice from a bottle in the fridge. "Let's go."

We started toward Buckets Pond. We hadn't been there since the day of the frogs. I had a hard time keeping up with him. "Wait up," I called every few minutes. My leg pulled with each stroke, not terribly painful, but there, pulling, hurting. We stopped at the picnic area, dropped our bikes, and started walking down one of the paths. We knew this area like our own backyards. "Wait up," I called again. He did. He stopped and turned around and waited for me to catch up to him. We walked to the grassy spot where you could see those bubbles, those mountains.

We stood, looking ahead at whatever was there, mountains, trees, bushes. Neither of us spoke. Just looked ahead. Kicked a piece of sod, bent down, picked up a rock, threw it into the bushes. I felt for his hand. He didn't pull away. He didn't move. We stood for a long time, Brian and I, holding hands. Or rather, I was holding his hand. He was letting me.

"Brian."

"Yea."

"You're my best friend."

"Yea."

"Did ya ever do it?"

"Do it?"

"You know, do it."

"I donno."

"You don't know? Brian. You don't know?"

I reached for his other hand and turned him toward me. I

could feel he was trembling, and his hands were cold and wet. His ears seemed to stick out even more than usual. His eyes looked straight ahead, not at me. I dropped his hand for a moment and pulled my tee shirt out of my shorts. When I reached for his hand again, I felt him pull away. I stepped forward and took his hand and pulled it toward me. I tried to catch his gaze but he continued to look straight ahead. With both hands now, I guided his hand up under my shirt and placed it on my bare skin. The nipple was hard. I could feel it. His hand was cold, so cold and wet. I tried to move his hand on me, but it was trembling and pulling away.

"Come on, Brian, please."

Finally his hand began moving on its own, not much, just a little. His other hand felt for the other breast. They were so small. I wished they were bigger, so he could hold them. I wanted him to put his mouth on them. Brian looked at me. He began to pant a little, his hands moving faster and pinching my nipples hard, so they hurt. He started to blow air out of his mouth, through his closed lips, making a funny sound. Then he grabbed me around the waist, hard. We stood there together for a few minutes.

"Shit." I said nothing. I stepped back and looked at him. His face was flushed, red, and he had a wet spot on his shorts. "Oh, shit," he said again, as he looked down at his shorts.

"It's OK. Did you like it? Did you? I mean, your hands there, did you like that?" We stood facing each other with our hands at our sides. Brian was looking at the ground and I was looking at Brian. I took his hand and shook it a little. "Did it feel good? It doesn't matter about the shorts. Did it feel good?"

"What'll I tell Mom? About the shorts?"

"Do you want to do it again?"

"No, not now." Brian finally looked up at me. "Maybe not ever. Can we go home now?" He turned to go back up the path.

"Brian." He turned, and I could see his eyes were teared up. "I'm sorry," I said.

He nodded, and I knew he couldn't speak without breaking. Our friendship had changed. We could still be friends, I was sure of that, but it would be different. Frogs and marbles and bike riding were things of childhood, and I felt we would never share them again.

"I'm going to Grandpa's today," I said as I picked up my bike. "I won't be home 'til next week. One whole week. Can we do something when I get back? Not, you know—something fun, maybe go to a movie, something."

Brian looked at me. "Sure, call me. Are you OK? I mean, well, is it OK?"

"I'm fine. Are we still friends?"

We nodded to each other and pushed our bike pedals down and were off. The wind was at our backs all the way to Brian's house, and I felt as if I were flying, hardly having to pedal at all. With Brian it wasn't what I had expected. It didn't even feel good. I thought of Maria, how soft she was, her breath, her smell. I remembered how she smelled. Like flowers. That last morning when I slipped my arm around her neck as she put on my white socks and Mary Jane patent leather shoes. She smelled like flowers. It should be like that. Like flowers.

Brian and I parted at his house, and I went on home. We seemed to be alright with everything. His shorts had dried by then, leaving a slightly stiff spot only noticeable to someone looking for it. Brian saw me looking and turned away for a moment. Then he grabbed my hand, and said, "Have fun at your grandpa's."

"Thanks, I'll call you."

I hadn't thought about Mama for most of the morning but now that I was alone the image came back and came back and came back. I thought about Brian's hand under my tee shirt and

I knew it wasn't the same, not that same stuff that Mama was doing with Simon. I didn't moan and scream and neither did Brian. My nipples hurt and my eye socket ached. Suddenly I hated that eye. Stupid glass eye. I thought about how it would be to wear a patch, a black one, or maybe fluorescent pink, or maybe Grandpa would make one out of raccoon skin. Some tourists on the road passed my bike and honked as I swerved off onto the shoulder.

What if Grandpa wasn't at the house yet, wasn't there to pick me up? Mama would be there and Daddy, and they would be talking about stuff, weather, the garden, maybe even Simon. What if Simon was there? In his baby blue van. I hated him. He thought he was so great. I looked at the mountains. They were everywhere, but they weren't purple or red or blue, they were gray and brown, cold, hard, jagged. I stopped and stood with the bike between my legs. I tried to see the purple, the colors. Maybe if I had two eyes I would see them. But I didn't think so.

I shoved off for the last short ride home and pedaled very slowly. As I turned the corner I could see Grandpa's truck parked behind Daddy's. No baby blue van. No easel on the hill.

"Grandpa." I dropped my bike on the edge of the grass and ran up the front steps. "Grandpa," I called as I swung the door open. The door slammed behind me and there she was. Standing there in front of Daddy and Grandpa, smiling at me.

"There you are, dear," she said.

"I'll be right down, got to throw some stuff in my bag," I said to Daddy and Grandpa. I ran past her up the stairs to my room.

CHAPTER 5

The Passamaquoddy Reservation was small, with new wooden houses tightly clumped together. They had dishwashers and washing machines and some houses even had satellite dishes on the front lawn. The tribe owned the land and let the people live on it if they had Passamaquoddy blood in them. Some people owned their houses and could sell to other Passamaquoddies. Grandpa made sure everyone knew that he was almost full Indian. That his mother was one of the last full-blooded Passamaquoddies. He made sure that everyone knew his father was half-Indian, only half-white. His father's father was a blue blood named Charles Willoughby from a good and proper New England family, a lawyer who met my great-great-grandmother on a hunting trip. He brought her to Boston to live in a fine house with servants, but something happened. No one ever said. She came back to the reservation pregnant with Grandpa's father and never saw Charles again. Daddy once tried to contact the Boston Willoughby family, but they never responded. I think Daddy was embarrassed, and he never mentioned it again.

Daddy said it was a good historical name that opened doors. I think Grandpa always regretted not being named Silliboy or Francis or Socabasin, or some other Passamaquoddy name. He had to explain "Willoughby."

Grandpa grew up on the reservation and had lived there all his life except when he was in the army. After Grandma died, Daddy tried to get him to live with us, but he wouldn't budge from Indian Beach. I don't remember Grandma. She died when I was a baby and was buried right near their house at the Indian burial grounds. Grandpa said that's where he wanted to go, too. Daddy hated the reservation, and I overheard him tell Sam Haycock next door that his father lived in Machias. He hardly ever went to Indian Beach because he didn't have to. Grandpa came to visit us. Grandpa told me once that he was going to die there. "Remember, I am telling you of my wishes. I don't want to be in any hospital. Just bring me home and stick me in bed," he had said.

Every morning I walked to a small corner store a few minutes from Grandpa's house to get some things: candy corn for Grandpa, milk, bread. I pretended I was one of the People, a Passamaquoddy. I had Indian hair, and my skin was a little darker than most people's. But, of course, they all knew who I was and that I only had about a quarter Indian blood in me.

"You must be visiting your grandfather again, young lady," Stephen Francis, the shopkeeper, said as I came into the store that first morning. Behind him on the back wall was a large painted sign that said, "People of the Dawn." Grandpa said our people were called that because we were the first to see the rising sun, living at the most eastern point of the country. "Come to get some candy corn? My land, doesn't that old man love those things." He put his large brown hand on my head and stroked my hair. My hair was really too short to braid, but I'd tried anyway. The front stuck out under the beaded headband

Mama bought for me at the Indian crafts place in New Brunswick. My grandmother made stuff like headbands and sweetgrass baskets before she died.

Mama always gave me some candy to bring when I went to Grandpa's to visit. I hadn't even said good-bye to her this time.

"Hi, Mr. Francis, I forgot to bring his candy corn from home, so I better get a bag. He waits for it, you know, always expects me to bring it. You like my headband? It's Indian, you know. Do you think it's Passamaquoddy?"

"Oh, I'm sure." He smiled down at me but didn't look closely at the headband. The old people here were always nice to the children. Not like some of the old people at home, not like old Mrs. Manzer down the road who called the police if we crossed her yard. Here we could go anywhere, do anything, as long as we didn't wreck anyone's property.

On the way home from the store, I practiced walking quietly. We were going to climb up Scodouc Mountain today, so Grandpa could collect some herbs to dry for the winter. Scodouc Mountain, where the mighty trickster, Glue-skub, and his helper, Marten, walked. Grandpa said we might actually step on the same rocks as they did. The animals like deer and rabbits would be hard to see this time of year. In the fall they were breeding and careless, but in summer they went into the thicker woods to get away from flies and tourists. They were more alert and didn't let themselves be seen. But Grandpa always walked quietly and slowly, watching so he wouldn't disturb the forest floor, wouldn't step on some little creature's nest or crush a lady's slipper. This was the first time I had been out with him since the day we saw the old buck and his doe, the day I cut my braids.

I passed St. John's Catholic Church, the biggest building on the reservation. It was built about a hundred years ago, and Grandpa wouldn't go near it. He said it was no place for him.

I wasn't sure what that meant, but it was one of those things that I knew he didn't want to talk about. No one seemed to be around. The windows in front were all stained glass, but at the bottom of each one was a pane of clear glass that ran across the width of the window. I was just tall enough to peer inside. My eyes took a moment to get used to the darkness of the massive church. There were rows and rows of benches, and the windows, which from the outside didn't look like much, shone with pictures of men dying and women crying. Not very happy. No wonder Grandpa didn't go near the place. There were no Indian things anywhere that I could see. No baskets or feathers, or painted signs that said, "People of the Dawn."

The church bells startled me as they began their hourly clanging. Nine bells this time. I wondered if a real person was ringing them or whether they rang on their own. I looked around but still didn't see anyone. I thought I might come some other time to look again. I was sure I would never go inside.

Grandpa's house was pink on the outside, and he planted nasturtiums all around the front. He liked them because you could eat them in salads. I thought it was weird to eat flowers, but I would never tell him that. Sometimes he kept some in his pocket and he would take them out and smell them. That was pretty weird, too, but that was Grandpa.

Grandpa was waiting for me when I got back. "Well, Miss Brown, what've you got in that bag? Huh?" He tried to hide his amusement, but his eyes gave him away. He knew I had his candy corn.

"Guess."

"Oh, let me see, a Snickers bar?"

I shook my head.

"Ummm, a can of Coke?"

I shook my head again.

"Oh, no, not my favorite." He squatted down to my level. He whispered into my ear as if he didn't want anyone else to hear. "Is it candy corn?"

I opened the bag and took out the candy. "But you have to share, Grandpa."

He tried to pick me up like he used to, but I was too heavy for him. He laughed. "We'll take them to the mountain. It's a long hike, and we'll need some energy. I'll pack a lunch, too."

I sat down at the kitchen table and grabbed some cherries from the bowl. The table was almost empty. The bowl of cherries and a mason jar full of nasturtiums. Our table at home was always covered with papers, blueprints, magazines, photographs, projects. Grandpa's walls were light pink, bare, except for an old photograph of him when he was very small. He sat on his mother's lap staring at the camera. My great grandmother, full-blooded Passamaquoddy. She had beads around her neck and very black hair. Like mine. She wasn't smiling but from her eyes I could tell she was happy. At their feet was a little dog, and behind them was a wood cookstove with large pots on it. Probably full of moose stew or rabbit soup. Next to the woodstove stood my great grandfather, son of Charles Willoughby, a half-breed, who Grandpa had said looked a lot like Daddy. Grandpa told me once he was going to leave me that photo when he died. It had run in the newspaper when he was a kid. The newspaper clipping was in his scrapbook. The headline said, "Indian family lives in squalor." Grandpa said he couldn't understand why they said that. They always had plenty to eat and warm clothes. And I could see from his parents' eyes that they loved him.

He made us both a white-bread sandwich with Cheez Whiz and pickles. We never had store-bought bread at home and certainly never had Cheez Whiz. "Grandpa, can I have two of those?"

"Do you want to take an apple, too? Gives you energy when you're walking around in the woods." I saw everything again. Mama in the woods, Brian in the woods, me in the woods. "Blue, do you want an apple?"

"No," I forced out. I wasn't sure I wanted to go to the woods. I wanted Grandpa to be able to pick me up like before. Carry me around. Maybe I could stay here on the reservation. I could go to school here in the fall. I had Indian blood in me. They would let me stay. And I would just tell Mama and Daddy that I was staying. Daddy would hate that I chose the reservation, chose to be with the Passamaquoddy people. Mama and Daddy couldn't do anything about it. They would have to listen to me. I would talk to Grandpa when the right time came.

We loaded our lunch and baskets for collecting into the truck. I sat next to him, holding the sweetgrass and split ash basket that his mother made. I never knew her because she died of pneumonia way before I was born, but I thought about her making the baskets, gliding through the marshes harvesting bushels of sweetgrass from her canoe. She sold them to tourists, but there were not as many in those days as there were today. I bent over and sniffed the basket. The sweetgrass was still sweet, after all these years. I wanted to learn to make those baskets, something that would outlive me as this one had my great-grandmother.

Our trek took us along a narrow path that meandered up the small mountain. Grandpa said that his mother's family gathered herbs from the mountain since before the white people came. We gathered raspberry runners to chop and dry for Grandpa's stomach and sweet flag root to prevent disease in the winter, and put them in a burlap sack. Grandpa found a lady's slipper off the path and after he had made sure there was another, he carefully pulled it so the root came out intact. "Steven asked me to get one of these for his mother. Good for nervousness."

We both laughed because we knew how Mr. Francis' mother was. We were very careful not to take them all, Grandpa said to always leave enough for someone else to pick and enough to throw out seed for the next year.

The top of the mountain was bald granite with a few low shrubs of juniper and blueberry. Lichen and mosses covered parts of the granite, and Grandpa searched carefully before we chose a spot. "This lichen took hundreds of years to grow. We don't want to squash it in a minute, just to have our lunch," he said. He took out our sandwiches and Cokes and the bag of candy corn. We sat where we could see everything around for miles and stretched our legs out in front of us. The reservation was easy to pick out, and I thought I could even see Grandpa's house. I could certainly see St. John's Church. Suddenly I felt so close to Grandpa, like we were each part of one big whole. We sat the same way and ate our sandwiches at the same pace. I watched him carefully and wondered if you could inherit the way you eat a sandwich. I thought of that day in the woods when he let me choose the way.

"Grandpa, remember the deer that time in the woods? Do you think she liked it, the doe?"

There was a pause. He didn't answer right away. "It's, well, it's something that she has to do."

"Why, if she doesn't like it, why does she do it?" I brought my legs up close to my body. I wasn't looking at him. I thought he might be embarrassed. I don't think he was looking at me either.

"That's the way they get babies, fawns for next year. If they weren't driven to it, they would stop having babies and the deer would be gone."

Grandpa was so wise. His deep voice echoed around the mountain even though he wasn't talking very loud. Like Glueskub when he stood here speaking to his people.

"Are fawns made the same as human babies?"

I knew he was looking at me now, but I stared down at my sandwich and took a big bite. I wished I hadn't brought it up.

"People are different. People like mating, they're not just driven to it. I read in a magazine once that that's what separates people from other animals. People like the act of mating and animals are just driven to do it. They don't really enjoy themselves. It's instinct. It's just something they have to do." Grandpa turned toward me and crossed his legs in front of him. "It's a natural thing, Blue. All plants and animals have a way to join the male and female together so that they can conceive young. People get close to each other and touch each other because it feels good to them."

"Do all people like it?"

"Well, not all people like candy corn or turkey, I guess not all people like being close to someone else, but I don't know anyone who doesn't. Don't you feel better when someone holds you? Hugs you? Well, mating is kind of like that."

I felt full of courage all of a sudden. "Did you like it, you know, with Grandma when you were first married?" I took another bite of the sandwich.

"I loved your grandmother so much. Yes, we liked being close or having relations as we called it, both of us, right up until she died." There was silence for a long moment. "I still miss her sometimes. I never made love to anyone else after that. I miss her and I miss the closeness and I miss the passion." I couldn't answer. Cheez Whiz stuck in my throat. "Never settle for less than that. Never settle for something that has no passion. Never do something because it's easy and comfortable and expected if there's no passion."

I swallowed over and over to get rid of the sandwich. Grandpa passed me a can of Coke. I drank almost the whole can and looked up at him. Something was different. He had allowed me through a window, trusted me enough to tell me all this. I felt like a grown-up, a real person, and I knew that I had not experienced passion. I also knew that my mother had.

"Do you think I will have passion?"

"Passion isn't just about a husband and wife. It is about a feeling of one person toward another, of a person toward a job or an art or even a religion. It comes from inside. It just comes. You can't make it come."

"What about Mama and Daddy? Did they love each other before they had me?"

"I think they love each other still. They have difficulty trusting each other. That gets in the way. Here, Miss Brown, take this and bury it somewhere, and when you find passion, you can dig it up. Do you think this feather wants to stay in the ground forever?" I turned toward him. He was holding a large white feather.

"That's just an old turkey feather."

"Maybe it's the feather of a white eagle, or a passion bird." I smiled up at him. "OK, Grandpa. I'll take it."

"When you find passion, you will understand the power of the feather." I took the feather from him and stuck it in my pocket. I didn't even ask where he got it.

We went to the woods almost every day during the week. Once we went back to the mountain to find some more herbs, and the other days we took long walks through the woods in back of the reservation. We found a bunch of juniper bushes, and we gathered about a quart of juniper berries. Grandpa dried them for the winter and made a tea if he got a cold. Said it worked better than any of those things in bottles at the Super Drug. He had mason jars full of plants and berries lined up on a shelf in the kitchen. He called it his own free drugstore. Hemlock, jack-in-the-pulpit, blueberry leaves, sweet flag. He said he could cure just about anything.

"When your daddy was a small baby, he screamed for hours one hot August night. Grandma tried everything. Then I remembered my mother using sweet flag root for a neighbor baby. I had some in the jar, for colds. I chopped it up and made a tea for nqoss, my baby. Your grandmother was exhausted so I carried your daddy down to the edge of the sea where I sang songs and offered him sips of the sweet flag root tea from his baby cup. The screaming slowed and finally he fell asleep on my shoulder. We sat on the granite until dawn, until the fishing boats appeared. I will remember that night always." Daddy was too young to remember that night, but I felt sometimes that he wished he were small enough for Grandpa to carry.

My leg seemed to be getting stronger, and I could walk farther than I ever could before. On my last day we paddled Stephen Francis' canoe out onto the marshes. Mr. Francis made the canoe from birch bark, and it didn't even leak. Grandpa pointed out the sweetgrass and said we could gather some later in the summer when I came back, and he would have Mrs. Francis teach me how to make a basket.

When we got back to the house the neighbor kids were there, on my steps. I hadn't seen much of them this visit, but we had been friends for years.

"Hey, want to come play Ha Ha Gigugiez?"

"Grandpa?"

"Sure, go ahead, be careful on those rocks."

We raced down to the shore, five of us. From Grandpa's house the dirt road went directly to the edge of the ocean, and if the church hadn't been in the way, we could have seen the beach from the kitchen window. The others were barefoot and could run faster than I could with my sneakers, even over the small round rocks on the beach, but they stopped and waited for me when I fell behind. Last year we were children and played with all ages. This year we were teenagers and played only with kids who were our age. I took my sneakers off at the water's edge. The water in the bay even this time of year was cold, but that was part of the excitement. We followed the wave as it went out and hugged it as it came back in. "Ha, Ha," they yelled if we got splashed by the waves. We teased the water, taunted it, "You can't get me, Ha, Ha." But of course it did get us, and we got wet.

Anna was the smallest and the bravest, dark and quick. She darted back and forth, daring the waves to come to her. "Ha, Ha, Gigugiez," she called to the ocean. And then she threw back her head and laughed a laugh much bigger than herself. I followed her but was afraid to get too close. The waves could be rough, crashing onto the rocks, pounding their surf onto us. The boys, of course, thought they were the bravest of all, but Anna was the best.

After we had all been chased by the waves, we collapsed onto the pebble shore to allow the sun to dry our clothes. Vincent took a couple of red dice out of his pocket and shook them. He let them fall on a flat rock. "Two fives." He picked them up and shook them again. "Three and a five."

"Can we play?" I said.

"You don't even know what I'm playing. You're too young. You're not even Indian."

"I am too, my great-grandmother was full-Passamaquoddy and I have Indian braids. Anyway, that doesn't have anything to do with playing dice."

"Come on, Vinnie, let her play, she's decent."

Vincent nodded and we all formed a ring around the flat rock.

"Anna, what do you call?"

"Evens."

He shook the dice again and threw them on the rock.

"A three and a five."

Anna smiled smugly and sat back on her heels.

"Melvin, how about you?"

"Odds."

"A two and a two."

"Oh, God." Melvin stood up and put his index finger on his forehead as if he were thinking.

"Come on, Melvin, you lost. Take something off."

Melvin rolled up his tee shirt and pulled it over his head. He threw it on the beach stones and sat back down.

I began to realize what we were doing. We didn't have many clothes on this time of year, and I had already taken off my sneakers and socks.

"Joe, you're next."

"Odds."

"Three and three," Vincent said.

"Ohhhh," rose out of the group in unison. Joe had already taken his shirt off when it got soaking wet. They started to clap in a rhythm, incessant and progressively louder. Joe had a smirk on his face as he stood up. I think he was glad he lost the dice roll. I started to clap with the others and Joe did a little wiggle. His hands went to the snap on his shorts and pulled it open. We continued to clap. Then he pulled down the zipper very slowly, wiggling all the while. I thought back to Brian and how awkward he had been. Joe let the shorts drop to his feet. His underwear was soaking wet and clung to his body. I could see the outline of a bulge through the underwear. Everyone was watching as he snapped the elastic with his thumb. "Stay tuned," he said, and sat down.

"OK, Miss Blue, you're next."

They all looked my way.

"Well, aren't you old enough? Maybe we shouldn't have let you come with us."

"Yeahhhh," the rest said in unison.

"Evens." I figured that would give me an even chance.

Vincent rolled and threw. "Two and three."

Their heads all snapped in my direction.

I had four things on. I knew everything was wet and I was sure you could see through them, like with Joe. My breasts were just starting to grow and Mama bought me a bra with a little padding. Maybe it wouldn't look too ridiculous, maybe the padding would make it less transparent. I pulled my arms out of the shirt so that it was just around my neck and my arms covered my bra. I felt a tug at the back of my neck. "Here, I'll help you." It was Anna. She pulled the shirt off and put it in my lap. I sat with my arms crossed. I had done it. Well, the shirt was off.

"Here, Blue, you roll for me." Vincent threw me the dice and I grabbed for them while keeping the other arm across my chest. "Odds."

I shook and threw.

"One and three," I called out.

Vincent stood up and looked around at us as if judging the audience. He had a very wet sleeveless tee shirt and a plaid bathing suit. His hands went to the waistband of the suit. I think I wanted to look away but I watched along with everyone else. He pulled the suit down with difficulty because it kept sticking to his legs. We followed the suit and when it was around his feet, I allowed myself to look up at his thing. It was sticking out, all swollen and bobbing there at the edge of his tee shirt. I couldn't take my eyes off it.

"What's the matter, never seen one of these? Bet you never saw one this big before."

I continued to stare. I wanted to look away, wait for the next dice roll, laugh with the others.

It was Anna's turn again. This time she lost. I could see her nipples through her wet shirt. She stood up slowly. "Come on,

Anna, take it off." Her thumbs hooked her purple shorts and she lowered them there right in front of me. No underwear. Maybe she hoped her shirt would cover her, but it didn't quite. She stepped out of the shorts and held them up in the air. I could see the hair, dark but just beginning to grow. I felt something move between my legs. Something I hadn't felt before except alone in bed. I forced myself to look away. "Yeah, Blue, throw the dice again for Anna."

They laughed in unison. All of them. Even Anna. Joe looked at his watch. "Christ, I gotta be home, we're going out for supper." He grabbed his shorts and put them on.

The boys started ahead of us. I put my shirt on and stood up. She stood in front of me like that, with no pants on. "Did you have fun?"

I could barely answer. "Yes."

She stepped into her shorts and pulled them up. I looked at her hair, between her legs. She turned around as she pulled at the shorts. Her rear end was so smooth and dark, small, I wanted to touch it.

"Come on." She put her arm around my shoulders and steered me toward home.

Blue holding up her first basket. Taken at Indian Beach.
Dad took this with his little Instamatic.
August 1992

CHAPTER 6

That same visit that Grandpa gave me the passion feather and I played strip poker on the beach, I started learning about baskets. I begged Daddy to let me stay longer than the usual week. I promised to work in the garden extra hours to make up. Grandpa got on the phone. "Blue wants to learn about baskets. Mrs. Francis is going to teach her. Why don't you and Mattie come up for dinner on Sunday and she will probably have a basket to show you."

I stood in front of him shaking my head and mouthing "no."

"Oh, well, that's too bad. I'll bring her back the end of next week. I love having her around."

I mouthed "yes" this time. Grandpa pointed to the phone and then to me. "No," I mouthed again.

"No, Blue can't come to the phone. I'll tell her."

As he hung up I wanted to jump up into his arms, but I knew I was getting too big for that. I hugged him and ran to get ready for my basket lesson.

Mrs. Francis and I had a deal. I would cut ash strips and

prepare sweetgrass for her for an hour and she would help me with my basket for an hour. She said I could come every day until I had to go home. The Francis' shed was stark and bare except for the basket forms and tools, scraps of wood, sweetgrass, and piles of ash strips. The strips had already been gathered and pounded by Mr. Francis. That was a man's job, she said. Mr. Francis had the biggest arms I had ever seen, even bigger than Grandpa's, thick as a tree.

"Blue, come," Mrs. Francis said. "You will sit here and cut the ash strips. 'Wikp.' You must learn the real words for things. Ash is 'Wikp.' Brown ash. Only brown ash is good for baskets. The strips must be all the same width. That is your job."

I sat in the chair with strips all around me. They were different widths and some had ragged edges. She stood behind me and reached around to take my hands in hers. Her hands were rough. She transferred a gauge to my hand. "Likp-beh-wa-zar-gon," she said. She left my other hand to pick up a piece of the ash. She held it in front of me without proceeding, without moving. I knew she expected something of me, but Indians have patience, at least Mrs. Francis and Grandpa did, so she might stand for a very long time holding the ash in front of me. I could smell her closeness, soap, cooking grease, sweetgrass.

Blue, I said to myself, *breathe slowly.* What should you do? I touched the strip. It was rough, like her hands. "Wikp," I said. "Wikp." Not quite the way she said it.

She placed the strip in my hand. She covered my small hands with her thick brown ones and pulled the strip through the gauge. All the way down the length of the strip, a bit at a time, but smoothly, all the way until the strip was gone from the gauge. The edges fell away as if they were piecrust or clay, fell to the floor in soft curls. She dropped my hand to pick up another, held it for a moment until she heard. "Wikp." It sounded louder and more like what she had said this time. Again the strip slid through the gauge, peeling away the rough edges. And it went in the finished pile. She still stood behind me with her hands on mine. She held up the hand with the gauge in it. "Lip. Lip . . . keswakon."

"Likp-beh-wa-zar-gon," she said.

I knew I would say it right the next time. She dropped my hands and pulled a small leather piece out of her pocket. "Here, for your finger. Mine is so old and tough I don't wear one. But you, very young, soft, you will bleed. It is called 'pheed-law-wun.' " I wanted to bleed, to toughen my hands, to look like I did real work. She went over to the table and began to gather the tools and strips together for the potato baskets. I sat in the chair with the gauge on my lap and the leather thing on my finger, the pitolawon. She looked over at me and nodded very slowly.

This looked very easy, slick, fast. I could probably get through all the strips in the hour. Then she would show me how to make my own potato basket. Wikp, likp-beh-wa-zar-gon, pheed-law-wun, wikp, likp-beh-wa-zar-gon, pheed-law-wun, I repeated to myself. Next time I would be ready. I picked up a strip and positioned the gauge on the end. I pictured Mrs. Francis doing it, her arms, hands, fingers, gauge, and began to pull the strip through. It went about two inches before it stopped. I jerked it a little and a piece of the ash separated from the strip and drove itself into my hand. Not deep. Pulled it out. I looked up at Mrs. Francis. She was working on the strips, but I knew she could see me. She didn't look at me. I closed my eyes and thought about what Grandpa would do. I looked at the gauge. It was not quite centered over the splint. I pulled the splint out and turned it around. I held the gauge and looked down the length of the splint, my arms and hands poised and ready. I pictured the peeling away in my mind. The center of the gauge pulled to the center of the splint like a magnet. I began the cut. The wikp caught my hands and drove in some small splinters. Next time my hands wouldn't be in the way. The strip slid through, catching only a few times and just for a moment. It freed itself from the likp-beh-wa-zar-gon with a jerk as my arms sprung apart. But I had a cut strip in my hand. I looked over to the basket table. Mrs. Francis was still weaving the strips, looking at the basket, but could see me out of the corner of her eye. She was not going to run over and look at my strip and say, "Oh what a wonderful strip, so straight, so smooth."

I dropped it in the finished pile and picked up another. I centered the gauge on the strip and imagined what was going to happen. Willed it to stay centered, to be straight, to cut. The strips got straighter and smoother. I became faster. I sat up straighter. The image of the centering stayed in my mind. And my hands started to get rough. Well, some of my fingers had splinters, and one was bleeding a little. I was not ready to take off the pheed-law-wun.

The cutting began to have a rhythm to it. Pick up, center, pull, pull, pull, drop, pick up, center, pull, pull, pull, drop. Well, not quite that easy, but it stopped being a struggle, and I knew that the more I did it the easier it would get. The pile of finished splints grew. I got up and began to gather the strips left to be cut. It felt good to stand up and move my arms in a different way. I had almost forgotten about Mrs. Francis. She was still there, weaving her strips, tapping them in, watching me out of the corner of her eye.

"It is time," I heard as I sat down again with the pile of strips. "Your time to learn about making a basket." I knew not to ask how I'd done. I should know that myself. "First, some lemonade." I removed my pheed-law-wun and moved to the basketmaking table. She filled two glasses with lemonade from a thermos. "There, drink." I think that was her way of saying I had done a good job. We sat together, facing the baskets, sipping our lemonade, one old and brown, one young and soft and not terribly brown. We were quiet, breathing, sipping. There was more quiet time with Passamaquoddies. They weren't scared of the quiet, didn't need to fill it up, to talk about weather and stuff. There was time to just be, to think about things. Mrs. Francis and I thought about the baskets and the coolness of the lemonade. I sat back and sighed.

"Now we are ready," she said. She laid out the strips in front of us, just a few to start, and showed me how to weave them together to begin the bottom of the potato basket. "I must tell you, now most of these are for tourists. A few years ago they were for potatoes. Horses went down the rows and plowed up the potatoes. Tossed them up onto the surface. Our people would work alongside the French and the English-speaking people and pick potatoes into those baskets. They need to be beautiful for looking at, as well as strong, for potatoes." She tapped the strips tighter. I watched, storing the steps in my mind, so I would know when it was my turn. When she was finished with the bottom of the basket, she took a form and placed it on the woven strips. "Now all that is done by machinery. Big tractors with air-conditioning and radios. People never touch those potatoes. The baskets? Tourists." She tapped the mold firmly, and said, "Dwe-tik-nul, dwe-tik-nul."

"Tuwit, no, tu tuwihtik nol."

"Dwe-tik-nul, dwe-tik-nul."

"Dwe-tik-nul, dwe-tik-nul." I tapped the mold. "Dwe-tik-nul, dwe-tik-nul."

At the end of the hour, I had eight strips woven together to start the bottom of my potato basket. They were uneven and a little loose. I could see that. The next day they would be better. And they were better.

For the next few days we worked on cutting the splints and weaving the basket. We had lemonade every day, and I learned more words.

The last day there were no ash splints to cut and she showed me how to comb sweetgrass. Grandpa had gathered it for her, and it lay in piles on the floor around my chair when I arrived. The smell came not only from the piles but from a smoldering bowl on her basket table. Mrs. Francis sat on the floor and motioned for me to follow. Between us was a pile. "Sweetgrass is sacred. Let your lungs feel it," she said. "Your grandfather left this for you. It was your great grandmother's. I remember your father playing at her feet while she used this comb, collecting the fallen bits in his pocket. You will use it today to comb the sweetgrass." She placed the comb in my hand. I had seen it at Grandpa's, in the basket with the other tools. I never knew what it was used for. With my finger I traced the six wooden teeth and imagined Grandpa's mother using it, the family in the old photograph around her, the sweetgrass near her on the floor.

"Nuz-koo-whun, nuz-koo-whun." Mrs. Francis always said the hard ones twice. She held the sweetgrass up to her face. "Nuz-koo-whun," she whispered to the bundle, her old brown face caressing the grass. She held my hand with the comb and we began to stroke the grass its full length. Over and over, as the roots and other debris that didn't belong fell to the floor. She would stop and feel the grass and then begin again. A pile began to grow on the floor under our hands. She felt the bundle again. She held it out to me. "Silky and smooth. Let your face feel it." She brushed my face with the grass, and the gentleness made me feel faint.

"Nuz-koo-whun," I whispered.

"Yes."

The hour of work for Mrs. Francis went by in what seemed

minutes. My hands felt soft, like before I started working with the ash. When I brought them up to my face the smell filled me. I could barely pull myself away from the sweetgrass piles to work on my basket. I swept up the trash from the sweetgrass and put it in a grocery bag and went to the table. My potato basket was going to be for Grandpa, and it was almost done.

The weaving was almost finished and looked fairly even. I stepped back and squinted at the basket. The sides appeared straight. It wasn't perfect, but it was my first one. It was time to put the handle on. We had cut it with a draw knife out of white ash, and it lay on its side beside the basket, waiting. Grandpa was taking me back home the next day. I didn't want to cry about it, but it was sure hard not to. Mrs. Francis and I sat together, facing the basket, breathing, sipping lemonade, waiting. After the lemonade, we put the handle on and finished the potato basket. "Blue, I have things for you. You must continue with the baskets. Look over by the door."

I sat, looking around the room. I wasn't sure what she meant.

"Go, over there, look." She gestured to several shopping bags. Ash splints, sweetgrass braids, my great grandmother's likp-beh-wa-zar-gon, I sat down on the floor and began to empty the bags. A mold for the potato basket, one for a small work basket, new sweetgrass. I looked over to the table. Mrs. Francis sat, back to me, sipping and breathing and waiting. "You must take them home and practice until you can make a very very good basket. Better than mine." She still had her back to me.

I felt like crying again but began to put the things back in the bags. "Thank you," I said when I returned to the table. "I will practice. And when I see you again, my baskets will be almost as good as yours when you were my age."

She laughed. I had never seen her do that. She smiled a lot. But never laughed.

When Grandpa came for me, I said, "This is for you." I held the basket out.

"Thank you. I will always treasure it," was all he said. And I knew he would.

Mrs. Francis kissed my forehead and held my head close to her chest. I smelled the soap and the sweat and the sweet-grass, and I breathed in as big a breath as I could. She held me at arm's length and nodded. "New-gee-buz-new-da-ked, new-gee-buz-new-da-ked." I hadn't heard that before. "New-gee-buz-new-da-ked," she said again, as if that was all she was able to say. I knew there was no use asking her what it meant. She never told me the meaning of the words. Only hinted or gestured. This time she did neither.

Grandpa and I gathered up everything. I carried two bags, and Grandpa carried one bag and his basket. I could not imagine going home. Home to what? Well, Daddy, but he wasn't always really there. He was oblivious when he was behind the camera. All he knew was what he could see through the lens. Nothing else touched him. The trees could all fall down around him, and he would keep clicking. Mama and that guy? I shook my head so that the image would go away. I hadn't thought much about it the last few days, but now it was there, strong, vivid. I wondered if she gave him enough time to answer her questions. The several blocks back to Grandpa's usually seemed so short, but this time it took forever. We dragged all the bags into the kitchen. Grandpa wanted to just put them in the truck but I didn't want to leave them there all night.

"Lemonade?" he asked as he opened the fridge.

"Grandpa, what's new-gee-buz-new-da-ked? You know, what Mrs. Francis said before we left. Do you know?"

"Basket maker. It means basket maker."

He poured lemonade into two glasses, and we sat at the kitchen table, sipping.

Four of Blue's potato baskets — 1992, 1993, 1994, 1995.
My mother would be so proud.

CHAPTER 7

I buried the passion feather as soon as I got home from Grandpa's. Because I thought the feather might rot in the ground before I was ready to dig it up, I put it in a hand-carved pencil box that Brian's family brought back from the Far East as a present from Brian to me. I chose a place behind the pumpkins where we never planted anything because it was all clay. After the box was covered with earth, I mounded small stones over it so that I could find it later. I didn't tell anyone about it except for Berry and, of course, she couldn't tell anyone. Of course, it wasn't really a passion feather or even an eagle feather. Maybe a cattle egret or seagull or turkey. But it meant something to Grandpa and me.

I lugged all the basketmaking materials except for the likpbeh-wa-zar-gon to the shed. Great-grandmother's gauge I kept in my room in a basket of special things. My old Beautiful Blue eye patch that I wore before I got my artificial eye was there, along with hair ribbons from Maria and some blue sea glass that Grandpa found on the beach. I worked almost every day for the rest of that summer on the baskets and when I went back to Grandpa's in the fall, Mrs. Francis said that my baskets were as good as hers were at my age. She showed me how to braid and work with the sweetgrass and how to dye the grass and ash strips for decoration. Over the years my technique improved so much that basket makers at other reservations wanted to see them. I sold a few but gave most of them away as presents. Teachers, neighbors, Mama and Daddy, Brian's parents, and, of course, Grandpa, who now had rows and rows of "Blue's Baskets."

I would have given everything to have lived with Grandpa and gone to school with the other Passamaquoddy kids, but, of course, that wouldn't do. I wouldn't even have mentioned it. My next few years were filled with blueberries, baskets, avoiding Mama, trying to get Daddy to view me without the camera, and school. In my mind I was attached to Indian Beach by an elastic band. If nothing was holding me away, I bounced back to Grandpa's. But people and responsibilities pulled at me and kept the elastic taut.

I didn't seem to fit anywhere but Grandpa's and sometimes with Brian. I slunk around the house lifting up papers, opening drawers, looking under beds, thinking that whatever was missing might appear.

My baskets pleased Mrs. Francis more each year. Something was missing from them, too, but I thought it was all in the big missing package that I might soon find in a cupboard or a locker.

"Savage barbarian—fucking Injun." Lipstick on the inside of my locker. The afternoon after my presentation on basket-making and the Passamaquoddies for my history class. "I am part Passamaquoddy and make baskets in the traditional way," I had said to my classmates. I showed them a picture of my great-grandmother and brought in a small sweetgrass basket half-finished. My hands flew as I wove the braided grass around the vessel, proud that I could work fast and efficiently. "I did it, they were impressed," I thought as I pulled the locker door open. The red lipstick sprawled over the inside of the gray metal door and my little basket lay on the shelf, cut into pieces.

Daddy knew something was wrong when he saw me get off the bus at his construction site. I held the basket up. "Look, look," was all I could get out.

"It's easier to be white," he said after I told him about the words on the locker. "There were many kids from the reservation who went to high school in town, and there was a group there that hated that we were different. Even though my name was Willoughby and my skin was light, they knew." Daddy led me away from the men working on the house, back to the trees, where they couldn't hear me sobbing. I felt small that day, too small to shrug off the lipstick, too small to fix the basket, small enough for him to hold. "Grandpa went to school to confront the troublemakers, the ones who called us savages. It wasn't just the white kids; the Indian kids called the few that were mostly white half-breeds. We didn't really belong anywhere. Your grandpa cried in front of the principal and the next day there was a big assembly about prejudice. Grandpa talked about differences in people and how that made the world interesting, that we are all people, with the same feelings inside. I loved him for that. I could do that at your school," he said as he held my face close to him. "When I went away to college, I never told. They never knew about my background."

Daddy never did go to my school. I didn't want him to. Brian and I discussed the lipstick words and the cutting and how hurt I had been. They hated me for being Indian and they hated Brian for wearing glasses and being smart. I never took my baskets to school after that, but I didn't stop making them. I threw away the little sweetgrass basket with the cuts.

Mama told all her friends that we were Passamaquoddy. I heard her talking to a real-estate client, someone she hardly knew. "Oh, yes, Robert is part Indian. Blue has straight black hair, looks like her Grandpa." Sometimes I wished Mama's tongue would fall out, wished she would stop telling people things. She never listened. Just babbled out information that was either true or false, didn't matter which. Just went with the wind. Thought it was neat to have Indians in the family. Daddy told her about the lipstick. I heard them that night, up late, discussing. "Just ignore them," was all she said the next morning as she played with her amber beads. She had an appointment.

Mama and Daddy talked past each other, like they were each talking to different people who weren't even there. "Robert, put the camera away. If you hadn't had that damn camera at the movie set, well, it gets in the way, causes problems. Should we ask the Masons over for dinner?"

"Pretend you're watching the eagle flying over. No one will know that you're looking at nothing. Now, hold still."

"What do you think about Blue raking blueberries this summer? I have a client this afternoon. Someone to look at the Sutherland house."

"Did my pictures come in the mail today?"

Mama asked questions and answered someone else's. Nothing made sense. Nothing was what it was, and I no longer even pretended to understand their relationship. Mama wanted me because she didn't have anything else, but she would have preferred twins or a younger child. One of us didn't seem like enough. She had the empty womb syndrome, Daddy said. But her womb disappeared with Berry, down the hospital refuse chute, so she didn't even have a womb to be empty. It was like someone said to her, you can have Berry, Blue, or a working womb. She picked Blue. But she thought she made a mistake, and now it was too late. I wondered if she ever saw Berry in her mind, all grown-up, perfectly beautiful, how I would have been.

I raked blueberries for three summers in a row. It was a race, our lanes marked off with white string, kids, old people, Indians, Mexicans, stooped over with their rakes, sweeping through the plants, keeping within the string, making sideways glances into the next row, watching to see who needed a new bucket first. But I was outside, I could see the mountains, and it only lasted a few weeks. Money was good—better than a store job or working as a camp counselor for the whole summer. My day wasn't as long as some of the others because my limbs would protest. I worked past the pain for a while, but I knew it would be worse the next day if I didn't listen to my body. One foot then the other, crouched down, swinging the rake, dumping into the bucket. A certain rhythm developed like when I was learning to walk after the accident. Step, step, swish, swish, step, step, swish through the bushes, berries falling plump and blue into the bottom of the rake.

When I'd been out of the hospital a few weeks, Mama made me walk in my bare feet across the kitchen floor. She had placed old cereal boxes and bottles and junk mail here and there and the job was to maneuver to the other side of the room without touching one of them. Bob Dylan sang about blowin' in the wind or sometimes it was Peter, Paul and Mary harmonizing, lemon tree very pretty. Daddy taking pictures, Mama instructing.

"Pick up your feet dear, that's right, up and down and up and down. Now turn around and come back to Mama." I watched my toes, flapping down, curling under on the right side, splaying out on the left. Flap, 2, 3, 4, flap, 2, 3, 4, curl, 2, 3, 4, splay, 2, 3, 4. I could count pretty well by then, at least in my mind. I wouldn't have dared say the numbers out loud.

Left and step and right and step. Great, Blue, you're doing it now. Keep it up. Flap, 2, 3, 4, flap, 2, 3, 4, curl, 2, 3, 4, splay,

2, 3, 4, in my head, in my head. It seemed to me that the object of all this picture taking and stepping around obstacles was to get me in some condition to go on living. I certainly was never going to be the perfect little doll that I was before the accident, and I really didn't care. But they did. They cared.

The rhythm switched back to the blueberry field. My browned arm swung ahead of me. The bucket filling faster, berries, bouncing onto other berries, placing the full one on the side, picking up an empty bucket. The sweat trickled down my chest, soaking my tee shirt, cooling my body. Most of the others were ahead of me but I wasn't back with the children and old people. Just behind the Indians and Mexicans and other high-school kids. No talking on the barrens, no time for that, only weeks to get in the harvest before they dried up on the bushes or the frost turned them to mush.

If the blueberries were wet in the morning, there would be no raking. A friend of Brian's parents worked in the blueberry factory and got me a job sorting if the berries were too wet to rake. The berries were frozen and came down on a conveyer belt. We stood at the conveyer and picked out the green berries and rocks and anything that wasn't a ripe blueberry. The tips of my fingers numbed so that I couldn't feel the berries as I picked them up and dropped them in the reject pile. I tried to get a rhythm going, but sometimes there would be no green berries and sometimes my hands blurred in front of me. The berries would be made into canned pie filling after the raking season was finished. Daddy's pies were better.

Brian worked as a caretaker's helper for some rich summer folks, but we saw each other on weekends unless I went to Grandpa's, where I worked with Mrs. Francis. I didn't have any other close friends except some of the Indian Beach kids. Sometimes Daddy took me to a construction site. He was a contractor and designer, not just a carpenter. He designed houses that complemented the environment, like ours. He taught me how to board up and shingle walls so they wouldn't leak. "This is my daughter, Blue, and she's going to work with us," he would say to the other workers. I think he was proud that I, a mere girl, could master carpentry skills. He stood behind me, hammer in my hand, my hand in his, and swung the head onto the nail. "Let the hammer do the work. Let it fall onto the nail. That way, your arm won't get as tired." I learned to hit the nail home in just a few strokes. Some of the men still hammered with their arms and needed more strokes to finish the job. "Grandpa taught me when I was your age. Taught me to throw the head to the nail, let the head follow your arm, not be dragged behind it."

Daddy and I never talked about their marriage. I guess parents never tell their kids anything about their relationships. We need to be detectives, put the clues together. With Mama and Daddy it was easy. They slept in the same room, ate breakfast together, but talked to the air. I hadn't seen Simon around in ages, so I figured he was out of the picture. She never again picked those white roses from the field or even mentioned them. Brian thought my parents were great together. "They look like movie stars," Brian would say. Mama's hair was golden and always seemed to be blowing in the wind, even in the house. And Daddy, tall and stately, dark and bearded with a little distinguished gray, not Indian dark, just a little exotic. They held hands when they walked together, but it looked like they just needed to balance themselves, not that they needed to feel each other's skin. That day in the woods with Simon, she had wanted their skin touching, screamed for it. And she lied about the roses.

The summer before my senior year in high school, I was working on a large hamper at Mrs. Francis' basket shed. She sold some of my baskets along with hers. I began to see shapes in my mind, shapes made out of pounded ash, strange shapes with feathers and sea glass and shells. My weaving followed the shapes in my mind. My hands worked as if independent of the rest of me, tying glass to the top with sweetgrass, moving and shaping the basket, until its symmetry was long gone, its center of gravity shifted. Mrs. Francis came into the shed. I could feel her looking at the basket from behind me. My hands stopped and hung in the air. I knew she would not understand. I turned to face her.

"I've tried something new."

There was a longer than comfortable pause. "We Passamaquoddies have been making the same kind of basket for many years. This is not a traditional Passamaquoddy basket. But it has something. It's different. Are your baskets almost perfect?"

"Yes. Almost."

"Well, then, work a little harder. The time will come for this other thing. Now you must strive to make a perfect basket. You will know when you are ready." She turned gently and left the shed.

She was right. I was good. But I wasn't ready. I went back to potato baskets and hampers and sweetgrass sewing baskets and fish-scale baskets. They were sturdy, well made, beautiful, strong.

CHAPTER 8

✍

My senior year was so busy I had little time for the baskets. College applications and term papers took up most of my week-ends so that I didn't go to Grandpa's very much. I felt I had no time to learn anything. Mama decided to leave us for good that spring.

The air-talking had gotten worse during the year. I think Mama forgot what was true and what was fantasy. "If only we could have had more children," she would say to Daddy, as if I weren't quite good enough to be the only one. Perhaps if I hadn't had the accident. Maybe then she would be content with just me. She spent time brushing her hair. She said she wanted it to shine like gold.

The night before she left, she knocked on my door. I'd heard them talking about Mama getting her own place, but just hummings through the house about it, no real talk, no calling it what it was, light insinuations. I thought if I didn't answer the door, she would think I was asleep and go away. She knocked again. I knew it was Mama, not Daddy, because he always called along with the knock. Knock, "Blue," knock,

knock. But Mama just waited, knocked, waited. My term paper on early Maine poets was due the next day, and I was going over it for errors. I heard her on the other side of the door, shifting her weight, shuffling, touching the door. She wasn't going away.

"Come in." I sat at my desk, scanning the paper for errors, not really seeing anything at all. She stopped at my bureau for a moment and then made her way over to my chair. I sat, feeling her behind me, expecting questions, excuses, reasons for leaving, reasons why it wouldn't be too bad.

She started at the nape of my neck with the brush, slowly and more gently than I thought possible for her. "Blue," she said, taking another stroke with the brush, this time from higher up on my head. "I'm sorry about Daddy and me. I know this is hard for you, and you must be scared." She brushed down the length of my hair, and with the other hand, followed the brush, both hands in my hair. I didn't want to turn and face her because I thought that she was crying. My face flushed and my heart pounded too loud as I sat pretending to be reading my paper. "It's not you. It's us. Me and Daddy. Maybe with some time apart." She rested her hand on my shoulder and continued to brush with the other, starting at the very top of my head, drawing the brush deliberately and methodically down the length of my hair. "There's no one else. We still love each other in a funny sort of way. But it's not working." Continuing to read became impossible to even pretend but I sat still, looking at the page, feeling her hands on me, wanting to turn to her, knowing I couldn't. She must have felt the pounding in my chest. "Blue, I love you," she said, pulling aside my hair and kissing the back of my neck tentatively. She laid the brush down on my desk and stood behind me, breathing on the back of my head, waiting for something I couldn't give.

As she finally removed her hand from my shoulder to leave,

I wanted to turn to her, to touch her hand, to have her hold me, but my body stayed still, watching the words on my paper swim around on the page. Please, Mama, make me speak, make me show you my tears, I shouted inside my head. The heat of her hand spread on my skin. My mouth tightened as I waited to hear the door shut behind her and her muffled footsteps fade. Only then did I turn toward her. "I'm sorry, Mama; now you can be a dancer, travel, have a boyfriend, be free of us."

She wasn't going far, only to town, to an apartment attached to the back of an old Victorian house on Elm Street. She had a new job as the manager of an art gallery and was going to start school in the fall to finish up her degree in art history, which she'd abandoned when she became pregnant.

"Hold still and look at that tree over there," Daddy said from behind his camera and tripod. Daddy insisted on taking a picture of me and Mama saying good-bye.

Mama had her arm around my shoulders. It was her fault that they were splitting up. Daddy didn't want her to leave. "I love you," she murmured into my ear. She wasn't crying this time. She was always doing that, kissing me, whispering at me. I had to go to town and stay with her on weekends. She was probably going to see Simon again. Or maybe she had some new man. "Look, this isn't forever. Maybe just for a short while." She held my face in her hands and tried to make me look at her. Daddy was taking pictures. "Robert, please, stop." She looked toward Daddy, and he stood up behind the tripod, backing away from it. "I'll pick you up on Saturday morning. Ten o'clock?" She looked at me with her eyebrows raised and her azure eyes permeating my wall, waiting for me to answer. I knew she would wait and wait and wait for the answer to this one question. I hated her eyes.

"Fine, that's fine." I still didn't look up. She cupped my chin and raised it, and it was hard to avoid looking at her.

"Oh, my Beautiful Blue." She kissed my cheek and didn't comment on the tears. "Good-bye, Robert. Keep in touch. If Blue needs anything, call. The number is on the wall by the phone." Daddy walked over to us. No camera. He stood beside me and took my hand. She turned and walked toward her new little Honda. We could never be enough for her, but I wanted to be.

"Bye, Mattie," he called to her. Those were the only words he said. He put his arm around me and brought me close to him. He smelled like sawdust and photo chemicals, but I kept my face pressed into his shirt, close to his chest. We stayed like that for a long time, until I was still, quiet, dry.

"She isn't going far."

"I don't care where she goes."

"We're going to be fine here, you and I."

But I knew he wouldn't be fine. I watched his chin crumple under his beard. He pulled his hat off and threw it in the closet. It wasn't yet time for that. But Mama was gone. I wondered if the accident hadn't happened or if Berry hadn't died or if Mama had been able to have more children, would she have left him? I felt as if I were losing control of everything around me, and then I realized that I never really had it.

Suddenly I felt the need to put them together, the real Berry and the one in my mind. Perhaps Daddy would talk about it now when he was vulnerable, exposed. "Daddy, can we talk about Berry?" That was the first time I remembered asking about her. The times I had tried before, I felt Mama getting tense. Now Mama was gone.

"Yes, sure, we can. Come on," he said, as we walked into the house.

"Tell me about her. You saw her, didn't you?"

We sat in the kitchen, the best room for real talk. Daddy made some lemonade and put some mint leaves in it, and a straw.

"She was just like you, same size, same hair. But she didn't cry or stretch like you. You know about her, why she died?"

"Yeah, no brain. But was I with her? I mean, did I lie down beside her? Was she near me?"

"Mama insisted that you be together. Mama held you both in her arms, both together." Daddy took a long sip of his lemonade, perhaps to think about what he would say next. "Why do you want to know all this now?"

"Are you crying?"

"No, not really, well, it's still hard. It's hard to lose family. When Grandma died, we buried her on the reservation. Your grandpa sat at the grave through a whole day and a whole night and his pain hung over him like a large umbrella. The pain never really disappears, it shrinks over time, but it's always ready to resurrect itself. Toward evening, I sat with him there, no need for talk. The pain never goes away but there is some comfort, it brings the memories back. With Berry, there are no memories. You never really get over something like this."

"But I thought unless you know someone, you can't feel bad. You know, like on TV if someone dies and they have it on the news, I don't know them and I feel a little bad but not real bad." I knew I was rambling, but I couldn't stop, for fear there would be silence. I wrapped my legs around the chair. "Sometimes I think I can remember her. Do you think I could remember her?"

"I don't know, honey." He touched my arm lightly and took another sip of his lemonade. "What do you think you remember?"

"Just something. A baby. What happened, I mean, did she just starve or stop breathing or what?"

"They just told us that she wouldn't live, just a matter of days. I don't know exactly why she died. She was so lovely. Beautiful Berry—like you. You could hardly tell the difference. Two beautiful little baby girls. But she didn't really have a chance. They told us she would die. It was a matter of waiting."

I looked at him, at his salt-and-pepper beard, at the lines in his face. His face was pained. He loved me, but I could see it was too much for him. The image of his face just before the accident loomed up into my consciousness. Behind the camera, waving at the director to leave him alone, watching me say my lines and Mama yelling at him to step back. That's the last thing I remember before I woke up in the hospital. I know he thought it was his fault. "I'm sorry," he would say, over and over at the strangest times. Since then he had retreated farther back into his camera. But we all needed a filter. He had his camera, and I had Berry. I took a chance.

"I see her sometimes. Sometimes I talk to her."

"I know, sometimes I remember her lying there, so inert, so lovely, so like you, but unlike you. She was umm, tiny."

I wanted to say, "No, I mean, she's big, like me, my size, and she has no brain," but I didn't. He would think I had gone insane. And his life would be finished. No Mama, Blue gone bonkers. Berry dead. "I miss her. I read about twins. They say one twin can feel the presence of the other twin. Do you have a picture of her? You must have taken pictures of her."

"I took a picture of you. Mama didn't want a picture of the other one."

"Berry, her name is Berry."

"Yes, Berry. Blue and Berry. She said if you were girls you should be named Blue and Berry—for the blueberry fields.

She went into labor in a field, raking. When we thought we were having just one baby, she wanted to name her Blueberry. Your mother thought the names would be unusual, fun. That was a time of girls named Rainbow and Salmon, and Karma. No, no picture of Berry. And besides, it was after you were born that I really got into photography again. I used to do a lot in school but then I met your mother and had you and that gave me something to take pictures of."

"Do you think the hospital would have taken a picture? Or the funeral home people? Did she have a funeral?"

"We had a very small private service."

"Was she in a box? Was it open? Did people look at her?"

"No one saw her. The box was closed. Mama and I wanted it that way."

"Was I there?"

"No, you stayed with Grandpa. Your mother and I went and a few friends and Aunt Marcia. She's buried at the little cemetery on the road to Brian's house. I guess we have never taken you down there. Mama and I go sometimes. We bring flowers on your birthday."

I swallowed hard. On my birthday? And I didn't know? Buried where I could see every time I went to Brian's? I couldn't speak, but I didn't want the talk to end. I got up and went to the fridge to get the lemonade. I poured some in my glass and my hand began to shake. I gripped it with the other hand and hoped he wasn't watching. He was. I poured him some, too.

"It's good to cry." His voice trembled. I was scared. They had gone to visit the grave without me on my own birthday. I didn't even know where it was. I thought I knew everything. I even knew about Mama and Simon. I had seen them. I knew when Mama and Daddy had an argument. I used to listen, to sneak to their door and put my ear on the thin part. I think I even heard them having sex a few times. But, this, I hadn't known about. Why didn't I ever think about it? Why didn't I ask where she was buried? Did I think they just tossed her away in the hospital garbage disposal like they did with my eye? Why didn't they tell me?

"Can we go there?"

"What?"

"Can we go there, to Berry's grave?"

"Oh, well, I suppose we could. Maybe we should check with your mother."

"I want to go there."

There was a long pause. I guessed that Daddy was thinking about it. He probably thought he would betray Mama if he took me alone, and that would be a scary step for him to take.

"Daddy, I want to go there. Please."

"Perhaps Mama would like to go with us. We could call her tomorrow."

"I'll go there myself and look at every stone and find it."

The cemetery was about two miles from our house. Brian and I had ridden our bikes along the cemetery paths for picnics, and once we crept in on Halloween night with flashlights, looking for vampires. We pulled up to the gate and parked on the grass by the side of the road. It was an old cemetery, stones lined the walkway, stones that had worn almost flat and bore only traces of names and dates and relationships. I walked behind my father like I used to do with Grandpa, before I saw the deer. The gravel made noise under our feet, but we walked slowly, like we were in church or in the hospital. We walked through the middle of the cemetery, toward the pond that I knew was on the other side. Some of the stones had been toppled and lay facedown so that the inscriptions were hidden. There was one large shiny granite stone with fresh flower arrangements and a newly turned mound in front. A body was down there, whole, with skin and hair and nails, probably still growing. I must have stopped there, for Daddy turned around and called to me. He waited while I caught up, held his hand out for me to take. I knew we must be near because we were almost to the far gate. There she was. I could feel Daddy's hand tense, and I stopped. In front of the gate was a small white stone level with the ground.

"There. She's there." He pointed to the stone.

I let go of his hand and knelt down to see what it said.

"Berry Willoughby, Daughter of Martha and Robert Willoughby, sister of Blue Willoughby," it read. "August 17, 1979–August 22, 1979."

Around the stone were purple and blue pansies newly planted, in full bloom, not a weed in sight. Someone had planted them. She was down there. In the ground. Now only little bones. Tiny bones like chicken's bones. She had only been the size of a chicken when she died. I wanted to dig her up. To look at her. To see what she wore, what they put on her, what her bones looked like, her head. To see if I could tell that she had no brain from her skull. My finger scratched at the dirt beside the stone, in amongst the pansies. She was my sister. My twin sister. Part of myself.

"Your mother must have been here. The pansies." Daddy walked behind a nearby tree and sat down under it. He knew I wanted to be alone. He didn't even bring his camera.

"Berry. It's Blue."

There was no answer.

"Berry."

She was there, beside her own stone. Big, grown-up. Her head lolled to the side. But she knew I was there.

"Berry, see. I've come. I've come."

I fell on her and held her and cried. Daddy sat under the tree, waiting for my grief to come out. My body crushed the pansies as the image of Berry slowly disappeared into the soil. My hand scratched where the pansies had been. Dug and scratched by the stone and the sobs grew farther apart until I was too exhausted to continue. My head pressed onto the cold hard stone, pressing my face into her name, and I knew I remembered her. I had touched her for nine months, lain with her, moved with her, was nourished from the same placenta, was born the same day. She was part of me.

I led the way out that day. Daddy knew I would go back alone, but we didn't speak of it.

Beautiful Blue with that nice young man on prom night.
Mattie pinning on the orchid.
June 1996

CHAPTER 9

I returned to the cemetery alone almost every day. Daddy knew, I think, but never let on. I could tell he was worried because he kept looking at me when he thought I wasn't looking at him. I was sure that he didn't tell Mama because she would have "had a talk." One of those sit down and be very serious talks that I hated because they were so full of crap. I usually packed a snack and went over on my bike after school. Brian wanted to know where I was going, but I wasn't ready to tell anyone else.

We were still close friends. No funny stuff since that day in the woods, the day I went to Grandpa's. Brian received a full scholarship to MIT, in Boston, to study mathematics, and I was going to Brown with my accident money. What was left of the settlement after lawyers took their share and we paid for the house and all my medical bills was just enough for my first two years at Brown. I figured I'd get some disability grants or, even better, an academic scholarship for the last two. Surely a person with only one eye, a deformed arm, and a gimpy leg should qualify for something. I wasn't sure I really wanted to go to college, but all the kids I knew were going and what else would I do? Grandpa wanted me to stay on the reservation with him. He'd done everything. He could teach me about passion and history and brown ash. He said he'd teach me the ways of the woods, and that would be better than any fancy education. That appealed to me, but of course Mama would think I was wasting my life. She always said that one of the biggest disappointments in her life was that she didn't finish college.

I didn't stay a long time at the cemetery. I sat quietly by the stone and ate my lunch. The caretaker got used to seeing me there and started making conversation with me.

"Hi there, deah. Good day for it." He scuttled from grave to grave, clipping grass and pulling weeds. I think he was a little off because he talked in a high singsong voice and made some very unusual faces, but he became part of the whole scene. The grass beside the stone was beginning to wear, so I switched to the other side. I wasn't sure if Mama knew I was coming, but I didn't want to leave any telltale signs. The pansies that I crushed that first day I came with Daddy had been replaced with new ones. Mama. Must have been. So I made sure to come only when I knew she was at work. I saw her most weekends, and it was tolerable, but I certainly didn't want her to catch me here. She never mentioned Berry and that she planted pansies at her grave, and neither did I. Most of what I knew about Berry came from Daddy, and that wasn't much. Grandpa would talk if I asked him, but he didn't know anything. He said it was one of those things that you knew you shouldn't ask about. An empty space surrounded Berry's stone, as if a whole plot of land was bought. I wondered if we would someday be there, next to her.

Berry didn't come to the cemetery after that first day, and I didn't call her. It was my time with the baby, the real Berry that died, not the Berry that kept growing, big, stupid, beautiful. Perhaps it was time to give up the imaginary Berry. I was almost eighteen and that meant almost adult. Old enough to vote, old enough to have sex. Old enough to get rid of imaginary people and dolls and teddy bears.

I had no time for baskets. I felt like I was working on an assembly line that was moving too fast for me to keep up with. Once Brian and I saw an old *I Love Lucy* show and Lucy was working in a factory putting twenty-five pills in each bottle. She put twenty-five in the first and twenty-five in the second and ten in the third and then just started throwing pills at the rest of the bottles.

We crammed for final exams, churned out papers, reports, term papers, arranged for records to be sent to Brown, planned for graduation, rehearsals, arrangements for the prom. Everyone was going to the prom. I thought I'd go with Brian. I mean, we were best friends. I was the only one who knew about the frogs and that he came in his pants that day. He was the only one who'd seen me take my glass eye out. He didn't know about the Berry in my mind or in the cemetery, but I planned to tell him.

Brian asked another girl. "Blue, I'm taking Sylvia Marshall to the prom. Who're you going with?" He said it just like that. Like he was saying it was raining or that his birthday was next month. We were walking home from school and he just came out and said it. "Blue, I'm taking Sylvia Marshall to the prom." Just like that. I wanted to turn to him and let him see how hurt I was. I wanted to say, "Please take me. We're best friends. You have to take me. No one else will take me." But, no, I just trudged along, dragging my leg a bit, shrugging my shoulders.

"I dunno. Dunno if I'll go." He was on my eyeless side,

which made things a little easier. "Couple guys asked me. Haven't decided yet."

I wasn't too bad to look at. The scars on my face had dimmed with the years and were hardly noticeable, and I always wore long skirts or pants and long sleeves to school to cover the scars on my arm and leg. A lot of kids didn't even know about the glass eye, and if I thought about it, I could walk without any limp at all. I scared off some of the guys with my good marks, but a few of them respected me, what I could do. I didn't jump in the sack like some of the more popular girls. No one asked, and the idea didn't really excite me much. After that day in the woods with Brian, he tried to make out with me. I kissed him a couple of times, but I don't think either of us enjoyed it much. I always had some excuse for leaving suddenly. That's probably why he was taking Sylvia to the prom. God. Sylvia. She was so stuck-up. What did she see in Brian? His apricot hair stuck up all over his head, his ears were still big and he didn't play sports.

"Who's coming to graduation from your family?" Brian asked. "My grandparents are coming from Chicago and remember those friends of my parents, the Fishmans, they're coming from outside of Boston. Your grandpa is coming right? And your aunt Marcia? Anyone else?"

I didn't want to talk because he would know I was upset about the prom. Or at least he would know I was upset.

Brian didn't really care that I didn't answer. I don't think he even noticed. I thought about the day I took his hand when he was crying about the frog. "Did you get your dorm assignment yet? How many roommates?"

"I dunno."

"I'm rooming with a guy from California. Another math major. It's a coed dorm, girls just down the hall. How about yours? My mother had a bird. Girls on the same floor. You're dragging a bit. You want me to carry one of your bags?" He stopped and grabbed my knapsack from my shoulder. "Jeeze, this sucker is heavy. What've you got in here?" He finally looked at me, at my face. "Hey, what's going on? What's the problem?"

I turned and looked at him. "Whaaaaaaa." Really. It sounded just like that. "Whaaaaaa." He was usually the crier, I was usually the hand holder. He looked scared. "Whaaaaaa." He couldn't reach out to me with a knapsack on each arm. Just stood there, looking scared. "Nothing, just so much work," I inhaled sharply. "Everything is confusing, the prom, graduation, Brown. Everything. I'm OK." I sniffled and wiped my face on my shirtsleeve.

"God, Blue, that's gross."

"Let's go."

We walked the rest of the way in silence. Brian stopped his rambling, and I stopped my crying. I couldn't believe he was taking Sylvia to the prom. Who was I going to go with?

The next day was my English final. I knew the questions would center on *King Lear* so I took the bus. That way I could go over my notes before the exam. The only seat left was next to Darrel Rayburn. He was OK. A jock. Went out with a cheerleader. He was in my English class and struggling with it. I slid into the seat next to him near the back of the bus. He smelled like aftershave. I wished my eye was on his side. I couldn't see him unless I turned all the way around.

"Hi," he said.

"Hi, ready for the exam?"

"I'll never pass this one. Stupid play about an old crazy guy. Can't even keep the daughters straight."

"You want to go over notes with me?"

"I guess it can't hurt."

"Can we switch sides? Make it easier."

He never asked why it would be easier, we just switched.

"You should be thinking about the subplot as it goes along with the main plot of Lear and the daughters. You can learn almost as much from the subplot as from the main one. Let's go over that." I opened my notebook.

"Blue," he said. I stopped and looked up. "Have you got a date for the prom? I know it's kind of late, but I don't have a date and thought you might not either."

"What happened to your girlfriend, Jennifer?"

"Jennifer? She's history."

I told him yes. That I hadn't really wanted to go but, well, maybe it wouldn't be so bad. He wrote my number on the back of his hand so we could make plans. I would get a new dress and look really good. I thought about Mama and the times she put my hair in rags to curl it. About Maria fixing my dress, combing my hair, putting on my makeup. I ambled home from school alone that day, thinking about Mama and the ripping of rags. She had combed out my hair with some curl-set stuff. I remember the smell. It was green and very sticky. I stood in front of Mama, naked and dripping from the bath. She rolled curls too tight and some of the hairs pulled. The next day Maria had eased the pinched parts of my scalp, released the tight hairs that pulled. I'm not sure how she knew which ones were too tight, but maybe her mother did the same to her when she was little. I wished I knew where Maria was.

"I guess I'm going to the prom after all," I said, throwing my books on the kitchen table. Daddy was drawing plans at his desk for a new house for some summer people. "This guy, Darrel, asked me and, well, I might as well go. Maybe we can go to Bangor this weekend. See if I can find a dress. Doesn't have to be anything fancy. I only have a week, not long enough to make one."

Darrel was picking me up at six o'clock for dinner at the Inverness Inn before the prom. A bunch of us were going, really fancy, expensive. Afterward we were all going to Randy's summer cottage to spend the night. The parents were trying to keep us off the roads. Darrel said Randy's folks would be there, but out of sight, just in case there was some kind of trouble. Brian and Sylvia weren't in that group, and I really didn't know what they were doing.

The morning of the prom, I washed my hair and tore up an old sheet from the rag box in the shed. An old Winnie-the-Pooh sheet that Aunt Marcia gave me when I was little and I kept it on my bed until it had so many holes my feet would get stuck in them at night and wake me up. I shredded the pieces into strips about two inches wide and a foot and a half long, lots of them. My hair was so black and thick and straight I wondered if it would even curl, and then I remembered the ringlets I had in the movie. Maria twirling them around her finger, murmuring things in Spanish that made me feel safe.

The large jar of green goo that I'd bought sat on the table next to the Winnie-the-Pooh rags. I started at the top, at the part. I combed the section and put the goo along the length of the strand. The smell. I remembered it. I rolled the strand up in the rag until it reached my head. I eased it back a little before I tied the rag. I remembered how it was back then, when Mama tied them too tight. It took me a long time to do all of my hair. When I was finished I sat looking at myself. I could hardly tell which eye was glass and which was real. Well, of course, I knew, but what if I didn't know? My tee shirt was wet with water and curling goo, but I couldn't take it off over my head because of the rags, so I threw a sweater over my shoulders and grabbed a book. No more *King Lear* or *Ship of Fools* or *Anna Karenina* for this year. I was reading trash, freezing to death with rags all over my head.

After an hour, I tried one of the curls. Soaking wet. It fell right out, straight, no curl. I rolled it up again and went out to Daddy's shop, looking for an old hair dryer that he used to dry glue and paint, one of those old-fashioned things with the big nozzle. I tiptoed back inside so Daddy wouldn't see me in the rags and plugged the dryer into my wall socket. It whirred and started to blow hot air at me from its perch on the table and began to move on its own, back and forth, like a toy snake. I snatched it up and dried my hair with one hand while I held my trashy novel in the other, occasionally switching sides so that I could dry my whole head. I unrolled a swatch of hair three times before it was dry and I could unwind the rags. The curls made me look like a little girl, especially when I twirled them around my index finger and they formed into ringlets. I wound them all into ringlets and flicked them so that they wiggled like a coiled spring. "Maria," I said aloud, watching myself in the mirror. I pulled my tee shirt off and threw it on the floor with the rest of my dirty laundry. The curls needed readjusting again, each one. "Maria," I said again. She had done that, made those ringlets move like little springs, as if they were alive. My nipples were hard. I was still chilled from the goo and my wet hair dripping on my shoulders. I watched in the mirror as I gripped my right nipple between my fingers. Then my other hand went to my left one. My fingers moved making them hurt a little, making them stand up. I wanted to make love to myself, but I wasn't sure how to do it. I had masturbated some, but I didn't mean that. I wanted to feel like I did with Maria, I wanted someone to whisper to me, to caress me. Not like Brian or the few other dates I had. But maybe Darrel. I thought he must really like me to ask me to the prom.

He was ten minutes late. Mama had come over to see me in my new dress. It was purple silk. The material clung to my body, and I could feel that Mama and Daddy were a little nervous about that. Good. She was fussing with the dress and my hair. She insisted that I wear just a little lipstick. "They will all have it on," she said. Even though I had never seen her wear any. I think she bought it just for me, just for tonight. I had brushed my hair for a long time, so that it no longer fell into ringlets, but waves, thick black waves. Mama gave me her diamond necklace to wear, and the diamond fell just into my slight cleavage. Daddy was behind his camera, shooting wildly. He had taken a whole roll and was putting in his roll of black-and-white when Darrel knocked at the door.

He wore a dark blue tux. Didn't go with my dress. Mama had opened the door and Darrel stood with his hands behind his back as he walked into the house. I could smell that aftershave again, and he had developed a few pimples on his chin, but Daddy thought he looked great. Daddy clicked and clicked before he even introduced himself.

"Hi," I said.

"Hi," Darrel said. In one hand was a box from the florist. "My mother said I should pin this on you."

He came toward me with a purple orchid that just matched my dress. Daddy had moved his camera around so that he was taking pictures facing me. Darrel's hands were cold as he tried to maneuver the pin through the orchid and my dress. I tried to smile for Daddy, but it was taking a very long time.

"Look, I really can't do this," Darrel finally admitted. He stood holding the flower, looking around for help.

Mama stepped forward out of the shadows and took the orchid from his hands. "Here, dear, let's put it on this side." She knew I could see it better on the right.

Daddy hugged me tighter than usual. "My little girl," he whispered, so that Darrel wouldn't hear. I think he was scared.

After the dance we all piled into Darrel's mother's car and took off for the summer cottage. Someone passed around a bottle in a brown paper bag. I don't know what kind of liquor it was, but I knew we were supposed to drink after the prom. Mama and Daddy gave me wine and beer sometimes, but this was like fire. The booze wanted to come back up, but I swallowed and kept it right there, didn't allow it to go any farther. I had seen Brian at the dance. And Sylvia. We hardly spoke.

There were no other cars parked in the lot when we arrived and the lights were all out. After all the dancing, my leg hurt on the short walk to the cottage from the car, but Darrel held my arm. This group of kids was the popular group, the group the other kids looked up to and talked about and aspired to become. I hadn't ever gone out with them but they all knew me. They came to me for help before an exam, and some tried to copy from my paper, which I usually let them do. I hoped Brian saw what a good time I was having. He and Sylvia danced by us a lot and I caught him looking at me a few times. I know the other kids thought Brian was weird.

Darrel fumbled with the switch after he got the door opened and illuminated a moose head with antlers big as small trees. No parents, no other kids, just Darrel and me and two other couples. The guys started a fire in the stone fireplace with wood already laid. I could have started it faster but didn't offer to. It was a cool evening but not really cold enough for a fire. Mama had loaned me her hand-knit silk shawl, so I pulled it around my shoulders and went up to the fireplace. Darrel was blowing into the small flame as I knelt beside him and pressed up against his back.

The other guys and their dates, Molly and Barbara, melted into the darkness, and occasionally I could hear a laugh. Darrel turned his head and gently kissed my neck, murmuring that I smelled good. I snuggled down on a pillow next to Darrel as he played with the fire. We touched each other in innocent ways and whispered words like, "great dance," and "you look good in the tux," and "your dress feels so soft." He turned toward me and kissed my mouth lightly, both corners, then full in the middle. His mouth pulled my lower lip into itself as his hands cupped my head.

"Wow," he said when he finally pulled back. I could tell he wanted me. His head turned so that his profile stood out against the yellow-orange of the struggling fire. He was much better-looking than Brian. Even had a small mustache. My silk dress hugged my skin, and I knew in the firelight that I looked like a woman. He turned and placed his hand on my thigh, over the purple silk, and I could see it in his eyes. He was glad he'd asked me to come to the prom.

"Wow, baby, have some of this." He held out the brown paper bag, and I drank the last little drop. It seemed to go down a little easier this time. "There's all kinds of booze over there," he said. "You wanna get me a glass of the whiskey with a little ginger ale in it? And bring those chips over here." Brian never told me to wait on him, but Darrel was Darrel. He was used to girls doing things for him. Randy's parents must have set up the table because it had a tablecloth and napkins with real glasses and an ice bucket. I lit the candles and poured Darrel his drink. I poured one for myself, too, weaker than his. It was better with the ginger ale in it. Someone put music on, not the usual fast electric stuff, but old songs, Willie Nelson I think, singing "Stardust." I sipped on my drink as I brought Darrel his. The flames covered the logs now and Darrel watched it intently. He took his drink from me and said, "Thanks, Beautiful Blue." I wondered how he knew. The lights from the fire flickered on his face, and the others seemed to have vanished. Darrel threw some overstuffed pillows on the floor and patted them gently. "Sit down here. I'll be right back." He went over to the table and got the whiskey bottle, no ginger ale. He held the bottle in the air as he sauntered back to me, singing along with Willie.

I really felt beautiful. I looked down at my dress, how it

clung to my body. Even Mama's shawl felt silky on my shoulders. My hair still bounced with a few curls. I pushed my shoes off and snuggled into the pillows. Darrel hovered over me, pouring more whiskey into my glass. It tasted better this time, went down smooth. He knelt onto the pillows and put his arm around me and brought me to him. I could tell from the way he held me that he really liked me, thought I was pretty. Willie singing "Stardust" came out of the tape player again. The music going around and around. I leaned my head on Darrel's chest, against his shirt. The aftershave was everywhere on him. I sipped my drink. I didn't really like it, but it felt warm going down, warmed me all the way down my throat.

"Where did everybody go?" I didn't really care, but I needed to say something.

"Dunno. The other rooms, I think. Come here, get comfortable." He filled my glass again.

He pulled me to him and kissed my hair. I swung my leg over his. He removed my shawl and touched my shoulders with his tongue. Little licks. He smelled like whiskey, but so did I. We put our whiskey mouths together and groped with our tongues. His hand pulled my dress up, searching between my legs. I helped him pull it over my head.

"Oh, baby,"

I fumbled for him, in his pants. He unzipped them for me, and I placed my hand there, on him. This was the prom, and there was Willie and "Stardust" all over again. As Darrel rolled over on top of me he started to pump. Up and down. His pants weren't even down. Not even in me.

"Shit," he said. I could feel the wet on my leg.

Not again, I thought.

He pumped a few times and collapsed on me. We slept, I guess it was sleep. I kept waking up a little, hearing Willie singing old tunes, feeling Darrel on me, thinking I was going to throw up. Everything swooned around me. I wondered if he re-ally liked me, if he thought I was beautiful, if he knew about my eye, if I would excite him when he was sober, if he would speak to me next week.

He woke me up in the night coming back into the room with a blanket. He settled down with me again and poured each of us some more whiskey. In a moment I was under him again and we were pulling off our underwear.

"Come on, you want it. Come on, baby." His mouth was on my neck, and I could smell the whiskey.

"Yes, I want it." I wondered if Brian and Sylvia were doing this. I wished Maria could have seen me all dressed up. I thought of Mama there in the woods with Simon. Darrel's hand fumbled with his erection. It pushed against me and my legs opened for him. His fingers slid into me and then back to him-self. His tongue sucked at my earlobe and I said, "Oh, Darrel," because it felt good and because I knew I should. I pushed my opened pelvis on him—toward his moving fingers. "Now," I said. It was wet down there, ready for him. The tip was against me. I felt his hand guiding it. My legs pulled him into me. The pain ripped through me for a moment, but he wanted me. This was it. The passion Grandpa talked about. I squeezed my legs around him again and pulled him close. It was prom night and the cutest guy in school was on top of me. I had a hard time fo-cusing on anything. Darrel was pushing and pulling, pushing and pulling inside me.

"Hey, we're doing it. I knew you would like it." His voice was too loud, loud enough for the others to hear if they were lis-tening. Darrel went up and down on me and Willie was still singing. He moaned and collapsed on me again.

"Nobody can say I didn't get laid on prom night," Darrel said. He smiled. I couldn't look away even though I tried. I knew that tears were running down my face. "Hey, which eye is glass? Do tears come out of glass eyes?"

Darrel pulled out slowly, pulling the blanket away from me. "Let's see how old Jennifer likes this," he said to no one in particular. I wanted to reach for the blanket but couldn't move. He looked down at me. "You weren't bad, baby. Let's do it again sometime." He bent down and kissed my cheek. I lay on the floor, naked, spread open, and it was prom night.

CHAPTER 10

I think Darrel drove me home alone. I only remember bits and pieces. "Oh, come on, don't whine, you wanted it. You had a good time, didn't you?" and "Don't worry about the guys. They probably didn't hear anything. Lighten up. Anyway, everybody does it."

It was almost daylight when we pulled up into our driveway. I fixed myself up enough so that Daddy wouldn't notice anything. The little bit of blood on my dress wouldn't show up in this light. "Hey, Baby, you look beautiful." His hand rested on my thigh. "Maybe we can see a movie sometime. I'll call you." I looked over at him. He kissed the air and lit up a cigarette. He idled the car just long enough for me to get out and shut the door behind me, then peeled out of the driveway. A note lay on the kitchen table. "Hi, honey, hope you had a wonderful time. You looked so beautiful, my Beautiful Blue, see you when you wake up. Love, Daddy." I picked up the note and took it with me. I think he must have been still sleeping as I tiptoed by his bedroom door to my room.

I opened my door, went in, and shut it behind me. It was

private here, my dolls, my basket tools, my rags on the dressing table, the rags from my Winnie-the-Pooh sheet. I picked up the torn rags and looked into the mirror. My Indian hair was straight, stuck to my face. I wanted Maria to hold me, to curl my black hair around her finger, to call me exotic Spanish names. I unzipped my dress and let it drop to the floor. I had nothing on under it. I guess my underwear was still at the house. I could smell whiskey, Old Spice, sex. My thighs were sticky with it. The worst part was that I liked it. I mean, it was OK. It was exciting. I needed a shower but didn't want to wake Daddy.

I clutched some shorts and a tee shirt in my hands and went quietly down to the bathroom. I remembered the woods and how quiet I could be so the deer wouldn't hear me. The shower was hot and I turned it up even hotter. My stink was hard to wash off even though I scrubbed. The smell of the Old Spice was all over my neck and in my hair and I had to wash it over and over and still there was a trace of it. The smell of sex, the blood, it stank like wallpaper paste, like my period, like the time Brian's dog had puppies. The water started to turn cold so I turned it off, still not clean.

Back in my room the stink hung in the air. Not powerful, just hanging there, permeating, incessant. I looked better. I burned a piece of sweetgrass in the smudge pot. That helped. The prom dress lay in a heap on the floor with the small blood spot standing out against the purple silk. I threw it into a plastic bag. The sun was rising. I could see the mountains, The Bubbles looking purple in the early-morning light, like my dress.

In the privacy of my bed I asked Berry to come. She appeared right away, and I kept her under the covers. I was too old for this. Berry wasn't real, but I would tell her soon not to come anymore. "He really did like me. He said I was beautiful."

I knew my words were hollow. Berry lay there, under my blanket, naked, alongside my body. Hers was perfect, no scars, no stink. "Do you think Brian and Sylvia did it?" Berry didn't respond. I snuggled as close to Berry as I could without making her disappear. "What about those other girls? Barbara and Molly. Do they think I'm pretty? Did they hear us? Could they hear me saying I wanted it? What the hell did I want?" I thought I could see a flicker in Berry, like she was trying to answer, but then her head lolled to the other side. "I could pretend nothing happened and hope they don't tell. How would that be? I could tell Daddy. Ask him what to do. I certainly wouldn't tell Mama. Grandpa would say, 'Come live with me on the reservation and I'll show you the ways of the old ones, of the woods.' And Brian. He wouldn't care. He had Sylvia. I don't have any other close friends." I heard myself talking as if I were in another room, another place, my voice bouncing around on the walls before hitting the blanket and coming to me all muffled.

Mama would say that I had sex for the wrong reasons. She always said that you should have sex when you're ready and responsible. I wasn't either of those. She would want to talk about it, discuss everything, ask me if I loved Darrel.

I pulled my knees up as far as I could without disturbing Berry and put the covers up around us. "Berry," I said, wiggling around to get comfortable, "I didn't really feel anything that great. Where were the fireworks?" I felt sore inside as if something foreign were still up there, pushing at me. I felt all open, exposed, full. I put my arm around Berry to get closer to her and she disappeared, melted into the bed like I knew she would. Hiawatha was there, too, so I pulled her to me. Just as I fell asleep I remembered that I was too old for dolls and imaginary people.

I woke to Daddy knocking on my bedroom door. "Your mother's here. She's dying to hear about the prom." He knocked again, this time a little louder. "Are you awake?" I could hear the door open and their footsteps coming into the room. Both of them waited for me to wake up. I didn't want them to pull the blankets off, so I groaned a little and pulled the blanket down myself, just enough so they could see me. Daddy had his hat on, and it was summer.

"Smells funny in here." That was Mama. She would notice. "If you're awake enough, come on down and have some tea with your old mum and tell me all about it. Daddy made sticky buns for brunch," she said as if she lived here. "It's almost eleven-thirty." She bent down and kissed me and I held my head still for it. Her amber beads brushed my face.

"I'll be down in a few minutes," I said after she stood up. I didn't want her to smell the whiskey stink in my mouth.

"I'll put the tea on. We'll wait in the kitchen."

I pulled the blanket up over my head again as they turned to go.

"Look, is that her dress rolled up in the bag?" I heard the bag crinkle as she lifted it up.

"Please leave it. I spilled some food on it. I'll wash it. Leave it," I lifted the covers off my face so my voice would go out into the room. My heartbeat sounded muffled under the blanket, too, muffled, but very loud.

I heard her drop the bag, and they left, shutting the door quietly behind them. God, he didn't even know about her and Simon. There were probably others that I didn't even know about. He thought she left because she wanted a change in her life. Right, change in her life. And now I had to go down for brunch and have sticky buns and tell them both what a wonderful time I had at the prom and all about Darrel and how much he liked me and how nice he was and how gracious Randy's parents were and hope to God that Darrel wouldn't tell everyone. Now the secrets were about me.

A week later, I won the English prize at graduation and Brian was the valedictorian. Grandpa and Aunt Marcia clapped very loudly when my name was called. Randy and David shouted, "There she is, Beautiful Blue," and sang "Did you have fun on prom night?" as they went by after the ceremony. Darrel blew me a kiss and headed our way.

He ambled over to our family group and kissed me on the cheek. "Congratulations on the English prize." I could smell his aftershave. "Hi, Mr. and Mrs. Willoughby, you must be so proud of your lovely daughter." He smiled at them. "And you must be Grandpa. And Aunt Maria." He shook their hands. "So wonderful to meet you. I took Blue to the prom. She told me all about you. She's quite a girl." And he winked at me and squeezed my arm.

"Come on, Darrel," David said. Darrel turned and sauntered back to his friends.

"What a nice boy," Grandpa said. "Seems to like you quite a lot."

"Everyone line up. I'll take the first few of all of us together," Daddy said. "I should've taken one of Blue and Darrel alone. Oh, well, go over by that tree and look natural. I'll set the timer."

Daddy clicked away, moving the tripod or us after two or three pictures. He gestured for Grandpa to come and take some pictures. Grandpa stood behind the camera with Daddy behind him, guiding his hands, talking softly about how the camera worked. I wondered then if Grandpa said the same things to Daddy when they went for walks in the woods when he was a boy. They were so close together. I wanted them to hug, to touch each other's faces. Grandpa took pictures of

Mama, Daddy, and me, looking as if she hadn't left and wasn't living in the apartment, as if they were still in love and living together.

"Mum would have been so proud to see this," Daddy said to Grandpa. He turned to me. "Your grandmother used to talk to you in the language when you were a baby about what you would be, a singer of songs, a weaver of baskets. She was right. She would have been proud."

"Oh, there's Brian." Mama waved over to Brian, who wasn't with Sylvia. "Brian, come so we can take your picture." She continued to wave until she saw that he was on his way.

"Great, Blue, you won the English prize. I guess we both did OK." He spoke as Daddy took a few pictures of Brian alone, with and without his mortarboard, and then gestured to me to stand beside him.

Brian's arm went around my shoulders and squeezed my arm. "My very best friend in the world." I slipped my arm around his waist, and we smiled at the camera. It was going to be fine.

It wasn't really fine, but I got up every morning and went to work and came home every night and went to bed. Daddy gave me a job shingling the house he was building. The money was great, and I saved the extra cash for school. The house was square, rather large and plain, a shingler's dream. I started at the bottom of the south wall with a large picture window in the middle which cut down on the amount of shingling. I strapped a leather hammer harness and a nail bag over my jeans and felt like a real carpenter. I had done this for Daddy before, so I knew what I was doing. I snapped the chalk line on the plywood wall. The blue line, perfectly level, was as good as anyone could do, and if you have a good level starting line, chances are, your shingling job will look even. Some of the guys on Daddy's crew watched, waiting for me to make a mistake. Daddy watched, knowing I wouldn't. The second row of shingles went directly over the first row to make a doubly thick row as a starter. I was careful not to let the cracks between the shingles line up at the same place. I snapped another blue chalk line a few inches from the bottom of the first row so that the second row would be even. It would be easy until I got to the window and then I'd probably have to cut some. I staggered the cracks on that row, too.

It was hot, especially on the south side. When I reached the window and the heat became unbearable, I moved to the west wall and started at the bottom. Daddy didn't care how I did it, he knew it would be a good job, as good a job as anyone could do. We often had lunch together if he wasn't involved in something else. At lunch the other men would pile into their pickups and head for the diner in town, and we would grab our lunches and position ourselves under the big maple that faced the mountains, The Bubbles. The tree trunk was large enough for both of us to lean against it and face the same way. And no camera. "Blue," he would say, "I climbed those mountains when I was a boy. Now there's a road right to the top."

"Did you climb them with Grandpa?"

"Yes." And then we would continue our lunch. "Your grandpa is very wise about mountains and woods. I wish I had paid more attention then."

Brian had a job taking care of the grounds down at the Hollis mansion. They didn't pay him much, but he had a full scholarship and the work was easy. We saw each other on and off, neither of us had time for much socializing. Mama still lived in the old Victorian house, and I visited some weekends. Things were tolerable between us. She always held me a little too tight when I left and really listened when I told her about Daddy and Grandpa. I think she missed us, missed living with us, but she wouldn't come back home.

Daddy always took pictures of the houses we were building. At the end of a job, he presented the owner with a photo album full of pictures of the building progress, from ground breaking to finishing touches and moving day. Grandpa came for dinner every week and tried to convince me to live with him on the reservation and learn the ways of the woods rather than start college in the fall. No one had really changed, but everything felt different, as if life were unfolding in someone else's mind.

All I wanted to do was get through the summer so I could leave for Brown. Things had to be better there. No one there would know about the accident, and about prom night, and that my mother left us. I didn't see Darrel all summer except for one glimpse of him in the drugstore early in July. No talk about us circulated that I heard about. No rumors ran through the networks. No one knew but me and those other kids. But people looked at me like they knew. Everybody. They watched me, not like before to guess which eye was glass, as if they knew my secrets. I burned sweetgrass in my room. If I didn't burn the sweetgrass, I could still smell Old Spice.

Most of the blood came out of the dress. I soaked it in cold water and scrubbed the spot with some dishwashing soap. If you looked carefully, you could see it, but I didn't think Mama would notice. Besides, I didn't intend to wear it again.

Berry slept with me every night. I knew I should give her up, that I was too old to be dependent on a vision. But she slept with me because I didn't know how to get rid of her. I stopped going to the cemetery and I'm sure Daddy noticed, but he didn't mention it. Every night when I got into bed, there she was, sleeping under the covers, naked. She looked fat and fleshy lying there. I slept on the far side of the bed. I didn't want to be near her. My old Indian doll, Hiawatha, slept between us. Sometimes I would watch her without moving, watch her for signs of life, anything that moved or an expression. I knew there was something in there, but I couldn't see any sign of it. She grew and grew, becoming soft and doughy. She came now even though I didn't call her. I began to sleep on the floor, and she stayed in the bed.

Daddy had a show of his photographs in the town library. There were pictures of me in the hospital, pictures of me learning to walk, pictures with Grandpa and one from prom night, with Darrel. I asked him to keep that one out of the exhibit, but he didn't. Perhaps if I'd made a fuss.

I was his date for the opening. Daddy bought a pair of brown pants and a beige linen jacket at Mortie's Second Hand for the occasion. His magenta silk fish tie cost more than the whole outfit and made the look bearable. Said he couldn't possibly wear that suit for real, needed the tie. The long magenta dress that I made to match the tie felt a little snug. Before we left for the opening, we took our picture in front of the house, using the timer. "Make a fancy pose," he said. "Quick, make like we're dancing." Running back and forth, swirling me around for an action shot.

The library sent out invitations to people in town and put a notice in the local weekly about the show. We arrived first except for the women setting out little egg salad sandwiches and bowls of red sticky punch. Daddy had helped hang the photos on one wall of the library in groups of time frames. The first group was all of me in the hospital with bandages around my face, a little slit for my eye, and the casts on my arm and leg. My doll, Ugli, was lying on one side of me, and there was something shadowy curled up on the other side. At first I thought it might be Berry, but I think it was just the shadow from the traction slings. My eye shone out from the swath of white bandages.

"Oh, Robert, these are just wonderful," said the woman who'd hired Daddy to build the house we were working on.

"Look at this one, George, she's on her first day of school. Look at the mother's face looking at her." She took another dainty bite of her egg salad sandwich and went on to the next group of photos. Later we learned that she bought a photograph of me against The Bubbles for two hundred dollars. You couldn't really tell it was me, but I don't think she cared.

"Oh, and here's a picture of that artist fellow who paints The Bubbles, Simon somebody. He's quite famous, you know," said the lady with the egg salad sandwich.

"Look at the old Indian. Put some braids on him and he could be in the movies. Wonder where he came from. Relative, maybe. The daughter is kind of dark," George, who must have been her husband, said.

"That must be Blue. She was a movie star when she was little, before that accident. Isn't she adorable with those ringlets."

"There she is, over there, in the pink, by the sandwiches. She only has one eye, you know. Isn't that a shame. But she is shingling the house. I saw her out there last week."

They turned to circulate in the crowd. I picked up all the radishes scattered in between the egg salad sandwiches and put them in my pocket. I hoped someone was watching.

CHAPTER II

The rest of the summer passed quickly. I saw Brian a few times and spent two weekends with Grandpa on the reservation, where we gathered blueberries for jam and wild herbs for drying. The work I did on my baskets impressed Mrs. Francis. I intended to take supplies to Brown and work on them. Darrel waved to me from his car once, but I didn't hear any rumors about us. Daddy let me take the truck whenever he wasn't using it, so I drove by the cemetery to the shore and sat and watched the mountains change color.

The beach near our house was rocky, like Indian Beach. The narrow path weaving its way to the open granite was lined with shrubs. Juniper, raspberries, blackberries, wild roses scratched at me as I pushed past them. Chunks of pink granite lay strewn around the beach as if Glue-skub had dropped them from Mount Katahdin and they settled where they fell. Sea heather stuck up at random through the piles of stones and sometimes I would pick some for the table. I sat on my favorite slab of granite next to a beach pea spot so I could eat without getting up.

Daddy and Mama both drove me to Brown in September. I settled myself in the front of Mama's car while one parent sat in back and one drove. They chatted about school and how proud they were of me and gave me lots of advice for making friends.

"You want to keep up with your work right from the start," she said when she was driving.

"Yeah, don't let it get ahead of you," he said from the back.

"See if you can get a ride home at Thanksgiving," she said. "Peter Blaney, I think he lives in Summer Harbor, he's going, too. He has a car. His mother stopped me in the health-food store last week. I'm sure he could give you a lift."

"Yeah, if he can't, there's a bus, at least to Bangor," he said. We stopped for lunch at the Miss Westville diner and I had fried clams and lemon meringue pie. "God, Blue, you have some appetite." Daddy noticed things like that. "I do think you've put on some weight."

"Don't tell her that, she'll turn anorexic. At least she isn't one of those thin sickly-looking wanna-be models who tries to look like a magazine cover."

"Just kidding." Daddy took a sip of his coffee and never took his eyes off Mama. She didn't seem to notice.

My roommate's name was Daphne and she was very black. I had never slept in the same room with anyone else before except for that long and horrible night with Darrel, and I wouldn't call that sleeping. Berry didn't count.

"I'm part Indian, you know," I said, trying to make her more comfortable. "My great-grandma was full-Indian, Passamaquoddy. My grandfather still lives on the reservation. I visit him there." I knew I was talking too fast, but I had never talked to a black person before, except for asking directions, or buying something in a store. Maine didn't have very many anythings but white waspy people except for a few Passamaquoddies, Penobscots, Micmacs.

"I never met a Native American before." She was long and fragile, but her voice was deep, full and deep. "All I know about Indians is what I learned in school, and that was mostly from a hundred years ago." She pulled her belongings out of her garment bag, dresses that looked like silk, cashmere sweaters. I wondered where she found such clothing. I presumed she lived in the city—New York, or Chicago, or Washington.

"Where do you come from? I mean, where do you live? You know, your family. Where do they live?"

"I'm from Concord, Massachusetts. You know, Paul Revere and all that. I went away to high school. Quaker school. In New Hampshire. How about you?" She turned to me. Her voice was like liquid chocolate.

"Maine, on the coast, past Bar Harbor. Up there, way up." I was rambling again.

"Do you have a squeeze?"

"A what?"

"You know, a guy, back home." She turned toward me, holding a long white silk dress.

"I have Brian." It was out before I could even think.

Daphne had chosen to be a political science major. Poly sci we called it. I was in liberal arts. Daphne wanted to be president of the U.S. She said soon it would be time for women and blacks to take charge of the country, and she was both. We talked about home and school and our parents. I told her about my accident and my eye. I even took it out to show her. Her parents were both doctors. Her mother did eye surgery, so she knew a little about glass eyes and wanted to see mine. I had never shown anyone before except for Brian and, of course,

Mama and Daddy. Even Grandpa hadn't seen it. She cradled it in her hand—her smooth, very black hand—and rolled it around.

"It's so big." She held my eye to the window light. Her fingers were long and slender. "I didn't realize eyeballs were so big." She cupped her palm and put her hand around it. "God, I can't believe you put this in your socket." She smiled. "Thanks for showing me." Daphne extended her hand to me. I took back my eye and went into the bathroom to put it in. It was a private chore.

I didn't want Berry to come to Brown with me. I was too old, and it was all too weird. Before we left home, I told her to stay there, that I would be home on holidays and for the summer, and she could come then. Of course, she gave no response. She did stay away. I had Daphne. At night I would look at her sleeping, her short curly hair cropped close to her head so that her ears showed. I tried to breathe with her, watching her rise and fall and trying to copy it, synchronize myself. I didn't even need Hiawatha, who stayed in the suitcase.

Daphne and I ran every morning before class. Sometimes some other kids from the dorm joined us, but mostly we ran together, just the two of us. I tried to match my breathing to hers, like when she was sleeping, but it was harder when I had to concentrate on my running and I couldn't always see her close enough. We didn't run very far because my leg would start to hurt, but she understood that. Daphne ran after class without me while I worked part-time in the library. She jogged two miles every afternoon and was going to try out for spring track. I had stopped menstruating, but they say that happens when you exercise too much.

Daphne dated a lot. Black guys and white guys both. But she didn't have anyone serious. A few times she even asked if I wanted her to fix me up. I didn't.

I bought some new clothes, the baggy style. My old clothes

were feeling uncomfortable. I usually hated shopping, but Daphne and I went to a new store outside Providence that had "comfort clothes," as they were called. We pawed through the racks grabbing shirts and pants off the rack to try on. There was only one dressing room, so we both squeezed in together. She didn't wear any underwear. Not ever. Even with dresses. I loved that her body was dark all over, not just where you might have a tan. Her belly, between her breasts, her lower back. All black, well, really dark brown. And her smell, not of deodorant or powder, something else. I had to stop myself from putting my face too near her body. We both got oversize violet-colored sweatshirts with pants to match. I got a few more of other colors. Grandpa had given me some money for clothes. "My beautiful Miss Brown," he said. "Buy yourself something pretty." He would love the colors.

My classes were great. English literature, world history, math, French, the regulars, but I got permission to take Native American studies because I was part Passamaquoddy. They wanted to have some Native Americans in the class for discussion.

Brian called a couple of weeks before Thanksgiving break. He left a message with Daphne that he was coming to visit on Friday for the weekend. He was going to stay with a friend of the family and would be by around six to take me out for supper.

"Well, what's up with this Brian. Are you sleeping with him?"

"God, no. Nothing like that. We've been friends for years. I think he has a girlfriend." I'd never seen Brian with Sylvia after the prom, but what did I know.

"You are a knockout, with that black hair and those long legs. You can't even tell about your eye." Daphne sprawled across her bed with her head dangling down the side. She was looking under the bed. "How come you don't have a guy? I bet you're even a virgin." She pulled out her snow boots and a bunch of books. "Do you know what I did with my red shoes?"

"I don't know." I squatted on the floor between the two beds and started to look under mine. "Here they are." I pulled them out covered in dust and candy wrappers.

"God, how did they get there?" She was sitting on the floor touching me. Her knees were touching mine. She brushed off the shoes, bright red pumps with little heels, and stuck them on her bare feet. "What do you think." Her legs were long, spread out to the side, and I was in between them. She plunked one of her feet on my lap. "Well? Will they go with that red-and-black dress? We're going to a grad party."

I could smell that smell again. I wanted to touch her leg, her foot. My hands touched the shoe with her foot in it. "It's fine. They'll look great."

I put it down very quickly and stood up. "Maybe you'd like to go to dinner with Brian and me. You'll like him. He's kind of weird, but, well, he's nice, easy to talk to." I began to braid my hair. Two braids, one on each side. I decided to wear the new violet sweatshirt and pants, not really "out to supper" wear, but my other clothes just didn't feel right. I was starving. We could go to the Mexican restaurant in town. Chicken molé. All that chocolate and hot peppers and cumin poured over chicken breasts. I stood in front of the mirror. I looked heavier than usual. But my face was the same. I brushed my hair a few times and turned to Daphne. "Do I look alright?"

"That outfit is great, for running. Are you going to do some running?" She laughed in her liquid chocolate way. She decided that she wouldn't go for dinner with us but she would stay and meet Brian. "I'm dying to meet this guy. You sure you don't have something going with him?"

We sat looking at each other, waiting for the knock on the

door. He was about fifteen minutes late. Unusual for Brian. He hugged me. He shook her hand. "You must be Daphne. I guess I talked to you on the phone."

"Right you are. Wish I could go out with you, but I've got a date."

"Let me look at you." Brian smiled. He held me at arm's length and looked up and down and then up. Then his face changed. Became all cloudy and wrinkled. He was making strange contortions with his eyebrows. He looked like he wanted to ask me a real important question.

"Well?"

"Whoa," he said.

I realized that Daphne was standing there watching us. Brian was looking at me. I was looking at him. No one was talking or moving. Just Brian's eyes moving down my body.

"Blue, you're pregnant, aren't you?"

Through the fog I caught a glimpse of Daphne moving. I couldn't look at her. I couldn't look at Brian. I tried to look at nothing but couldn't find it. I stared straight ahead, through Brian, out toward nothing.

"Um, guys, I'll leave you alone." She seemed to be taking a very long time getting her things together. My breath was making a louder noise than it should. I hoped there wasn't something wrong with me.

"How did this happen?" He was still holding me at arm's length. "Blue, are you with me?" He shook my shoulders a little. I was very aware of what he was doing. "You're going to sit over here and you're going to tell me about this." He guided me over to the edge of the bed and lowered me down until I was sitting. Then he pulled up the desk chair for himself and placed it right in front of me. I heard Daphne open the door. "Can you stay a minute?" I think it was Brian who said it. He looked in

Daphne's direction. The door shut. She sat on the edge of her bed.

They both looked at me. I could tell even though I was still looking through everything at nothing. Finally I looked down at my feet. They were turned inward, like a naughty child who has been found out. I watched my feet, waiting for something to move.

"I thought about it, but she didn't have anyone, a boyfriend, you know," Daphne said. "Blue, how could this happen? You're a bright girl. Who was it? Not that guy Darrel you went to the prom with?" I looked up quickly. "Oh, my God, it was." I knew it was Daphne's voice. I thought about the chicken molé that I probably wouldn't have for supper. I wondered why Mama hadn't been to visit me. And why had Berry gone away?

Dad carving the chicken. Just the two of us.
Thanksgiving 1996 First one without Mattie and Blue

CHAPTER 12

We never did go out for the chicken molé. Brian stayed with me, and Daphne canceled her date and went out to get a loaded pizza and some Cokes for all of us. While Daphne was gone Brian held me very tight. He didn't ask questions or give advice until I'd stopped crying.

"Tell me." He held my chin and stroked my hair. He loved my black Indian hair. "Please tell me what happened. Does Darrel know?"

I looked at him and tried to answer. "The prom. The night of the prom. I got drunk." And then I started in again. "I guess I should have known when I started gaining weight."

"OK, let's not talk right now. Daphne is due back. We'll eat some pizza and then we'll all talk." He turned my face toward him again. "I want to help. You're my best friend."

"Well, then, why didn't you take me to the prom? Why'd you let me go with him. I counted on you. I thought you'd take me." My voice was rising. "Why that stupid Sylvia what's-her-name? Shit, I figured we'd go together. Shit." Brian said nothing. Just held me.

A laugh was coming and I knew it was not good timing. I tried to think of something else, Mama when she found out that I had "irresponsible sex," Daddy when he found out that he was going to be a grandfather, my world history class. My shoulders began to shake. "It's OK, we're going to work it out," Brian said.

I hoped he would think I was crying, but he looked at me. "God, what is so funny at a time like this?"

"Remember." I gasped between words because I was laughing so hard. "Remember the time." I wasn't sure that I could finish or that I wanted to.

"Well, what is it? You've got to tell me now."

"Remember the time when you humped my leg and came in your shorts?" The laughter became hysterical, and I couldn't stop. I heard Daphne struggling with the door and knew she would think I'd lost my marbles. She came in and dropped the pizza and Cokes on the table.

"Oh, my God, is she alright?" Then the laughter turned to sobs, and I wasn't sure which I wanted to do. It seemed to be more appropriate to cry.

"She's doing OK. We'll get up and have some pizza. Come on, weirdo. Up you get."

Brian pulled me off the bed, my hair stuck to my face and my nose running. Daphne opened the pizza box and found some paper towels in the bathroom. She popped the Coke cans and poured three glasses. She hated drinking out of cans. "Come here, baby," she said with her arms out. I sank into them and she closed them around me. My head turned toward her neck and toward her smell. I wished I could stand there until I got tired of it. She patted my back and pulled away. I wiped my face with the sleeve of my new violet sweatshirt and sat down at the table.

"I called James about the party. He took a rain check.

Thought you might need me here." She put pizza on paper towels in front of each of us. "Eat, eat." She gestured at me. Why did everyone think that eating was the way to fix all possible problems? It actually did make me feel better. I stole Brian's anchovies and gave Daphne my mushrooms. Daphne didn't give Brian anything. The three of us chewed and chewed and knew that when we were finished, we would have to deal with my problem. That's how we first referred to it, my "problem." We discussed the pizza and my Native American studies class and Brian's smelly roommate. The really serious stuff would come after the pizza was gone, and I wondered why we weren't eating as slowly as we could.

Daphne picked up all the paper towels and empty glasses and moved them off the table. She folded her hands in front of her on the table, took a big breath and exhaled. They both looked at me, and I knew it was my turn.

"I don't know what I was thinking. I mean, I knew I was, well you know, having a problem, I mean, I guess I knew. I couldn't face him. Darrel. I never want to see him again."

Daphne gazed at me with patience. I couldn't see Brian very well because he was on my bad side. What I'd said was certainly not enough. Neither of them said a word, and the silence didn't seem to be a problem for them. They waited.

"It was a bad scene. I thought it was over. That it was in the past. But I guess not. Pregnant." I shrugged as if I had no idea how it had happened. It seemed so strange to be saying that word. Especially about me. I lowered my head.

"Come on, we have to deal with this." It was Brian. He moved over so that I would have to see him.

"I never want him to know. He's a piece of shit." My mind raced so fast I felt that I might not be able to keep up with it. "I haven't seen a doctor. It's too late for an abortion."

They sat and watched. Brian took one hand, Daphne, the other.

"Mama and Daddy, I don't want them to know right now. I don't think I can give it away." Tears came again as I thought of Berry and how lost she was to me. "I don't know what I'm going to do." The tears were dripping, but my voice was steady. I looked at their hands holding mine. Daphne's brown fingers were massaging one hand, and Brian just held the other one. I felt a flutter in my belly. *Oh, my God,* I thought, *what a family for the poor baby, what a family.*

We talked late into the night, sometimes holding hands, sometimes not, sometimes crying, sometimes laughing. Daphne said I could come to her house for Thanksgiving, if I wanted to avoid my family, said her folks wouldn't mind. Christmas was another matter, and after that, well, we'd try to make some decisions by then. Daphne said I should see a doctor right away. Maybe there was something that could be done. She would talk to her parents. Brian wanted to marry me. He loved me and wanted to be the baby's father. He said it only made sense. People would think he was the father anyway. He was sure my folks would believe him. His folks would go nuts, think he was ruining his future, but they'd come around. I'd always been the one to hold Brian's hand, comfort him, convince him that he would reach adulthood. Now he was doing that for me, and I loved him for that. But I couldn't marry him. Not that I didn't love him enough, just that we weren't lovers, where was the passion? "It's nothing if there is no passion." Grandpa's voice sounded in my mind. "Never do something because it's easy and comfortable if there's no passion."

The next day I called home to talk to Daddy. "I've been invited to Daphne's for Thanksgiving. Isn't that great? Aren't you happy for me. Of course I'll miss you but, God, it'll be such fun. Daddy? Are you there?"

"Sure, honey, that's fine. We'll miss you, too. Grandpa will be here. I know you'll have a great time. And of course we'll see you at Christmas."

"Daddy, you'll tell Mama. Tell her I'll call her after I get back."

We said our good-byes and Daddy blew me kisses over the phone. I, of course, had to blow them back with Daphne watching. I was glad I didn't have to lie to him, but I wasn't sure what would happen about Christmas.

Daphne's parents picked us up after classes on Tuesday afternoon. They were as attractive as Daphne, tall, dark, with mellifluous voices. Daphne and I sat in back and every once in a while, she would take my hand, as if she knew I needed her, and squeeze it. I left my hand out and easy to find.

In the few days since the fact of the pregnancy jumped out of the closet, I seemed to have grown enormously. None of my regular clothes fit anymore and my appetite was out of control. I pulled on my new violet sweatshirt and pants and packed the other sweatshirts I had bought. Daphne told her parents that I was coming for the holidays. That was all. Not that I was white or that I was unmarried and pregnant or that my parents didn't even know. They didn't seem surprised at all about my color or that I was pregnant, and they probably didn't suspect that my parents were in the dark about it all.

"Please call us Dan and Lydia," her mother said. She had that same voice that I loved about Daphne. I had never been in a room where I was the only white person. They talked about the turkey and about what kind of pies we would make and who was coming for dinner, just like we might do at my house, at least before Mama left. I told them I was part Native American. They said they knew about the Wampanoag's and the

Penobscots but had never heard of the Passamaquoddies. I said we were known as the "People of the Dawn," because we were the first to see the sunrise.

On Sunday morning, when grandmothers and uncles and cousins had gone home and the turkey was only an empty rack in the soup pot, we sat down with Dan and Lydia. Dan made waffles and sausage and had just given me my third waffle. I knew I was beginning to look like a whale, but I couldn't seem to stop eating.

Lydia spoke first. "Daphne tells me that you had an eye removed when you were very young. I operate on eyes, you know. How did you lose it?"

My mouth was full of waffle and the maple syrup was dripping down my chin. I held my finger up so she would know I had to finish chewing. They were all watching me, so I swallowed too soon and the waffle barely went down my throat. I finished my juice before I spoke.

"I was young. Before I started school. I was in a movie and a golf cart ran into me. The driver was thrown, but he was OK. I don't really remember the accident but I remember all the stuff afterward. The hospital, the nurses, the traction. I broke a lot of bones, and my eye had to be removed. I always wondered what they did with it." Suddenly I felt very foolish. What did I mean? They probably just threw it in the garbage. What did it matter anyway. "My brain went 'cou de cou,' they called it, so I had a lot of trouble with my speech. I had brain damage and couldn't talk right for a few years. It's not too bad now. Sometimes if I'm tired I still have trouble with my words." I didn't tell them about the swearing I did after the accident. About all the inappropriate words I used and that Brian seemed to understand them.

They all leaned back in their chairs, listening. No interruptions. "Sometimes when people lose parts of themselves, like eyes and legs and fingers, even breasts to cancer, they wonder what happened to them," said Lydia. "Sometimes they are used for research or transplantation but if they are damaged, they go into the waste stream, which is probably where yours went. I always tell my patients where their eyes went. It seems to allow them to continue feeling whole to keep track of their body parts."

"I have a twin, too. She died just after we were born. Her name is Berry." I realized that I was speaking in the present. "I mean she died, so her name was Berry. I know where she is."

"God, I didn't even know that," Daphne said. "Do you think about her?"

"Sometimes I see her, in my mind, grown-up. Lying next to me. I talk to her." I felt the tears coming but I continued. Daphne poured some hot tea into my cup. "She had no brain."

My tears didn't seem to inhibit anyone. It seemed to be acceptable in this family to cry. They cared that I was crying but they didn't try to humor me or offer me more waffles or tea or try to change the subject. I had never talked like this with anyone. "You mean anencephaly?" Dan said. I had forgotten he was a doctor, too.

"Daddy and Mama just said 'no brain.' I didn't know it had a long name. I guess that means that other babies have the same problem. Do they all die? Do they ever grow up?" I continued to cry, but Daphne pulled her chair closer to mine and held my arm.

"Some live a few days or even a few weeks. There haven't been any cases of anencephalic babies living longer," Lydia said. "Often they are stillborn or are aborted early in the pregnancy. Lucky for you that didn't happen." She smiled at me.

I wiped my face with a flowery cloth napkin. Daphne let go

of my hand and poured me more tea. I smelled the turkey soup cooking and suddenly felt hungry again. "I guess I needed to talk about this." My hands went to my belly. "The baby. Is there a danger this baby will be ancephalic?"

"Anencephalic," Lydia corrected me.

"Yes, no brain." I looked up at her and waited for the answer.

Dan answered for her. "Not really any more than if there had been no history in your family. There may be some genetic link, but in your case it isn't likely to affect the baby."

"Can you tell there's no brain right away. Do you know when it comes out? Do they look different?"

"Well, it depends on the extent of the problem. Every baby is different. Have you asked your folks these questions?"

"We've talked a little. But I know they feel funny about it."

"Do you have a doctor? Have you been to see anyone?" Lydia said.

Daphne hadn't told her anything. "No."

"This is none of my business except that I like you and you are a good friend of Daphne. And I'm a doctor. Where's the father? Is he involved?"

"No."

"Are you planning to have the baby?"

"Yes." It was out before I realized it. What would I do with a baby. I was barely out of high school.

"You have some choices. Abortion, adoption, keeping the baby. Some doctors will do abortions this late in your pregnancy if there are extenuating circumstances." Lydia's voice was kind. "Perhaps I could help you find someone if that's your decision. We'd like to help any way we can."

We talked until it was time to leave for school. We discussed what it took to raise a child. About giving a child up for adoption. About abortion. They didn't make judgments or tell me what would be best. That meant I had to decide myself, and I wasn't quite ready to do that.

Lydia drove us back late Sunday afternoon and I hugged her for a long time. She kissed my cheek, and said, "Call me if you want to talk."

Me decorating the Christmas tree. Taken with the timer.
December 1996

CHAPTER 13

❦

I wrote a letter to Mama and Daddy about Christmas. I also told them the biggest lie of my life.

Dear Mama and Daddy,

Had a great time at Daphne's house on Thanksgiving but I missed you both. We had turkey and cranberry and pies just like at home. How is Grandpa? I miss him, too.

Great news!!! I have been chosen to go to Mississippi over Christmas vacation and help build a new school for victims of the hurricane. They flipped when they heard I could do construction—a woman with a hammer—they loved it. Tons of people applied but they only chose six. Isn't that great??? I'll call you on Christmas day around 2:00 and save my stocking and presents for when I come home in the winter. I'll bring you something from here— they have great folk carvings. I never thought I'd be some-

*where else for Christmas but I can't pass up this oppor-
tunity.*

I'll be in touch. Love you both. Say hi to Grandpa.

Love and Kisses,
Blue

I knew they'd believe me because they trusted me. They
would have to know someday if I decided to keep the baby, but
if I had an abortion, they wouldn't have to know, ever. Daddy
would hug me and probably cry and croon, "My baby, my beautiful Blue," and I would get all blubbery and not be able to decide anything for myself. Mama would hug me, and say, "Blue,
my dearest, why didn't you tell me last June, when it happened,
where were your condoms? Where were your brains? You're
certainly much too young to have a baby. I'll find a good doctor
to deal with this."

I knew that was the best thing to do. Abortion. I had
written a term paper on that subject in government class my
senior year in high school. My stand was for the woman's
right to choose what happens to her own body. I still believed
that.

Brown University had a small dorm kept open over the
Christmas holidays for foreign students or students who
couldn't go home for the holidays, and they said I could stay
there. They closed all the others to save money on heat.
Daphne wanted me to come home with her, but I needed time
to myself. My belly was large, no more hiding it under my
sweatshirts. My due date was early March so I didn't have
much time to decide what to do. Dr. Simpson, at the college
clinic, scolded me for waiting so long to see a doctor but she
went over all my options. It seemed I had a lot. Have an abortion (she said she could set it up even though it was so late in

the pregnancy because she felt it was a rape situation), give the baby to some other couple, marry Brian and keep the baby, keep the baby by myself (hard to do with no job and few skills). She asked me how I felt about the baby considering its conception. She made me think about Darrel and prom night and my audience.

"Listen to me a minute, you need to think about this guy. Do you want to raise his baby? Will you love it when you look at it? What if it's a boy and looks just like his father?" We sat opposite each other in straight-backed chairs and Dr. Simpson held both my hands. I wanted her to tell me what to do, but she just raised more questions.

"Will you tell Darrel about the baby?"

"No."

"Do you think that's right? To not let him know he has a child?"

"Yes."

She knew she wasn't really getting anywhere, that I needed time to sort it out. She also knew that there wasn't much time left. I thought I had all the time in the world.

"Look, you're healthy. The baby seems in good shape. I want to see you in one week. And please make your decision. I know it's not an easy one, but you don't have much time, and when the baby comes, he or she will need a home."

My chin quivered, but I didn't want to cry in her office, so I bit my lip and swallowed the lump in my throat. "OK, I'm going back to the dorm and make some lists of possibilities."

She smiled. "Good, make an appointment with Ruby at the desk, and I'll see you next week." We stood up, still holding hands. She looked down and laughed.

The folks swallowed it, just like I thought. A letter was in my box when I returned from the clinic. And I moved to a private room for the holidays. Daphne helped me move across the courtyard, and we said good-bye. She begged me again to come home with her, but she understood what I had to do. She hugged me hard and long and I breathed deeply and tried to remember her smell, tried to identify what it was so I could recall it when I was alone.

"I'll call you on Christmas," she said.

"I will be fine. It'll be great here. I need this. Don't worry about me." I kissed her on the cheek and turned back toward my new room.

Brian called me every day from school and continued when he went back to Maine for the holidays. He loved me. He wanted to marry me. He wanted to help raise the child if that was what I decided to do. But I couldn't do that to Brian. It would ruin his career. He would get some dumb job that he hated, making nothing. He wanted to teach college math. He'd always wanted that. This wasn't even his problem. Besides, there was no passion.

I started my lists. I sat on the bed with my yellow legal pad leaning against my belly and had sharp pencils ready. The abortion was out. It was too dangerous for me now, and I didn't want to lose the baby like I lost Berry. It was selfish. I knew that. I could give the baby up. But what if she had a horrible home and someone beat her or didn't like her? God, I was calling "it" a "her." How did I know? My first choice was to keep the baby, so I began to make lists of ways to do that. Brian was out. Go back home to Dad. Move in with Mama. No to both. Not that they were awful or mean. But they would hover. It just wouldn't work out. I needed my independence now. Get an apartment and a job. What job? I could do some carpentry. And who would take care of the baby? I could go on welfare. No. That was totally out. With the handout, came the strings. Besides, I was strong and capable of work. Talents. What could I do? Put on shingles, simple framing, baby-sitting, painting houses, typing, yuk. What if I hadn't had the accident? What if I had made it as an actress? I could try out for the lead in some movie. I could make baskets. Maybe I could sell them to the tourists. I would have some money from the accident settlement if I didn't go back to Brown, enough to live on for a while, enough to get started.

My decisions. No Brian, no abortion, no adoption, no living at home, no welfare. It seemed I had lots of noes but no yesses. They would come.

"I'm going to have the baby," I blurted it out to Dr. Simpson as soon as I entered her office the following week. "I'm not getting married. Darrel won't even know about it."

"Well, you have been thinking. What are you going to do?"

"I'm working on it. I'm going to take a makeup exam the end of January and then take a leave. I might as well get some credit for all this. Besides, my grades are good, all As and one B so far."

"You have to deal with your parents."

"I know. I will." I didn't know how or when I would, but I nodded strongly as if that would help convince me.

"Well, let's see how this baby is then."

The fetus made the correct blips in the stethoscope, and I was enormous. My due date was only nine weeks away, and I could hardly walk. I couldn't sit behind the desk at my English lit makeup. The professor gave me her chair. I still didn't know what I was going to do. Mama and Daddy were coming to get me the day after the exam, supposedly for the break before the next semester.

Our room was empty when I got back from the English exam. Daphne's note on the table said she would be at the library until very late finishing her paper on "The Kennedy Years." I threw my book about early-American literature on the bed and pulled the sweatshirt over my head. I dropped the pants, kicked them off, and grabbed my nightgown from the foot of the bed. I say threw, dropped, kicked, grabbed, but they were slow, ponderous motions that took a long time to complete and I stood exhausted beside the bed, naked except for my socks, with my nightgown dragging on the floor. It wasn't just my belly that was huge. I seemed like a whale. A blue whale. My belly was lined with new marks just since yesterday. I traced them with my finger so I would remember when they appeared. At first I counted them, but now new ones appeared every day and I couldn't keep up.

My arms circled my belly and clasped underneath. The baby was heavy. I couldn't imagine giving birth to something that big. I dropped the nightgown and got into Daphne's bed with just my socks on. It wasn't cold in the room, but I pulled her covers up as high as I could and scootched down into them. Lying on my side was the only comfortable position now. Her smell was strong, and I breathed deeply. Underneath the blankets my breath mingled with the scent of her shampoo and the smell of our bodies.

"Berry," I said aloud, softly but loud enough for her to hear. "Berry," I called again. She had never appeared at Brown, but I had never called her. She was there, in Daphne's bed with me. She lay facing me, eyes closed, naked, with a pregnant belly. I cried then. Just a little.

We lay there together, not touching, for a long time. I knew if I touched her, she would disappear. "Berry, I'm glad you're back." No response. "I don't know what I'm going to do now. What are you going to do?" I half expected her to answer. I stifled a little laugh. It wouldn't be appropriate. But here we were, looking exactly alike, lying in a single dorm bed, facing each other. I hoped Daphne wouldn't come in now, but she said she would be late. "You need to help me." My voice was demanding, and I looked right at her. Of course her eyes were closed, so she couldn't see me. But maybe she could hear. This was serious and I needed her. "Mama and Daddy are coming day after tomorrow. They're going to see me like this and they're going to know. I have to decide before that." The baby suddenly shifted and stuck out something, a hand or a foot. I put my hand on the lump and held it there. "Grandpa will be happy." I looked at Berry closely for something. I thought I saw a small smile. Not really a smile like you or I would make. But a Berry-smile, a slight upturn of the sides of her mouth, barely perceptible. "Grandpa, that's it, Grandpa will let me stay there. I can help him. I can rake blueberries in the summer." My voice got higher and louder. I reached for her, my sister, and thought I felt her skin on mine just as she disappeared. "Grandpa, of course, why didn't I think of that. He's so lonely, and he loves me." I jumped out of bed with my socks on and threw my arms in the air, or rather put them there, nothing was fast these days. "Yes, I've got it. Eureka. I've found the answer." Brian and I used to say that when we discovered something amazing. "Yahoo," I said in my loudest voice. "Yes." The door opened.

It was Daphne. She shut the door quickly behind her and raised her arms in the air with her paper clutched in one hand. She ran toward me and grabbed me as a man might grab a woman to dance. And dance we did. Around and around, slowly. "'I could have danced all night, and still have begged for more.'" I started off in a very loud operatic not terribly good soprano voice. Daphne joined me in her smooth alto voice, and we went on and on until the song was finished.

"You're naked, and you have your socks on." She stared at my feet. "And you've been in my bed." She held me at arm's length. "I sound like one of the three bears. God, what a belly." I placed her hand on the little arm or foot or whatever it was that made a lump. The baby kicked when she felt the pressure of Daphne's hand. "I felt it. I felt it." Her warm brown eyes filled. "Thanks for letting me do that." I threw my nightgown over my head. "What the hell is going on. Have you discovered gold? Won the lottery? Well, what?"

"I know now what I'm going to do."

"Oh, Blue, come, sit down. Tell me," she said. "Can I help?"

Daphne and I had said our good-byes and promised to write and visit. She would come to Grandpa's when the baby was born. I readied myself for Mama and Daddy when they came on Friday afternoon. I received an indefinite leave of absence, packed everything, and was waiting at the entrance to the dorm. I figured it might be easier if we met in public.

Mama's car pulled up to the curb. "Blue, we're here." Mama waved out the passenger side and Daddy had hardly stopped the car before she had the door open. I waited until she was almost within touching distance before I stood up in all my blue-whale glory.

"Hi, Mama," I said.

"Oh, my God, you're pregnant. Robert, Robert," she called louder than she really needed to. "Oh, my God. Whose is it? Someone at school? Blue, you know better." She used to say that if I forgot to feed the goldfish or skimped on the vacuuming. Then, as if she had said "eureka," recognition flashed across her face. "It was that awful boy, Darrel, wasn't it?"

Daddy finished parking the car and walked toward us. "What have we here? Oh, baby, my beautiful Blue." His arms went out to me, and I fell into them, leaving Mama standing there by herself, shut off from our intimacy.

*Blue kneeling with deer we hit on the way home
from Brown. Taken with flash, January 1997*

CHAPTER 14

We were silent in the car all the way to the motel in Massachusetts. They didn't want to drive all the way home in the
dark. They had made reservations at the Suisse Chalet Motel
just outside of Boston. I had my own room. Said I didn't want
any dinner. That I was tired and needed to get some sleep.
They said we'd talk tomorrow. I watched Audie Murphy in *To
Hell and Back* and Elvis in *Jailhouse Rock*. They wanted to get
takeout and eat in my room, but I convinced them that I was
fine, that they should go out and get some dinner.

The room smelled of old cigarettes and disinfectant and
excited bodies. I opened the window, but the smell clung to
the drapes and the furniture and, most of all, the bed. Prints
hung on the walls. Famous paintings. Monet, Picasso, Renoir.
I stood on the bed to look at them up close and stuck my finger on the Monet. Cardboard. Flat. I slid my finger down the
length of it. No texture. I glanced at the TV. Elvis was still
rocking with the inmates, so I lowered myself into the bed and
found the remote. I found *Who's Afraid of Virginia Woolf?*, with

Dick and Liz. He is telling the guests that their son ran into a tree while trying to avoid hitting a porcupine. I couldn't resist watching again. I had seen it so many times. I pulled some pink perfumy Kleenex from the box in the bathroom to get ready for the end. God, they were good. There were some couples like that. I heard kids talking in school about how much their parents fought. One girl's father even killed her mother when we were in sixth grade. But Dick and Liz had passion. So did George and Martha. You could see it. You knew they pulled each other's clothes off and screamed when they were doing it.

But they were weak. Their lives were fake. They didn't even really have a child. They sat by the window. The company had gone. She was crying. He was holding her. "Who's afraid of Virginia Woolf?"

"I am, George, I am."

They had passion, but they were weak.

A pile of the pink flowery-smelling tissues piled up next to me, all soaking wads. I think it was a mistake to watch that particular movie in that particular motel room. Suddenly, the air felt oppressive. The mood from the movie, the stink of the old cigarettes. The one open window wasn't enough, but I couldn't open the others. They weren't made to open. There was nowhere for the window to go. Just stuck on the hole. Hammered in. I pulled a chair to the open window and sat for a long time, watching the neon blink, "Suisse Chalet, your home away from home."

The next day we got on the road right after breakfast. We had six hours of driving to do, and I was sure that we would "talk" this time. By the time we reached the Maine border, still not a word. Well, perhaps a "look at that old car," or "those kids don't have seat belts on." But not real talk. About my problem. They stopped to switch drivers. Daddy was driving when we got to the border and Mama sat up front with him, just like married folks.

"I am going to Grandpa's. I'm going to live with him for a while. I'm going to have the baby there." I had rehearsed these lines, and they came out easily.

"What's that, dear?" Mama said, looking back with some difficulty because of the seat belt.

"Nothing."

She turned around.

Silence again.

We stopped in Belfast for lunch. Mama went in and got tuna sandwiches and orange soda and a bag of chips to share while Daddy bought gas. Everything I put in my mouth just pushed out my belly more, but I was hungry. I ate the sandwich but begged off on the chips. "Heartburn," I said. The orange soda helped.

Daddy was taking a big bite of his tuna sandwich when I saw it. The buck. "Deer, deer, deer." I said it with a mouthful of sandwich.

Mama turned around and said, "What's that, dear?" just as we hit him. I jerked forward and banged my head on the back of the front seat. The screech of the brakes seemed to go on longer than possible. I held my breath and wrapped my arms around my belly as best I could. Daddy pulled the car over to the side of the highway and we bumped along on the gravel. The deer slid up the hood of the car with his head pressed up against the windshield as Daddy finally pulled to a stop. Blood poured from his nose onto the window and one eye was a mass of pulp. The other eye blinked twice before he slipped off the hood onto the ground in front of the car.

They sat there, looking straight ahead, as if waiting for something else to happen, waiting for someone to tell them that it was OK to go. Otuhk. I knew it wasn't the same buck, but it could have been. Shit. I undid my seat belt and heaved myself out of the backseat. A streak of red ran across the hood of the car, and the body lay directly in front of the bumper. I knew an injured deer can be dangerous, so I stood to the side, watching. A muscle spasmed on his hind leg and I could tell he was dead. He looked just like Otuhk except his antlers were new, small, just starting to grow, winter antlers. Otuhk had a full rack that fall. But that had been a long time ago.

Daddy trundled out of the car with his camera and tripod. He set it up facing the deer and the car. "Is he dead?" Daddy asked me.

"Yes, I think so."

He picked up a stick and gently poked at him. No response. Silence. He grabbed the legs and pulled the body over so that the head was facing the tripod.

I was starting to shiver. The snowflakes that had started in Belfast were turning to freezing rain and washing the bloody streak off the hood of the car, down on top of the dead buck. "God, Daddy, what are you doing?"

"I'm taking some pictures of the buck." Daddy started to click. He moved the tripod in for some close-ups of the face, of the bloody nose and the mashed eye. "Blue, go over and kneel beside the head."

"Daddy, it's a dead deer. What are we going to do with it? Shouldn't we field dress it and bring it home? Grandpa would like it. I could bring it with me, you know, for a thank-you present." I was rambling, but it didn't matter. Daddy ignored me, waiting for me to move.

"Robert." Mama called from the car. "Is it dead?" She had rolled down the window. "Should we call the police?"

"Blue, please, go stand by the head." Daddy was pleading. It was important to him. I knew we wouldn't go any farther until he had taken my picture with the dead buck. "Yeah, right there, now kneel down next to him." I went over to the head and knelt as well as I could. His eye was open, staring. I closed it and left my hand there, on his face. Daddy took pictures. He stopped to move the tripod in and repositioned his parka to protect the camera from the rain.

"Robert, what are you doing? Is it dead?" Mama's whole head was out the window now.

"OK, I guess I have enough." Daddy packed up his equipment and took it to the trunk. He slammed it and brushed his hands together. "Come on, Blue, let's go." He got back into the driver's seat and shut the door.

"Come on, dear, you'll catch your death."

I looked off into the woods to see if his mate was waiting, watching for him to stand up. Of course they wouldn't be running together this time of year, but I couldn't help looking.

"Daddy," I said, shutting the door and fastening my belt, "shouldn't we do something with him? Call the warden? The police?" I was shivering.

"Yes, call the police." Mama rolled up the window a bit. "We'll stop at the next phone."

"He came out of nowhere. I didn't even see him. We could have had a bad accident."

"Is there a dent in the car?"

"Blue, are you hurt?" Daddy asked as he turned around toward me. "I felt your head bump on the seat."

"I hope no one else hits him. We better stop at a phone."

"It looks like we got a crack in the windshield. I have insurance for that. Good we didn't take your car. You probably don't even have any insurance," Daddy said to Mama. At least we were talking now.

I pulled my knees up as far as I could and closed my eyes. I would call Grandpa to come and get me as soon as we got home. In Ellsworth, I went into a store with Daddy to call the warden and bought Grandpa some candy corn. It wasn't Halloween, and it could be hard to find this time of year, but I bought two bags on sale.

The rest of the trip was quiet, as if they were thinking about the world and death and birth. Maybe they were.

As soon as I got home I called Grandpa and told him what was going on. "Oh my, we have lots to talk about. I'll be there first thing in the morning."

There seemed no point in talking to them. Mama stayed for supper, perhaps hoping for an opening for discussion. We sat quietly through supper with a little chatter about the ride home and the dead buck. Halfway through the apple pie, Daddy stood up and aimed the camera at us.

"No, Robert. Sit down. Haven't you done enough?"

Daddy placed the camera on the table. "I'm sorry, Mattie. I don't know what to do. I just wanted to do something. Anything." My courage was all used up on the baby decision. I calmly left the table, left the pie, left Mama to handle him, and walked to my room.

Grandpa picked me up the next morning. The bags of candy corn in my sweatshirt pocket made my protruding belly look even larger than it actually was as I lumbered out to meet him. It was my offering in return for his taking care of me—shelter, food, love, money, everything I needed to have my baby. I knew it would be enough. "Come on, Miss Brown, let's go home and talk about this."

Daddy stood in the doorway taking pictures. "Bye," he said, waving. "Call us."

Little Marten, age four days. He squinted at the flash.
March 1997

CHAPTER 15

Is there a father?" the doctor asked after she examined me. *Of course there is a father.* Did she think I didn't know about how babies were made?

"No," I said.

Brian arrived the day before I went into labor. March break. I was overdue. He didn't call. He just arrived at Grandpa's house in his father's car.

"I want to be there, to help you through it."

"But, I don't want to marry you."

"This isn't about marriage." He placed his hands on my cheeks and kissed me, softly, on my forehead. I felt so loved. He kissed my closed eyelids. "I love you and want to be with you." And he did love me. Good old Brian. Brian who got everything right in math class and didn't even know that the kids were laughing at him. Brian who cried when we killed the frogs. Brian who came in his shorts. Brian who took Sylvia to the prom. He loved me. There was no passion, but there was love.

"Wait, let me get my bag. Grandpa, is it alright if I stay for the baby?" Brian always called Grandpa, "Grandpa."

Grandpa was watching Oprah and nodded. "Sure thing. She needs someone with her. I think I'm too old." His attention went back to the show.

Brian ran to the car and came back with a knapsack full of books, his sleeping bag, and a paper bag overflowing with clothes. We stayed up until after midnight reading the books and practicing our breathing. He brought books about babies being born in water, about home births, about father's role, about having twins, and we read them all.

"Here's a good one," Brian said. "The father should bring a good supply of lollipops and Popsicles. Is that for the mother or the baby?"

"Listen, here put your head here." I was lying on the couch. Brian came over and knelt next to me. "Right here." I pulled up Grandpa's old shirt so that my belly was bare and brought Brian's head down to it. I cradled him there on my baby and tried to feel something. I wished this baby was Brian's. I wanted to tell him that, but I was afraid he would bring up marriage again. "If it's a boy, I'm going to call him Marten. Marten, help-mate to the gods. But I'm sure it's a girl. I'll call her Maria." The baby jumped.

"God, I felt it. Hey, I felt it move." He placed his hands on my bare skin and kissed the place where the baby moved. We slept there, Brian and I, until the sun came up around five-thirty. I was in labor. Not like the movies, when the woman screams, grabs her belly, makes a terrible face, and falls to the floor. I felt different. Full, crampy. Every once in a while a ripple flowed over my belly. I lay still for a while and watched Brian sleeping, half on the floor and half on me. He looked so different without his glasses, which were placed neatly beside the lamp on the little end table next to the couch. I didn't want to wake him, but I felt that my bladder would burst. When I moved out from underneath him, he snorted and licked his lips, but his eyes didn't open.

Grandpa wasn't awake yet either as I went by his room to the bathroom. I switched on the light, which caused the fan to go on, a loud sucking noise on the ceiling. The ripples again. I grabbed the edge of the sink and stood watching the faucet drip. Waiting for the cramp. Something dribbled down my legs. And then the pain came. I tried to hold my belly but it didn't help. The baby pushed against my hands, and I knew it was going to come out. After a moment, the pain subsided and I sat on the toilet. There was blood on my underpants. I thought of that first time, when I began to menstruate. I was so scared. Grandpa said it was for women to deal with. He told me later that when women bleed, they have power. Too much power to be in the common house. That's why they used to go off alone. I felt powerful. Scared and powerful both at once. The baby was right there. I could feel it waiting to come out. I pushed a little. Nothing.

"Blue, you in there?" It was Brian.

"I'm going to have the baby," I called from the toilet.

"What?" he said as he burst into the bathroom. "Now? Right now?" He stood near the door. His ears looked red and bigger than ever. "Come on, let's go. You can't have it there. You can't have a baby in the toilet."

"Go make me some raspberry tea, and I'll be out in a minute." He stood, staring at me. "Out," I yelled. "God, do you think I'm having the baby in the toilet? God."

Grandpa said he would stay home and get things ready. I wasn't sure what that meant, but that was fine with me. Brian did his deep breathing in the living room and calmed himself down. Grandpa placed the knapsack I had packed two weeks earlier in my hand. He kissed me on the forehead and smoothed my straight black hair. "I love you, Miss Brown." That's all. Nothing else.

The hospital was very small. Only three beds in maternity, and I was the only woman there. "You're from the reservation?" the nurse asked. I didn't get a sense of aversion, only curiosity.

The contractions continued all day. There was more blood, and my water broke on the floor of my hospital room. It splashed down between my legs during an especially hard contraction and spilled into my slippers. I started to shiver. I thought of Mama that day in the blueberry field when her water broke, down her socks into her sneakers and the flies that congregated around her feet, attracted by the smell. I looked down. No flies. Brian took my arm and walked me to a chair. He pulled off my soggy slippers and washed my legs and feet with a warm wet washcloth from the bathroom. Then he dried me gently with a towel.

"He's going to make some father," the nurse said as she poked her head in the door to see how things were going. "You keep walking if it feels good, and the doctor will be right in."

Brian took some warm wool socks from my knapsack and put them on. He wrapped a blanket around my shoulders and helped me to my feet.

"Won't be too much longer," the doctor said to Brian when she examined me. "Coming along nicely. You can push with the next contraction if you feel like it. Do you want your bed raised? Sitting up is more comfortable."

"Sure." I didn't really care what she did. I knew the next one was coming, and I knew that it was going to be bad.

Brian stayed at my side with a lollipop, breathing heavily out of his mouth. "Come on, honey, breathe with me."

"OK, push." Someone said it. I heard a guttural snarl and thought that there might be a monster in the room. Then I saw him. Darrel. My eyes were closed, and I tried to open them so he would go away.

"Keep pushing. Good."

What the fuck did she know? Darrel smiled and nodded. "Please God, go away," I said.

"Me?" That was Brian's voice. I didn't think I had spoken out loud.

The contraction was subsiding and I could open my eyes. No Darrel. Brian held the lollipop in his hand. He took a lick. I think it was raspberry. Another one was coming. "Don't let me see him again." I looked from one nurse to the other. They looked back as if I was just another crazed woman in labor.

"Now, push again."

I took a big breath and pushed. I struggled to keep my eyes wide-open.

"You can do better than that," Dr. Litten said with a stern voice. "Push."

"Fuck you," I yelled as I took another breath, pulled up my knees, and pushed. Brian clutched my hand and put a cloth on my forehead. I don't know what he did with the lollipop. With my next breath I could smell the birth, and I knew what Mama meant. There was nothing like it. I wanted this thing out of me. I clamped my teeth together, let the moans come out. Darrel was there, smiling, watching. "You goddamn pig," I spit out during the pushing. "You did this, you fucking pig."

"You don't really mean that. He's such a big help." There was no point in explaining. The pain subsided like a wave, with the next one coming in as the other went out. Brian wiped my lips with the washcloth. The nurse scurried around with metal instruments. Putting them on a table. Getting towels, looking alert.

"One more, I think." What did the doctor know? Had she

ever had a baby? I doubted it. I made a note in my mind to ask her after this was all over.

Brian had a fresh cloth and wiped my hair off my face. The doctor stuck her face inches away from the opening. "Come on, you can push it right out this time. Push it right out." Her voice was demanding, incessant. If I pushed it out, the pain would go away. I took a breath and pushed and pushed. "It's coming. Push."

What did she think I was doing?

"That's great, Blue, we're having a baby," Brian said as loud as I'd ever heard him.

I didn't give a rat's ass who I saw when I closed my eye. This baby was coming out, and it was coming out now. I pushed as if I was trying to push my insides out. Sound came through the clenched teeth.

"Stop. Stop pushing. There it is."

"Stop pushing." Brian's voice came through, and I could feel the body of the baby. Moving through the passage.

"Now, just a little snip, you'll hardly feel it," I heard the doctor say as she pressed something cold against me. I didn't feel anything at all but the cold.

Brian and I panted together, like two exhausted puppies. I was beyond the pain.

"Here it is." I could feel the doctor's hands down there. I pushed longer than I had before. The pain changed.

"God, there it is. Wow, it's coming out." He was crying. He took off his glasses and looked up at me.

"It's a boy." The doctor placed it on my chest. Still wet and bloody. It couldn't be a boy. A small whimper. He looked just like him. Little ears just like Darrel. I wanted him off me. They were all watching, Brian, the doctor, the nurse. Watching for me to love it, to cry, to smile, to say, "Oh, my beautiful baby."

"You can put him on your breast." The doctor seemed anxious.

"Please take him away. Please give me a little time." I looked at Brian. He would understand.

"He's a beautiful baby, Blue, you don't mean that. Just hold him a minute, and you'll see," he said.

Blue nursing the baby. Used her camera.
Not really very well focused.
Spring 1997

CHAPTER 16

I named him Marten after Glue-skub's helpmate. Helpmate to the trickster god of the Wabanaki. Wabanaki Native People included the Penobscots, Micmacs, Abenakis, and Maliseet people as well as the Passamaquoddy, living from Quebec through Maine into the Canadian Maritime Provinces. Koluskap named our people Wabanaki because they were the ones who lived "where the day breaks." People of the Dawn, we called ourselves. I called him "the baby." They all said that it would come, the love, the closeness that a mother feels for her own child. I sat in my room at Grandpa's, holding him. Brian had gone back to school, and Grandpa was playing cards with some of the older men on the reservation. We were alone. The baby was on my breast. I looked down at him, his mouth circling my nipple and his tiny lips sucking and sucking and sucking. He was taking my milk out of me, draining me, exhausting me.

Mama gave me a rocking chair made by a man we all knew well, Josh Kantner his name was. It had a little sway to the left every time I rocked back and a little sway to the right when I rocked forward. It gave me something to think about. I knew I had made a mistake. I should have had an abortion or given him away to some nice family with a six-figure income and a full-time nanny. They all watched me with him, Mama, Daddy, when they came, the public health nurse, even Grandpa. They must have talked to him about me and the baby, asked him questions about how we related.

The nurse had come every week for the first month. "Hi, I'm Susan," she said the first day she appeared at the door. "May I come in? I'd like to talk to you and answer any questions you might have about being a mother." She was very white, blond, young, rich, sacrificing her years for the unmarried Indian mothers who didn't know anything about raising babies. "Oh, isn't he cute, Indian babies are so adorable." I couldn't tell her that I wished he would go away, that sometimes when he sucks on me I wanted to pull him off, put him in the other room, shut the door. "Sometimes it takes a while to bond. Do you think you are bonding with Marten?"

I didn't answer her. Just made tea, said what was necessary, told her we were doing just fine. What would she do if she knew anyway? Take him away, find me a shrink?

And Mama. "Aren't you just thrilled with him? We have a new show opening next week, young artist from Ellsworth. I wish I could have had another baby, but I couldn't after you, you know. You can't have a baby without a uterus." She looked right at me. "Cuddle him, Blue, he needs to be cuddled, everyone needs to be cuddled."

I rocked back and forth slowly and watched him. I pictured him in my uterus, growing and moving. I remembered the bumps in my belly and how Daphne loved touching them. I closed my eyes and thought of love. Of how much I loved Grandpa. And Maria. And even Mama and Daddy as weird as they were. And, of course, Brian. When I thought of them that feeling would well up in my stomach. Maria, when she brushed my hair. I knew what love felt like. Passion, I wasn't so sure. But love and closeness, yes. I looked at the baby. The fluttering feeling in my stomach was gone. Instead, I felt as if my whole life force was being sucked down his throat, my very being, me, Blue Willoughby, disappearing down the gullet of a newborn. I knew it was wrong, that I shouldn't feel that way. But what is wrong if you feel it? Isn't wrong something you do knowingly? What if you can't help it? Is it still wrong?

I rocked and he sucked. I would feed him and change him and take care of him. It was my duty. I wanted to love him, too. His fingers grabbed around my shirt, that same old violet sweatshirt I had bought in Providence. They were perfect hands, like Grandpa's, strong, thick, but they grabbed at me and I had to peel the fingers to get them off. I named him Marten to be strong and good. His face was contented. But I could still see Darrel in him. The baby inherited his genes. His lip turned up a little, even when he was nursing. He couldn't help it, but that's the way it was.

He stopped sucking, and I looked down at him. He didn't have black Indian hair. Just wisps of light brown fluff. When I breathed, his hair would move, like seaweed in the ocean. I pulled him off my nipple and covered my breast with the sweatshirt. I continued to rock slowly, not enough to sway to the right or left. He didn't seem to notice that his source of food was gone. I thought of my milk in his mouth, on his tongue, down his throat. He was living off my milk, and they said at the clinic, "Don't feed him solid food until he is at least three months old." For three months everything would be from me, from my body, my breasts. My milk. I looked at the baby's throat, at the pulsing blue artery just under the skin, bringing my milk to his brain, exposed as his head lolled to the side. Down his tiny throat, coating the sides, down into his stomach.

I pulled up his undershirt and watched as his stomach rose and fell with his breathing. Inside all that skin and tissue and stomach lining was my milk, being broken down by his enzymes, making it ready to send nourishment to his brain. His mouth made sucking motions, and his foot kicked up. He must have been dreaming. Dreaming of sucking on me. What else could he dream about? He didn't know anything else.

I undid the side of his diaper and pulled it down. His navel was healed up. His abdomen was not moving, but I knew it was working on the milk. Inside I knew my milk was working its way through the long corridors of the intestines, the best parts taken for nourishment. I stopped the rocking and undid the other side of the diaper, curious now. A bowel movement lay in the diaper, yellow, left there for me, the remains of the milk, the stuff he didn't want. His penis moved. It wasn't cut. I wasn't sure if Darrel was circumcised, but I guessed that he was. I pulled the foreskin down and the head of the penis peeked out, nestled there, protected, small, harmless. I wasn't quick enough to move as the urine hit my cheek. The force of it was more than I thought possible from such a small thing. I pulled the diaper up to catch the last few dribbles and waited until he was finished. The urine dripped down my face and I left it there as I pulled the diaper down again. Piss and shit. That was what was left of me after he was finished. Piss and shit, waiting for me to deal with, to dispose of, to clean up.

His eyes opened, and his mouth began sucking again. I pulled up the sweatshirt on the other side and turned him. His head twisted, looking for the nipple. His mouth was searching as his head moved back and forth. "See, my baby, see it?" The nipple stood out as if asking to be taken. His lips covered it and began to suck. I felt my nipple being pulled into his throat.

"Rock a bye baby, on the treetop, when the wind blows, the cradle will rock, when the bough breaks, the cradle will fall, and down . . ." I stood up, got out of the rocking chair, stopped singing. How could someone sing that song to a baby? It was the only lullaby I knew. Everyone knew that song. I just want to sing to him. How could anyone sing that song to a baby? I would ask Grandpa to sing me a Passamaquoddy lullaby. Something his mother sang to him. Way back in my memory there was a song, but I couldn't quite touch it. I looked down at him. He was fine.

My baby grew and I took care of him. I found other songs to sing as I nursed him. They weren't all lullabies, but they were kind songs, not cruel, not violent. Grandpa sang Passamaquoddy songs and I tried to learn them, but I only got bits and pieces of the words. "Kuhkukhahs, kuhkukhahs," and then something about "kakskus." An owl in a tree, Grandpa said. "Whooooooo." He danced around the living room, holding the baby and singing "Kuhkukhahs, whoooooooo." We were so happy, Grandpa and I. As soon as the frost was out of the ground and the mud was gone, we would go out in the woods and look for brown ash trees. Mama gave me a backpack for the baby, and Grandpa would carry him on his back. He would learn about the woods early. I decided that I was going to be a basket maker. I was good. Mrs. Francis had said so. Sweetgrass and split brown ash. I could support the baby if I worked hard, and I had that insurance money to get me started. I could do it. I could do anything with my hands. And I was Passamaquoddy, so making baskets was in me somewhere.

The morning of the day I met Leonora, I sat at the kitchen table with my hands spread out in front of me. They were soft and smooth like the baby's skin. I spent the morning with Mrs. Francis talking about sweetgrass and weaving it into baskets. The baby had fallen asleep on the way home, so I put him on the floor still in his backpack. Mrs. Francis' hands were brown and covered with lines as if her skin was too big for the bones.

Her nails were broken and ragged from working the ash. Stains of blue and red and yellow from dyeing the sweetgrass were embedded in the wrinkles and cuticles of her fingers. She had real hands, working hands. I looked at mine, counting the fingers, surprised to come up with ten. Ten white soft fingers with smooth nails and half-moon cuticles. They looked manicured, pampered except for a few little scars from the accident on one hand. I picked up a piece of split ash she had given me and ran it across my fingers. My great-grandmother's picture was too blurred to detect detail in her hands even when I moved up close to it. I remembered when I made a lot of baskets, my hands were tough. They would be again.

Mrs. Francis had gone home, and I was weaving the handle onto a potato basket when I heard squealing brakes and then a loud thump right outside on the street in front of the house. I sat still, holding the ash, waiting for the next sound, afraid of what it might be. A car or a small truck sped off almost immediately. Certainly if it was a person, an old Indian man, someone would have stopped, especially here on the reservation where everyone knew everyone else.

I checked to see that the baby was still sleeping and went out the front door to see what happened. I could hear a whimper coming from a dark form on the side of the street. Jesus, someone had hit a dog and left it there to die in the gutter. One of those black-and-white Border collies used to herd sheep and cattle. It wasn't from the reservation. It lifted its head and whined at my approach. The first thing I could think of was a blanket. There was an old one in the shed by the side of the house. I ran as fast as I could, as if the blanket could make all the difference. The blanket in my hand, I knelt to look more closely. I knew I shouldn't approach an injured animal, but it looked so helpless. A small stream of blood came out of its eye and ran down the white streak on its shoulder. I gently touched the paw closest to me as the dog raised its head again and made a small noise. I thought that perhaps it wasn't too badly injured and wondered if I should bring it to the house. I moved on my hands and knees around it to see how I could pick it up. Its hind end lay at an odd angle to the rest of the body. I crawled closer and felt along the back. It was broken, broken and twisted. The dog's hind end formed a right angle to its front end and a piece of the backbone stuck out through the black hair on its back. I could see that it was a female. I wouldn't have to think of the dog as "it." Her teats leaked a steady stream down onto the macadam. She didn't seem to be in terrible pain, but I knew she would have to die. She couldn't live with her back broken in half. I rested my hand on her head. She relaxed under me and stuck her tongue out as if trying to lick me. I placed the blanket over her and tucked it around her neck before I went into the house to get Grandpa's gun. Grandpa wasn't due back for another two hours, and the dog needed to be dealt with now. The bullets were in his desk drawer, and he had shown me how to load a pistol a few years back when we were walking in the woods. Grandpa always carried it in case he came upon a trapped or injured animal. I had never seen him shoot anything alive, but we used to shoot trash-can lids for practice. He said I had a good eye. The bullet dropped into the chamber effortlessly. I put one bullet in my jacket pocket in case I missed with the first one. But I didn't intend to miss. My hand with the gun shook as I held it out toward the dog's head. She lifted her head once more and dropped it back on the blanket. I lowered the gun and crouched down to her. "Don't be afraid."

The sound of the shot was not as loud as I expected. More of a "pop" than a "bang." She didn't look much different except that her head no longer moved and a small hole appeared above her eye. I picked up the corner of the blanket and pulled it over toward the grass, out of the street. A green-leather collar with several tags attached to it encircled her neck. "Hattie," it said. I closed her one good eye like I'd seen people do in the movies. She still felt warm under my hands. "Hattie." I said the name out loud. "Someone is missing you." I couldn't hold the tears back. They seemed to come from my guts, from way below my eyes, down deep where I could only imagine, as I sat holding her head. "Hattie." I began to hum to her. I'm not sure what the tune was, but I held her head close to my chest and hummed and rocked back and forth. Her body seemed for a moment part of my own. "Hattie." I murmured her name over and over to her and cried until I had no more need. The grass was cold and wet, and a spring chill was still in the ground even though the lilacs were beginning to bloom. The dog's body was cooling and becoming stiff, and I wasn't sure how long I had been out there. The dark settled over the house, and my legs were shivering. I remembered the baby, my baby, on the floor sleeping. I undid the green collar from her throat and pulled the blanket up to cover her head before I went into the house.

"Leonora Kausen," the dog tag said. I held it under the kitchen ceiling light. "Lighthouse Point Road, Green Harbor." God, that was ten miles away. I checked the baby, went to the bathroom, poured myself some peppermint tea, picked up a piece of split ash, and turned it around in my hands. The owner's phone number was on the tag, and I knew I would have to call, but it was hard to start dialing. I hoped she wouldn't answer. I thought of Hattie outside in the dark under a dirty blanket. I dialed so slowly the phone made that horrible noise telling you to hang up and try again. I tried again and almost finished. Then I grabbed a notepad and pencil and wrote down what to say. "Hello, this is Blue Willoughby. I live on the reservation. Your dog was killed by a car in front of my house." No, that wasn't really true. "Hello, my name is Blue

Willoughby. I live on the reservation. I shot Hattie. She's dead. I had to. I'm sorry." How would I want to be told? I would want someone to come to my house, bring the dog, hold me tight while the idea sank in. But I couldn't do that, and Hattie was outside dead. The puppies were probably crying and Leonora was probably out looking for her. "Hello, this is Blue Willoughby. Your dog is here. I held her head before she died. She was a beautiful dog, and you must have loved her very much. Come here, and I will tell you about it." That sounded better. I practiced it while I held my hand on the phone. I didn't make any allowances for her to say anything. She would have time when I was finished.

The phone was ringing. A voice said, "Hello."

"Hello, this is Blue. I . . . your dog. She . . ."

"Hello. Who is this? Do you know about Hattie?"

"She's here. I'm sorry. She's dead." I couldn't say anything else. There was no sound from the other end. I thought that she had hung up, but there was no dial tone. I waited.

"This is Leonora. Did you find my dog?"

We talked, and I gave her my address. She said she would be right over. I went out again to the street, to Hattie. It started to drizzle, so I picked her up and carried her into the house. By now she was very stiff, and her hind end stuck out at an odd angle. I laid her on the floor, wrapped in a clean blanket, in the living room and waited. There was no blood from the bullet hole, and I wondered if I should tell the owner about the gun, that I had shot her.

Leonora's pickup truck pulled up in front of the door about fifteen minutes later. I watched from the window. She stopped at the spot where Hattie died and looked down. I wasn't sure how she could tell. Crushed leaves or perhaps a spot of blood or urine. Her red rubber boots kicked at the place as if to mark it. She walked very slowly up to the front door. Her head down.

I felt that she was usually very quick. That this was hard for her. That she was wondering if there was another way to handle this. I looked at them both on the floor. The dead dog and the sleeping baby. Not close to each other, but both on the floor. Hattie was near the kitchen door, but the blanket covered her head.

I opened the door just as Leonora raised her hand to knock. She stood in the drizzle, tears and rain mingling on her face. "Come in," I said.

She stepped into the kitchen. I'm sure she could see the blanket-covered mound in the next room. "I'm Leonora." Even through her grief, she was lovely.

"I'm Blue. I called you." Of course I called her. She had a bit of an accent. I wasn't sure what kind. Not from Maine. Not from the U.S. "I'm so sorry. The driver sped off. I didn't get a good look."

She didn't move. Just stood, like she needed to be taken care of but didn't know how to ask. "This is hard for me. Her puppies are whimpering. I've had her for seven years." There was no longer rain on her face, only tears, just a few. She brushed her cropped brown hair back from her face. "She jumped out of the car at the vet's. Got confused, I guess. Oh God." She smelled like fresh rain and flowers. Not perfumy flowers. Real ones. Lilacs or apple blossoms. "She was probably trying to find the pups."

And that's when I met Leonora. I told her about the gun. I told her everything. I insisted she take the blanket and watched from the window as she left. At the spot on the road, she hesitated again. She put Hattie in the passenger side rather than in the back of the truck. I wondered if the back was full of something or she just wanted Hattie with her. A few days later she arrived at the door at lunchtime, to return the cleaned wool blanket. Framed by the doorway, she held a bouquet of dried flowers, mostly sea heather with some purple statice mixed in. "I wanted you to have these. And I wondered if you would like to come out and see the pups. They are weaned now, of course." Her voice reminded me of Daphne. I could feel Grandpa behind me, holding the baby, waiting to be introduced. I took the flowers and the blanket and invited her in for lunch.

Blue and her new friend, Leonora.
Spring 1997

CHAPTER 17

⤜

Leonora reached across me for a roll. Her arm touched my shoulder. I could smell the flowers. Her hands were dry, cracked, her fingernails ragged and torn, the skin on her fingers ingrained with lines of dirt. She saw me looking at them.

"Dirt," she said. "Garden. I've been weeding all morning. Can't really scrub the dirt off." She smiled at me. "Getting ready to put the onions in."

"Do you sell eggs?" Grandpa asked. "Nothing like a real fresh egg."

"Sure. I keep thirty layers. I don't sell a lot. Sometimes folks from Indian Beach come to buy them."

"Perhaps we'll come out and get some."

"Call me in the morning. I can tell you if I have any. Sometimes I'm working on the computer and I don't hear the door. I do freelance editing and some English to German translating. For a publishing house. I try to do it only on rainy days. Haven't had many of those lately, so sometimes I work at night."

She reached again. "Excuse me. Great bread. Did you make it?" She looked at Grandpa.

"I made it," I said.

Flowers and sweat. Lilacs and apple blossoms and sweat. Like the smell of the sweetgrass. All over. In the air. Her legs and arms were long. Her limbs seemed to sprawl, as if they were too long for the rest of her. Too long for our table and chairs. She looked at Grandpa. "When you come to get the eggs, I'll show you around the farm. It's small but lots happening. Goats, chickens, and two pigs I'm raising, one for me and one for the man next door. His wife just died, and I thought it might be a diversion for him. He comes to look at it every day, calls him Hamlet."

She left right after lunch to get back to the garden.

"Seems like a nice woman."

"Yes," was all I could say.

"Might be a good friend for you. Seems to like Marten."

"Yes." I carried the dishes to the sink. Rattled them around. Made some noise. Brushed crumbs off the table. "I'm going to help Mrs. Francis get ready for the museum show. She's letting me make the lids for the small sweetgrass baskets." I couldn't talk about Leonora.

The afternoon went by quickly. The lids piled up. I had almost enough for all the baskets. Our lemonade break, which I usually looked forward to, was the hardest time. We had to talk, and I just wanted to sit and work with my hands.

That night Marten was restless. Finally he drifted off and I was wide-awake. I carried him from the bed to his crib. I needed to have the bed to myself.

"Berry." I knew I'd have to give her up soon. It was all too weird. But not quite yet. "Berry. Come on." I pulled the sheet over my head and made a tent for her. I didn't really have a friend here to talk to. Brian came to visit when he could, but he needed to make money for school. I knew Berry would come if I was patient. She did. Lying on her back. I felt sad for a minute when I thought that she wasn't real. Just in my mind. But she had been real. And I knew where she was buried. And nobody knew that I still talked to her.

"I like Leonora. Well, I mean, I guess I like her. I love the way she smells and moves. Her arms are so strong. Longer than most people's. I wonder if she's got a boyfriend. She must be at least thirty. Older than I am. She smells like sweetgrass." Berry lolled her head. Not much response but that was OK. "Grandpa likes her. I think we'll go out there, to her farm. Take Marten. Berry, why do you have no brain? Such a small thing. You have everything else. How could you have no brain?" She was flawless. Just like me if I hadn't had the accident. Her mouth was open a bit. I wanted to hold her, but I knew she would disappear. So I held myself. My hand between my legs.

I woke up in the morning with my hand still there between my legs. Berry, of course, was gone. It was early. Marten was still not awake. I had fed him around two, so I hoped he would sleep another half hour. Berry had not been in bed with me for a long time.

When I was little, just after the accident, I thought Berry gave me ideas, suggested words for me to say. I really believed she talked. But she'd been silent now for so long. My words had been wrong for others even though I understood them. I tried to say "school" and it came out "kak" or "lunch" became "slurp" or "cat" became "bitch." I usually said nothing for fear of saying the wrong word, most probably, a swear word.

That day in the first grade we practiced vowels after lunch. A-E-I-O-U, A-E-I-O-U. We said them over and over and over. A-E-I-O-U. I practiced them in my mind until I had confidence I could say them with the class. My voice began to say the same letters as the rest of the first-graders. The right ones this time. My voice grew louder. A-E-I-O-U. Marty Cullen in the desk next to me, began to stare. "Mrs. Booth, Mrs. Booth,

Blue is talking." Marty shook her hand up in the air and bounced up and down in her seat. "Mrs. Booth, quick."

The class stopped and looked. "A-E-I-O-U, A-E-I-O-U." Over and over, louder and louder. I was afraid to stop. Afraid that I could never do it again if I stopped. Mrs. Booth put her hand on my shoulder. "Blue, that's very good, dear." Her hand rested on me, quiet, waiting for me to stop on my own. I couldn't see Berry, but I knew she was there, surprised that I could say something without her help. I stopped slowly, so as not to change anything, so you might not even notice. Just slowed down, "A-E-I-O-U, a-e-i-o-u." When I was no longer in-canting, I looked up with my one beautiful brown eye and smiled. I felt that I could do anything. I could write those letters and read them.

That was the last day I even thought that Berry said some-thing. I couldn't remember her talking, just remembered that I thought she did. Anyway it didn't matter because she existed only in the cemetery, dead, buried, years ago. But if only she had been normal, with a brain, and hadn't died, I could talk to her about Leonora.

The next few weeks were busy. Mama came to visit. The next day Daddy. Their visits were like slogging through a ma-nure pile.

"Blue, dear, the baskets are lovely. Maybe we could have a show at my gallery. I'll talk to the owner. But, you mustn't hold your hopes up."

"Mama, I can do this myself. I don't need any help. I'm doing fine."

"The baby should be able to play with other kids," she said. It took me a minute to follow her leap. I should have been used to it by now. "Soon you'll meet a nice man and settle down and have another baby. You're lucky. You still can."

"Can what, Mama?" She didn't respond to my question.

"My daughter, the Indian basket maker." She spun around with her delicate hands clasped, like a small child realizing that her dreams had come true. I had failed in the movie-star slot, and she had found a new one for me. We didn't discuss the baskets again that visit. It had been a momentary amusement.

And Daddy—almost worse, setting up scenes, clicking, endless poses of Marten, talking only when he looked through the viewfinder. Daddy. He came after breakfast to spend the day. Leonora dropped in with some sorrel from the garden and Daddy took our picture. They were so different, Grandpa and Daddy. Grandpa was dark and thick and wise. Daddy was tall and pale and bearded. Their heads almost touched when they talked about my baskets and Grandpa's herbs on the shelf. Two grown men with nothing in common except love. How could Daddy have come from Grandpa? And then me from the two of them?

"Oh, my Beautiful Blue, I've missed you," he said, trying to hug me with all the equipment around his neck. I thought about telling him not to call me that. It sounded like he was talking to a baby. "So, how was the visit with your mother?"

"Fine." I didn't want to get into it.

"Does she seem happy, I mean, content. Does she need anything?"

I could see that he needed to talk about it, and I remembered the day he talked to me about Berry. How kind he was. And patient. "Yes, and no. Yes, she seems OK. Talks about work and all. And no, she doesn't seem to need anything."

Daddy played with his fingers, one at a time, on the table. He looked awkward, like he was too big for our little house, like he needed his high ceiling and long rooms and big windows. Grandpa and I looked at one another. "She asked how I was when we met at the post office," Daddy said. "She said we should have coffee sometime. Don't you think that's a good sign, Dad?" It was less of a question than a statement needing affirmation.

"I guess it's a sign that she is concerned about how you are, son."

"Do you think she would go to counseling with me? You know, maybe see if we could patch things up. We really didn't get along that badly. Something happened. I'm not sure what. We had everything going for us." He stopped playing with his fingers and looked up at us. First one, then the other. "Right?"

"I guess so."

"Sometimes relationships just don't work out," said Grandpa. "Your mother and I were lucky. In those days you had no choice. You just worked at it and stuck it out. Today it's too easy to quit."

I knew what Grandpa and Grandma had together. I knew they had passion, talked to each other about real feelings, and hurts, and needs.

"Mama loves you so much," Daddy turned to me. "Maybe you could talk to her. Tell her that maybe we need to try harder. I'd do anything. We could go on a trip. She always wanted to go to Europe, Greece maybe." His voice rose. "God, that's it. We could go on a cruise of the Greek Islands. What shots. Oh, God, the scenery, the people. I'll buy a new lens. It would be perfect." He looked pleadingly at me, as if he were trying to convince his mother to let him go to a Saturday matinee.

"I'll talk to her, but I don't think it'll do any good. You know Mama. She's created a new life now." Daddy winced when I said "new life," as if the words gouged his face. His hand went to his mouth. I thought he might cry in a minute. "I'll talk to her," I said, so that he wouldn't. Later, I watched Grandpa walk him to the truck, arm in arm, heads together, Daddy's head so much taller. But why did he look so small?

"What do you say," Grandpa said the next day. "Should we go out and get some eggs at that farm?"

It was like a picture book. The house. The barn. Chickens clucking in the grass. A goat grazing with a brass bell around her neck. And Leonora in the garden. She came toward us, arm raised, wiping her forehead. Her scent wafted ahead of her. Her legs, bare until the shorts. Long, browned from the soil and the sun. Tufts of curled underarm hair, stuck together from the sweat.

"Oh, come and see all my babies." She guided us to the barn. Old, I could see, but fixed up. Old lines, timbers. But new roof, doors, stalls. Marten bounced and kicked in his sling as if he were excited as well. "Only two left. The others have been sold." She stood back so we could lean over the wall into the box. Black-and-white, just like Hattie, but fluffy and cuddly.

"Oh, may I pick one up?"

"Please, they'd love it."

I held them both together, Marten and the puppy, about the same size. The puppy smelled the milk on Marten's mouth and started to lick around the edges.

"Let me," Grandpa said as he held out his arms. "We used to have a dog, before your grandma died. Not a Border collie, just a plain old dog. Fanny, we called her. I don't think I ever told you that."

"And look," Leonora said, "Francine just had kittens again, her last I think. She's very old and kind of worn-out." Grandpa had to hold the pup very tight because it was trying to get at Francine and her kittens. "She's got a bad ear. Something tore it, and I think it's infected."

"Looks like you grow plenty of fir trees around here," said Grandpa. "Just score the bark of a tree and scrape up some of the resin. Stick that on the ear. Probably clear right up." He winked at Leonora. "Old Indian custom."

"Yes, try it. Grandpa's cures always work." I looked at him. "Well, almost always."

She asked if we would come the next day for lunch. Grandpa said he was going to a meeting at the reservation community center and wanted to take Marten. "Why don't you come," he said. "It'll be good for you to get away by yourself. You can take the truck. We can walk, can't we, Marten?"

Blue in the Indian skirt I gave her
for her 18th birthday.
Spring 1997

CHAPTER 18

Leonora waited for me on her stoop. She looked odd, different, like she'd changed somehow. Her face had lost the few lines of the day before and she wore a light green cotton sundress. Just straps over her bare shoulders. Bits of garden soil and witchgrass clung to her tanned feet. Francine lounged in her lap, tail flicking left, then right, kneading at the pocket of the dress.

"Blue, hi, come sit with us." Her hand touched mine, and I took it. She eased me down to the stoop next to her. "Look, Francine's ear seems better already." She lowered her head to purr back to the thin orange mama cat, and continued to hold my hand. I wanted to pull it away, wasn't sure how to. "Come, let's put her back in the barn."

"Good," I said, eager to change position. I withdrew my hand from hers to balance myself as I stood up. "Here, I'll take Francine."

I reached for the old cat and brought her close to look at the ear. The sore was beginning to close. Francine had been with

Leonora for years, and I wanted so badly for the cat to recover. We brought Francine back to her kittens in the barn. They mewed for their milk. She leapt out of my grasp toward the tiny mouths, and I heard the faint sound of sucking. Leonora stood behind me, very close. I felt her leg pressed against mine. I was very conscious of my clothes, that I wore my new Indian-print skirt, that it moved gently with the breeze blowing through the open barn door.

We stood for minutes, our breathing the only sound audible over the sucking and mewing of the kittens. Leonora sighed. I was aware of her breath on my neck, aware of my own breath, afraid to move. I felt frantic inside, but continued to be still, breathing slowly with her, waiting. She touched my waist and the breathing continued, both of us together. Her hand made its way slowly up toward my breast, but I could not see her. She was still behind me. I knew she could feel my nipple hard against the silk of my blouse, and she made a sound. I felt my milk rush.

Her hand held me there, barely moving, as she placed her mouth on the back of my neck. She brought me closer to her, and her body pressed against mine.

"Oh, Blue."

I wanted to speak. There were no words. Her hand left my breast and she turned me toward her. Again I tried to speak. Instead, it was Leonora's voice.

"Oh, Blue, your neck. Your mouth. Everything. Beautiful. So beautiful." She looked at my body, at my mouth.

Me, beautiful, Beautiful Blue, beautiful. I could do nothing. She began to unbutton my white silk blouse and noticed the buttons weren't buttoned right. She smiled and opened the next one, and the next, pulling the silk out of my skirt as she descended. I watched her, conscious suddenly of my face, my drooping mouth, my eye. She finished the buttons and my breasts were there, behind the silk, pushing the material away.

"Don't be afraid, Blue."

She slipped the blouse off my shoulders, and it fell onto the spilled hay like a parachute. As she lowered her mouth to my breast, I again became aware of the kittens sucking. Her tongue touched the nipple of one breast as her hand held the other. My milk began to drip. I was afraid she would go farther and terrified that she wouldn't. I turned my good side toward her as her mouth opened on me and she moaned again. Her hands slid down to my back, to the button and zipper of my skirt, her mouth still on my breast, sucking slowly. My skirt fell, and I was naked except for my sandals. I closed my eyes, unable to take any more without reacting somehow, but now unsure what to do. My hands went between my legs but Leonora gently removed them.

"No, Blue, I will do this," she said, barely lifting her mouth away.

We sank to the hay together and she sucked at me and groaned so that I could hardly bear it. I turned my good side to her again and I believe she must have noticed. She lifted her mouth and looked at me. Her fingers found the scar running the length of my body and she traced it up to my glass eye as she kissed it with tiny kisses.

"It's alright," she whispered, moving her weight onto my body. "Please let me do this."

"Yes," was all I could say. And I closed my eyes.

I sensed her fingers were near, near that place that no one else had touched in a sexual way since that boy so long ago, that place where my own fingers went in the night. Leonora's hands made little circles up my thigh as her mouth went back to my breast. My hands went to hers and moved rhythmically in circles, moved with her fingers. She tried to shake me away.

"Please," I said to her in a whisper.

She made a noise in her throat and fell back on my breast, her tongue circling my nipple. Her fingers stroked the hair in that place down there before they entered, her thumb stroking the outside, touching the nub so familiar to me, two of her fingers inside, moving ever so slightly. Her fingers responded each time to my squeezing. Her tongue wet the surface of my skin all the way down to the hair. Our breath came in gasps, no longer in unison, but held together by its purpose. My hands stopped moving, and I gently pushed her down just that little bit more until her tongue found the place and she sank into me.

I knew then, I knew after that day, that I was a sexual being, that I could feel passion, that I was beautiful, and that I would do it again and again.

CHAPTER 19

Mama called first. "Blue, honey, I'm going away for a while."

"Oh."

"I thought I'd tell you. We're going to South America. Painting. You won't be able to reach us."

"Who?"

"Well, dear, you probably don't remember him, but many years ago Daddy and I had a friend who was an artist. He's been living in South America for years, but now he's back. Of course we were just friends when he was here, but now, well we have been seeing each other. I've taken this semester off from school and Rachel is going to take care of the gallery. It's only for two months. He loves my work. Isn't that exciting? How's the baby? And Grandpa?"

It had to be Simon, the guy in the woods.

"Blue, are you still there?"

I wondered if he still had his old blue van.

"I wanted to talk to you about something," I said, remembering Daddy at the kitchen table.

"One of my friends is staying in the apartment, and I told her to call you if she needed anything. You know Daddy isn't very reliable and the way he feels. Well, I hate to ask him."

I heard Simon's fly zip in my mind. They never knew I was there.

"Blue, please say something. Are you upset I'm going away? I remember you liked Simon. Remember, he was the one with the scar on his face. Remember?"

"Yes, I remember. Have a good time. I'll tell Grandpa."

"I'll send you a postcard, but we'll be on the Amazon. Can't reach us there. No phones. Simon says we could have a joint show when we get home. We'll get together then."

"Does Daddy know?"

"Well, you know, we aren't married anymore. I thought maybe you could tell him. He always liked Simon, too. We were all just friends then. Marten will be so big when I get back. First thing I'll do is come right over and give him a big hug. Now don't forget to call Daddy. Love to Grandpa. Aren't you excited for me? This is the biggest moment of my life."

"Have fun. I'll call Daddy right now."

"No, wait an hour. We're just leaving now. I wouldn't want him to think he has to come and say good-bye. We fly to New York and then direct to Montevideo. Bye, darling. Simon sends love."

"Bye."

The dial tone seemed louder than I had ever heard it. I listened for a moment and dropped the receiver in its cradle. I hadn't even had a chance to tell her about Leonora.

Daddy seemed surprised when I called. "She went with Simon?" he said. "He was that mediocre painter. He painted The Bubbles from our house. Do you remember?"

"I tried to talk to her. You know how she is. She said we'd get together when she got back."

Daddy promised to come for dinner soon. I promised not to worry about him.

I did worry about him. He was weak. He knew they were divorced, but there would never be anyone but Mama for him. On Saturday afternoon he called to say that he would be away overnight. Going off with one of the guys working on the new house. Maybe do a little fishing. He sounded fine. Said he would take his camera. Maybe get some shots for his new show. He was sure they would ask him to do one for the opening of the new bank in town. Be back in the morning, he said. Asked how the baby was. Said he would see us soon. Said he loved me.

Grandpa was off playing cards with his friends. With the baby on my back, I walked to the edge of the reservation to gather some greens. Dandelions were just starting to bud, so the leaves would still be good. I knelt in the grass and cut off some leaves with my knife. From the oozing milk I could tell that they would be slightly bitter. Should have cut them last week, but Grandpa would love them in salad. He would say, "My beautiful Miss Brown, you know just what I like. A real Child of the Dawn." Marten tried to grab the greens from my hand and laughed when I pulled them away. He loved the crinkle sound of the paper bag where I put the leaves. I could hear his little attempts at laughter, so I crinkled louder each time. After I'd picked a full bag I stood and stretched my legs. They ached for the first few steps. It seemed that since the lovemaking with Leonora everything hurt more, ached more, felt better, sounded louder. On the way home I sang some blues for the baby. The blues had more guts to them than lullabies. He put his head down on my neck and fell asleep.

Upon our return, we found Grandpa sitting at the kitchen table. Hamburgers and spring greens for supper were his favorite. Marten slept in the backpack, his head cocked to the side. "Now, how many youngsters in this day and age would know how to pick dandelion greens?" he said when we were al-most finished with supper. "Now, you tell me."

"Grandpa, I'm no youngster anymore. I'm a mother. And Grandpa?"

"What's that, my little Miss Brown." I looked at him. So dark and so thick. I could see how much he loved me in his hands. They seemed to caress each other sometimes when he looked at me. I knew I could tell him about Leonora.

"Let me put Marten in his crib first." Marten stayed asleep as I lowered him into the crib and kissed his damp curls. On the way back to the kitchen I wondered if I were making a mis-take. "Grandpa," I said again as I sat down facing him.

"This sounds serious. I better get some lemonade. You too?" I always wanted lemonade. He dropped a sprig of mint in mine and lowered himself into his chair.

"I want to tell you about someone." My gaze shifted to the little pile of greens still left on my plate. I felt his finger under my chin, lifting it up.

"You should always look at the face of the recipient of the news or else you cannot tell how he feels."

The baby stirred. "Let me check him. I'll be right back."

His hand moved gently to my shoulder. "You have started. Now finish. I want to hear about your someone."

"It's passion. I found it. I understand what it is, what it is that you had with Grandma, what we read about in school. *Romeo and Juliet, Wuthering Heights,* Elizabeth Barrett Brown-ing's sonnets." I realized that I was playing with my greens, twirling them around with my fork. "We did it. Remember that day with Otuhk and El in the woods. Not like that. It was like nothing I could have imagined." I looked down at the salad that was left on the plate and again felt his finger under my chin. "Remember the feather you gave me? Years ago? The time we talked about passion?"

"Yes, I do. A white turkey feather. We made believe it was from an eagle. I told you you would understand its power when you had found passion."

"I buried it in our yard, at Daddy's. I said I would dig it up when I found passion. I marked the place so I could find it again. All these years I have been waiting and looking at the marker, wondering if it was still there, still down in the earth."

"Perhaps it's time to dig it up."

"I know it's only a turkey feather, but in my mind it's become something strong."

"Can you tell me about this person?"

"I don't know." I avoided looking at the greens again because I knew the finger would come, so I looked through his eyes. He waited.

"It's the woman, isn't it? Leonora. The woman with the puppies." This time he looked down at his plate. I lifted his chin.

"Grandpa, can you understand?" We looked at each other without veils.

It took him a moment to respond. He breathed a big breath. "No one said that passion comes only with man and woman together. Passion comes in death, in anger, in sex, in birth, sometimes when you don't even expect it and sometimes when it is painful. Many people never experience it. But now, my beautiful Miss Brown, you have had passion, and I am so very happy."

Grandpa kissed my forehead with a tenderness usually reserved for a mother toward a child.

"Tomorrow I'm going to Daddy's. Check on him. Make him some lunch. And I think I'll dig up that turkey feather. I mean eagle feather. Do you want to come?"

"No, I'm going with Frank to get some ash. He found a good spot, near a stream, but on dry ground. Won't tell me where it is but said he'd take me there. I'll split it for you. I used to be pretty good when I collected it for my mama. You take the truck though. Frank's picking me up."

I knew it wasn't the right time to bring up the idea of my relationship with Leonora to Daddy. Whether he approved of her or not, he would want to take pictures.

The next day I pulled Grandpa's truck in behind Daddy's. I noticed "Robert Willoughby, Contractor," was newly painted on both sides in red with gold shadows. The baby was sound asleep, head drooped over to the side of the car seat, so I decided to let him sleep. I opened the car window on his side so I could hear him if he woke up. His head cocked at such an odd angle. I reached in and straightened it. His voice squeaked, but he kept on sleeping. The fields were white with blueberry blossoms, and I saw that Daddy had hired the bees again.

Daddy's camera and tripod were visible through the window. It flashed suddenly, causing me to trip on one of the stones. He must have had the timer going because I couldn't see him near the camera. Asparagus had come up in the little garden along the walk up to the door. We could have them for lunch. I picked a few out of compulsion and went into the house.

The camera flashed again. I almost stepped on the smashed photograph of Mama and Simon, but I didn't stop to pick it up. "Daddy, where are you? It's Blue and Marten. We've come for lunch." Then I saw him. My Daddy. My poor Daddy. Swinging ever so slightly, as if a light breeze were moving him back and forth, back and forth. Swinging from the ceiling. I gripped the asparagus and stood very still. The light flashed again. I jumped. Bile welled up in my throat. Same as when I was pregnant. I swallowed, trying to keep it under control.

"Daddy?" I'm not sure why I spoke. Tips of the asparagus broke off the stalks and fell to the ground. I knew the flash would go off again soon, and I couldn't bear it. I turned off the timer and disconnected the flash and camera. From the tripod the view was too clear. I looked through the lens into the purple face of someone I loved. The vomit, when it finally came, covered the camera. I couldn't bear to get close enough to cut him down. The smell, the excrement on the floor, his bowels, fallen out of him, fallen out of his shorts. Still covered with vomit, I called the police, threw the picture of Mama and Simon in the trash, and sat down in the kitchen to wait.

The baby slept through everything, the police, the funeral-home people, the neighbors wanting to see what happened. Grandpa wasn't home yet. I told the Carsons that I was fine, I would wait for Grandpa to get home. I would call some friends, Brian, Brian's parents. I would really prefer to be alone, I told them. They said they'd come back in an hour.

The marker. A cairn of garden rocks stood directly over the place where I buried it. After removing the stones, I slid my fingers deep down into the earth. I felt something on my fingertips. The hard piece, a piece of something that didn't belong there. Not earth, not rock, not someone's long-forgotten trash. Something that belonged to me. Something that I was ready for. My fingers wrapped around it. Wet earth pulled hard, as if holding my fingers there, protesting against the pulling. I held tight. The damp clay soil settled around my body, folded around my legs, my feet. I worked the box free. The old pencil box with the feather. Some dirt had worked its way in through the top. White. White under the brown of earth and age. I held it up in my hand. Up to the light with a tight grip. Mud oozed out between my fingers and dropped back to its source.

Rain began and mud smeared down my arm into the sleeve of my jacket. Cold ran in rivulets past my wrist down my arm and settled around my elbow in a cold pool. The wet earth seemed to invade my clothing, moving through my cotton skirt onto my skin, through my underwear to my body. I clutched the feather tightly, unable to stop the mud from coming so close to the bone.

CHAPTER 20

I stayed at Daddy's house with the baby and finally reached Grandpa on the phone. As soon as I told him to come right away, he knew something terrible had happened to Daddy. I wanted to tell him in person, to look into his eyes and hug him and cry with him. But he knew, guessed, that Daddy was dead. "Yes, Grandpa," I spoke into the black plastic of the mouthpiece. "He's dead. Please come now. Now. I need you." I sniffled between the words.

That night the baby and I slept in my old room and Grandpa slept in the little guest room that used to be Mama's office, where he used to stay on holidays. I moved a chair over the stain on the living-room carpet, but it was obvious, a child's attempt to cover something up. He knew what it was but left it there, perched over the brown stain, concealing the evidence, the proof. He could see it from his room.

"Berry." I didn't want the baby to hear me. "Berry," I whispered. "Please come, I need you." Just the words I said to Grandpa earlier. I pulled the covers over my head and waited for her. I didn't bother wiping the tears. Every once in a while a strange sound, like the imagined monsters of childhood might make, emanated from my throat. Growls. Growls that Daddy used to make to scare me. Raarrr . . . And it was me. Coming from my throat. Like the sounds I had made in labor. Daddy's face came and went minute after minute. The tongue, out to the side, black. Daddy's tongue. He used to touch his nose with that tongue to make me laugh. He said his tongue was long enough to touch his ear, but he wasn't in the mood to show me. I knew he couldn't really do it. It was pink then, small and pink. I wanted to push it back into his mouth when they took him down, but I didn't know how to ask. So he went to the funeral parlor with his tongue like that. I couldn't think of what they might do to it there.

"Berry, please come." It began to sound like a chant. Every few minutes I repeated. "Berry, Berry." I had taken the film out of the camera before anyone came. Black-and-white film. Thirty-six exposures. Set to click every minute. I hadn't decided if I would develop it or not. "Berry, please come." She was there, lying next to me, and for the first time, she was crying, too. Very softly, with little noises. It was her Daddy, too. Her Daddy and my Daddy and where was he? Where had he gone?

Her head lolled to one side as usual, but I heard her making noise, and the tears oozed out of her eyes.

"Daddy, he's dead, hanged, hanged." As if saying it aloud would make me believe it. "Why, Berry? Just because Mama left with that old painter guy?" We had all tried to reach Mama. It would have to wait until she came home. There was no note, just the film. And I would have to decide what to do with it.

I watched her lying next to me. She was flawless. I thought of the real baby, the real Berry, lying next to me for all those months inside our mother. How did they feel when we came out? Did Daddy know right away. Did he say, "Oh, my God, Mattie, she has no brain. Maybe the other one will be better." Could he tell when he looked at her? Right away? Did they cry when they saw her? When they saw me? I realized that I couldn't ask Daddy any of these questions. That day we talked about Berry and went to the cemetery. I could have asked him then. Now it was too late.

I couldn't tell Daddy about Leonora. My hand went down to the place she had entered with her tongue. Just rested there over my underwear, gently. But I could feel the pulsing. I looked at Berry, tears still oozed from the corners of her closed eyes. I awoke with my hand still in the same place. The baby was making noises from his basket. It was morning, and I had slept, but I saw that dead face all night. I woke up and saw it in my mind a hundred times, flashing like a slide projector, the same image over and over. Berry stayed with me. If she knew anything at all, she knew that I was hurting and Daddy was dead, so she stayed.

Grandpa made breakfast. His face was older. The night must have been long for him. I sat at the table nursing the baby. I wasn't really hungry. It was the ritual. Grandpa would say, "Now, you must eat something." Then I would say, "Try to eat a little of that." And the neighbors would come in with casseroles. "You must keep your strength up. Try to eat this chicken soup. It's good for you."

Grandpa put a pancake on each of our plates and sat down in Mama's chair. "Frankie from next door brought this syrup. Said he made it himself." The baby finished on my left side so I turned him around to the other breast, which he took eagerly. He didn't seem to have any trouble eating. Grandpa watched me.

"I remember when your daddy used to nurse from your grandma. Just like that. She'd strap him on with a shawl or something and work in the garden. And he'd suck and suck, just lying there in the shawl. Course, in those days you didn't nurse too long. A few months. Then the doctors said they needed cow's milk. That was the modern thing. Funny." Grandpa speared a piece of pancake with his fork. He held it up above his plate and watched it as if it was going to do something startling. I could see that if he spoke any more, he would cry. "How could he have done this?" He looked at me as he dropped his fork. His dark face sagged as if pins holding it up were pulled out suddenly. "He was my baby." I reached for his hand. He never looked away, even when the tears flowed.

The pancakes went untouched as Grandpa and I sat at Daddy's table, our hands touching. The baby looked up at him, frightened of his expression, his fear and grief. Grandpa took him from me, held him close to his chest and began to sing in the language. Over and over he chanted softly into Marten's ear as he walked around the room. Words I didn't know. Old Passamaquoddy talk. I felt like an intruder, like it was a private thing. Grandpa saying good-bye to his son, my father. He didn't notice that I stood there, awkward, embarrassed to watch. I turned slowly toward the screen door leading to the yard. My hand felt for the knob, and, as I left, a car slowed down and the passenger hung her head out to get a closer look at the house. They had been driving by ever since it happened. Neighbors, people I recognized from town, even some people I had never seen before. Everyone wanted to see the house where Robert Willoughby hanged himself.

I waved, and the car accelerated away. The garden showed different shades of green. Daddy had planted some lettuce and carrots but never got to the tomatoes sitting in a box to the side, wilted and brown. Mama would be upset when she saw the tomato plants. She probably brought them over for him to plant.

When the next car slowed I was ready to wave again but it pulled up into the driveway. I walked over thinking it was a friend with another casserole. "Brian," I said.

"Oh, my God." He seemed to fall out of the car and grabbed me, pressed my head into his neck, held me very tight. He sobbed against me. "Mom called last night. I was out on a job. Got here as quick as I could." His arms tightened around me until his own sobs lessened.

"I found him. Swinging from the ceiling. I couldn't cut him down."

"Oh, baby," he said as he kissed my face everywhere. I needed someone to do that.

"The funeral home took him. They're going to cremate him. Will they fix him up or anything first? What about his face?" The questions didn't make sense, but I needed to ask them. Brian knew that they didn't need to be answered. I wanted to say how I felt, but I didn't know. Brian and I always told each other the truth, but I couldn't find the truth. My Daddy. Hate. Anger. Love. Passion. My link to living. My link to my sister. He fucking hanged himself from the goddamn ceiling joist. For me to find. Well, who else? My Daddy. His camera. His last picture was of himself. My Daddy cooking my breakfast on Sunday mornings. Putting up with her. Showing Simon where he could paint. Asking me to talk to Mama. Sorry about my accident. He always thought it was his fault. Did he have a secret life, too? But hers wasn't a secret. I knew about Simon. But if I didn't know, it would be secret. My hands worked their way around Brian's waist and brought him as close to me as I could and held on.

The next few days were a blur. Aunt Maria came and stayed

with us. The neighbors brought enough casseroles to fill up the spare freezer. The service overflowed with tributes. No one said, "I hate you," or "Why, you fucking bastard, why?" or even, "He was weak." Some of the people from the reservation came, and Daphne drove up with her parents. Leonora came just for the service. Grandpa hugged me every hour.

When everyone had left, I showed Brian the passion feather and said that when I felt a little stronger I wanted to tell him something important about it. He took it in his hand carefully and never said that it was only an old turkey feather. "I'd like to hear about it, when you're ready."

My grandmother surrounded by potato baskets.
Taken by a tourist, Summer 1950

CHAPTER 21

Grandpa had to drop some of the pieces of candy corn so he could take his hand out of the jar. Since Daddy died, Grandpa was never very far from the candy. It was summer, and the regular store on the reservation was only sure to have them at Halloween, so I was always on the watch for some to keep the jar filled. One, and then another, and then another. He caught me looking at him and put the rest in his pocket. "Need some energy if I'm going to get you some ash for those baskets." He took one more out of his pocket. "This is the very last one for now." His teeth pinched off the yellow tip. He held the orange bit up to me. "You want it?" I smiled back at him. "Oh, my Miss Brown, I'll save it for you." He deposited it in his pocket with the rest before he kissed me on the top of the head and went out to the woods with his saw.

We would be alright. I would make it alright. Mama would be home soon, and she would ask questions to fill in the air. "Did you find him? We'll have to sell the house. What did he look like? Who came to the funeral?" She would be tanned, bleached, glowing from lust. And she would want to know everything that was private.

The film was up on my bureau, next to the passion feather. I was almost strong enough to decide what to do with it. I'd thought of having it developed and leaving the pictures on her kitchen table.

Ash strips lay on the table. Just as good as Mrs. Francis' strips. They were good, even, so brown, so smooth. I held my hands in front of me. My palms were soft and pink. The backs a little browner. My fingernails filed and clean. No rings. No polish. I wanted people to look at my hands and know what I did, to know what kind of person I was. What kind of a person was the owner of these hands? Brian's hands were so white, with big cuticles and squared-off nails. I would look at those hands and say, "Mathematician." Grandpa's fingers were thick like sausages, brown, like sausages that were smoked for a long time. "Indian," I would say. "Works in the woods, cutting ash for his granddaughter's baskets. Had a hard life." I thought of taking a "before" picture of my hands and remembered Daddy. I would watch them change without taking pictures. I planned to work with the ash and sweetgrass as much as I could. Go further than tradition, create new tradition, a real business, not just a hobby. I would know when I was a real Passamaquoddy basket maker, a fine craftsperson, a weaver of ash strips.

The ash wanted to go where I put it. The bottom of the basket grew and I allowed it to go beyond the traditional. It seemed to want to be larger, to carry more. The basket turned up from the bottom. The sides gently sloped and curved back. Strength, Mrs. Francis said. The tourists want it to be strong so they can carry lots of sandwiches and fruit and cakes. The basket got a little higher than the usual potato basket, but the curve was strong. The handle and the edge needed to be done to stop the basket from growing any more, to limit it, to make it strong enough for bricks.

They piled up, the baskets, at first potato baskets, sewing baskets, pack baskets. Split ash and sweetgrass. The latest ones were different. Strong. Good lines. Better constructed than the first ones. Screaming for something to be put into them. They were symmetrical but off in some way. They were almost perfect but asked for more. I reached under the bench where I kept a box of feathers and stones and shells. I picked up a piece of sweetgrass braid and wove the strand around a clump of stones and shells. The smell of the grass reminded me of Leonora, sweet, sweaty, pure, clean. All of those things.

I sat back and squinted at the basket. One spot seemed empty, and that's where I put the group of stones and shells. They hugged the basket as if they were born there. I chose a small gull feather and juxtaposed it with the other pieces. It was no longer a traditional Passamaquoddy Indian basket. It made me want to put something in it. Pulled at me. I laughed. "For Christ's sake, I'm passionate about my own baskets." I said it out loud to no one in particular.

"Leonora?" I said into the phone when she finally answered. "Can you come for supper? I made lasagna. I want to show you my new baskets."

She brought me a bouquet of delphiniums and kissed me on the forehead in front of Grandpa, right there on the steps with the front door open. "Blue flowers for my Beautiful Blue." She turned and took Grandpa's hand. "Here, I brought you something." From her bag she pulled an institutional-sized bag of candy corn and held it out to him. "Candy corn for a corny old man," she said, kissing him on the top of his head as she plunked the candy down.

"Thank you. How did you know?" He tried to stifle a grin as

he looked at me. My Grandpa. I think I loved him more at that moment than I ever had before.

"Let's see these baskets," she said.

Her hands rested on my waist as she followed me to the basket shed. At the door, I turned to her. "I want you to tell me what you think."

"I will."

I raised the latch, and she followed me so that our bodies touched lightly. At the table I stopped and stepped aside to allow her to see. There was silence and at first I wasn't sure that she saw it. She crouched toward the basket, her hands tracing the outline, then stepped back.

"You have something more than a container here. This makes me feel that the basket is crying out for something, and I need to find the proper piece to complete it. Something of mine to put into it."

"You like it?"

"You are here, in this basket. I feel you washing through the sweetgrass, parts of you lingering in the feathers and shells."

"Thank you."

That night I called for Berry. No crying this time. Just lolling. But that was fine. "I didn't tell Leonora about you. Well, that there was a twin, yes, but that you come when I call you and you are my size and so beautiful, no. I'm going to. Soon." Suddenly, I felt a little silly talking to my own illusion. The cover enveloped our heads and I spoke very quietly. I didn't want the baby to hear. "You would like her, Berry. She is so gentle and glides like a water creature when she walks. She kisses my eyeless socket like she knows it is my vulnerable spot." Berry's face seemed to turn toward me. Usually I complained to Berry. Asked her for advice. I traced my face with my finger and pretended it was Leonora. I could almost believe it if I closed my eyes, but I was afraid Berry would go away, feel left out. My index finger made the circle around my eyeless lid, and I could feel the hardness of the prosthesis. It felt different, harder. I traced down the side of my nose and down to my lips, which opened a crack to allow the finger to touch my tongue. When I opened my eyes, Berry was gone and that was alright.

Mrs. Francis came the next day to see the baskets. We sat cross-legged on the floor. She must have been well over seventy and still loved to sit on the floor.

"Blue, these are almost perfect. You see these splices? A little rough. But very good. But the last one. Oh, my, nul-lee-dar-huz." I was beginning to learn some of the words. That was Passamaquoddy for "I am happy." She reached in front of her for the last basket I had made. "This one. Your skill is better here. You see the splint here and the rim?" Her rough brown hands ran over my basket. I heard the sound of skin catching. "Much better. Soon you will be better than old Mrs. Francis." She smiled so wide that I could see her two lone top teeth. "But the lines. The People of the Dawn. The Wabanaki. They may not like the lines. They are not Passamaquoddy. The technique, yes, the skill, yes, but the lines. They make me feel, well something different. This will make you famous." She picked up one of my hands and turned it over and back and over. "Yes, soon they will be better than mine, yes?"

"Yes."

"You know, Passamaquoddy men and women didn't make these before the white people came. We made birch bark vessels. But not the split ash. Not the potato baskets. They are considered traditional Passamaquoddy, but we learned about them from the white people. We had the skills, but the white people didn't want our designs. They wanted baskets they were used to. We needed the money. Our people, we made the baskets to sell to them."

Afterward, we sipped mint tea I made from Grandpa's herb

garden at the kitchen table. Mrs. Francis' earrings were heavy and hung down almost to her collarbone. Her earlobes were stretched, and the hole was about an inch long. "I will leave you with a list of things to improve. You will work on the splices. They will soon be perfect?" She smiled again, and I could see her bottom teeth. Three of them. "Well, yes or no?"

I pulled my gaze away from her teeth and nodded. "I want to make baskets. Will you come again next week and see what I've got?"

"You call me when you have some more. And tell that Grandpa of yours he does a good job of splitting. Tell him if he goes for the ash up higher on the bank, the grain will be straighter, strips will be stronger. But it is good ash, not great, but good." She kissed my forehead as she left. "You give that kiss to your little boy. Kisses should never stay with the receiver. The sooner you give them away, the more will come." I watched her walk down the steps, her thin housedress clinging to her old body, still thick, but no longer straight.

After supper I remembered the kiss. I kissed Marten on the forehead. He held on to my finger and pulled it to his mouth. When would he be able to kiss me back?

Mother and Dad in the canoe.
Taken by Bobby Willoughby with his first camera,
August 1954

C H A P T E R   2 2

Isn't this maaarvelous?"

"I especially like this one. Look at the lines." The woman tilted slightly to the left, so that she would be in line with one of the baskets. She waved her radish sandwich to indicate which basket she was gooing over.

"You've got to try one of those lemon tarts. Then we'll go and look at the other baskets. They say they're more traditional. More Indian-like. What you think when you think 'baskets.' "

"This one kind of does something to me. I mean, what would you do with it? But, you know, it talks to me."

I wanted to skulk around in the dark corners all evening and listen to their comments. The art appreciators, the idle rich, the buyers. Most of them had no taste of their own, but relied on the museum to tell them what they liked, and this was my night. "New England Native Arts Exhibit," the Boston Museum of Art called it. I represented Maine. Mrs. Francis was chosen originally, but she said she'd never been out of Washington County and didn't plan to start at her age. She told the Arts Commission people that my baskets were good. That I was Passamaquoddy. That I had my own creative flair. And they wanted me.

Anna, my old childhood friend from the reservation, braided my hair and loaned me a deerskin dress her grandmother had made. The bodice was worked with porcupine quills and the waist needed a tuck, but otherwise it fit. They wanted an Indian, and they were going to get one. I pumped my breasts for a week so that I would leave enough milk for the baby. Anna and Grandpa were looking after him together, and Mrs. Francis said she'd come in and help get him ready for bed. It was difficult for Leonora to leave the farm because of the animals.

"I understand she's quite striking for an Indian." The woman with the radish sandwich now had one of the lemon tarts in her hand. "You know, they're usually so, well, heavy-featured." She reached over and plucked my business card out of the little Plexiglas holder. "I've heard this kind of stuff is going to go through the roof." She saw me then. Standing there in all my Indian regalia. She tossed me one of those "Hello, dear," smiles and turned back to her friend so that I wouldn't see how red her face was. She was still waving the lemon tart when she and her friend glided off into the next room.

Then I saw him. Coming in through the revolving door at the entrance of the museum. "Brian." Brian in a suit. I waved.

"Blue? Wow. It is you." I could see he was resisting the urge to run toward me. Each step was measured. Calculated. As quick as he could take them without looking too anxious.

Brian was no Indian with his red hair. He kissed me softly while the art enthusiasts watched, trying to figure out whether we were lovers, or friends. A flash went off. I thought of Daddy. Newspaper maybe. Neither of us really cared. "God, Blue, these . . . wow, these are yours? God." Brian strutted over to the baskets and leaned over the rope as far as he could. There was a pause. A pause for everyone. No one spoke or moved. They were looking at us. Brian almost falling into the basket exhibit. Me, Indian Blue, watching adoringly. We stood still, waiting for someone else to move when the flash went off again. People picked up where they left off, and Brian turned to face me. "You look beautiful, and I'm so proud of you."

We'd seen each other only once since the baby was born, at Daddy's funeral. Brian had finished his first year at MIT and was back early for a special math course. "God, I missed you. Can you believe this? Remember that first year I came back from Grandpa's with my little baskets? Who would have thought." I grabbed his hands and jumped up and down a little. I knew it looked silly, but I felt like it.

"Let me look at you." He held me at arm's length and looked me up and down like Daddy used to do before I went to school in the morning. Daddy. I thought I might cry if Brian didn't move or change position soon. But he kept looking and the tears came out. I bit my lower lip to keep the crying under control. "Come on. Come over here." He steered me to a corner, past the salmon in aspic and the baked Brie. He held me there in the corner until the tears stopped.

"I don't know why I'm crying. I really am happy with this."

"I think I understand."

"I'm OK now. Let's get a plate of silly hors d'oeuvres and mingle with the rich. And Brian?"

"What?"

"Thanks for coming."

"Sure. Wouldn't miss it."

Brian piled his plate with meatballs. The table teemed with highly garnished food. Radishes made into little roses. Nasturtiums filled with herb cheese. And the salmon. Covered with aspic shimmering like its original scales, layered with cucumbers and dill with pimento for a mouth and more radishes where the eyes had once been. Grandpa would laugh at the attempt to recreate the original live fish with vegetables and gelatin. The fish hadn't been touched. I picked up the serving fork and stabbed it near the backbone, knocking off one of the cucumber slices. The fish fell away from the bones and I brought a chunk to my plate. God, Grandpa wouldn't believe it. Daddy would though. Daddy would have been proud of me. He might have been jealous. I know Mama was jealous. She didn't come to the opening. Too far. Just got home from the Amazon. Daddy's death had been too upsetting. Needed to get settled. Move Simon in. See about the house. Sell? Rent? Move into it. Didn't think she could live in the house. All that. "Baskets? You're making baskets to sell? Do you think you can support yourself and the baby with baskets? Oh, life is just too much sometimes. Being away so long. So much has changed." God, she'd only been away two months.

We mingled, me with my salmon in aspic, Brian with his meatballs. "So, what do you think of this basket? Phenomenal, right?" It was Brian's voice. I turned. He was speaking to a group of blue-haired women in tweed suits. For God's sake, it was summer. Tweed suits? "I have known the artist for years. We're good friends." He looked my way and winked.

"Yes, it's a beautiful piece. Indians usually make such boring baskets." She didn't get it. That she had said something rude. I thought of using my fork as a slingshot and catapulting the salmon chunk still left on my plate.

"Ms. Willoughby combines the craftsmanship of the skilled Native American with the artistic creativity of a genius. That's why this basket speaks to you. It's perfect and it's emotional. She will be famous someday." Brian tilted back on his heels and cleared his throat.

The ladies looked at the basket again and huddled together. One of them broke away and took some cards from the plastic holder on the wall beside my name. "We'll take some of these," she said to no one in particular.

"Blue"—the curator of the show tapped me on the shoulder—"people love your baskets. What a success." The women had moved on. "I'm sure you will get a good review. The paper comes out in the morning. The arts critic just left, and she spent a long time at your display before you got here." His smile was very white and straight. "Good luck, daahling." He kissed me first on one cheek and then on the other.

"Thanks, Mr. Creston. I feel it's been very successful. This is my first show. Well, I mean my first real museum show." I didn't want him to think I was a complete misfit in the crafts world. "My friend, Brian. He's come to see it." They shook hands.

"You must be very proud of your girlfriend." He was searching. I could tell.

"He's not . . ."

"I sure am, Mr. Creston," Brian said, more loudly than I had been talking. "Someday I'm going to be Mr. Blue Willoughby, and proud of it."

"Good-bye, my little Pocahontas. And good luck with the show." I waved with my fingers. When I became famous I would not wave with anything, and no Passamaquoddy was ever named Pocahontas.

"Let's get out of here," Brian said through clenched teeth, managing to smile. "I have to be back to finish that statistics project in the morning, but I am yours 'til then. Do you have to stay here any longer?" Smile again. Looking at the next batch of elegant ladies.

"I'm staying at the MacKenzie just across the street. Want to come up and have a glass of wine? I've been here most of the evening. Come on." I grabbed his hand and led him through the groups of fine-craft enthusiasts. Several people stared.

"There she is. That Blue Willoughby. Look, in the Indian dress. Her stuff is great."

I strained my ears to hear everything that I could, but we were both anxious to get out. I looked around the crowd and smiled. But no waving. I want to leave I want to stay I want to be Indian I don't want to be Pocahontas I want to swear I want to wave I want to smile. Finally we jammed ourselves into the revolving door and were spit out onto the sidewalk. I looked at Brian. I loved him. Brian. Brian who creamed his pants over me. I wanted to tell him about Leonora. And the passion feather. To share it with him. But something in his eyes made me hesitate at even the thinking of the telling.

We held hands all the way up to my room on the seventeenth floor. I felt uneasy. I wanted to hold him. I didn't want him to hold me. We both avoided talk until we got to my door. I dropped the key on the carpet. Brian picked it up and opened the door. I followed him in. The champagne that Leonora gave me was in an ice bucket, the note still around the neck of the bottle. I pulled the note off and jammed it into the drawer of the desk. "Wish I could be there to drink this with you. I will dream about you. Love, Leonora."

After I had two drinks and Brian had four, I pulled out a bottle from the hotel's fridge. Not quite as good. But they say that after a few glasses of Moët then Ripple tastes the same. We sat opposite each other. Me on the couch. Brian on the chintz chair. I poured a glass of the cheap California into his glass, spilled a bit on his pants, and had a flash of prom night. I didn't usually drink much. And Brian certainly wasn't anything like Darrel. I poured myself a glass of club soda.

"To the girl of my dreams." He held up his glass. I clinked with my water. He still looked like he was trying to grow into his body.

"Brian."

He was looking up at me, sipping his champagne.

"Well. We need to talk."

He patted the couch beside me. "May I sit here?" I didn't answer for a moment.

"Please." God, those ears and the suit that didn't really fit. "OK, talk."

"I'm different. I've changed. I've found something that makes me feel whole." I looked ahead.

"The baby. I know." He moved closer to me and draped his arm around my shoulder. "Blue. Someday I'm going to marry you. You're my girl, right? Right, Blue?" I wished I hadn't opened the second bottle of champagne. "We've known each other for so long. I always knew. I couldn't love someone else. I couldn't do that to you. That girl I took to the prom? Nothing." He played with my braids, caressed the back of my head. He moved closer to me on the couch. His breath in my ear was hot and loud. I wasn't really aware when he first started to move back and forth on me. Thought he was just moving, maybe a little drunk. Then I realized what he was doing. That day in the woods long ago. It was the same. I didn't know how to stop him.

"Oh, Blue, you love me, don't you. You said you loved me." I wanted the scene to be over. The thrusts became more urgent. I held him against me. I wanted him. I didn't want him. I loved him. I felt sorry for him. I didn't want to make love with him. He wanted to make love to me. I owed him something. I turned toward him and brought his body down on mine. It didn't take long.

"Shit." He lay very still. "Shit, I did it again. I came in my pants again."

We lay there holding each other. "Brian."

Nothing.

"Brian."

Finally. "Um."

I put my head back on his arm for a second. No. That was too easy. "Brian. I have found someone. Not the baby. Someone you don't know." I still didn't have the guts to look at him.

"Found someone? You mean? That's crap. That's really crap. What do you mean 'found someone'? That isn't true. You're really full of shit."

I had to look. His chin was trembling. I put my hand on his cheek. "Brian, I have found someone. I am in love. I love you, but it's different."

"It's different all right." He didn't say more. He couldn't. His chin was trembling too much for words.

"Come here." I pulled him close to me and held his head. It was all familiar. But different now. "We are going to lie here and I am going to tell you about everything and I am going to hold you very tight and love you while I'm telling you. And I want to love you always. But I have to tell you about this. And you have to listen." I told him about Leonora. I told him about Grandpa and the feather long ago. I told him about Mama and the artist in the woods.

"Oh my God, you should have said something."

"It was the day before you creamed your shorts."

I was glad we weren't looking at each other. It was all easier talking to each other's bodies.

"And here I did it again. Oh my God."

"It's OK."

"I want to make love to you so badly. Do you think that will ever happen? Do you?"

It would have been easy to say "yes." Easy and comfortable. I could do it. And it would make him so happy. And there might be kind of a quiet passion, a comfortable passion. Christ, what was I thinking.

"No. I don't." I started to explain. To think of a way to make it easier. But Brian deserved to know. Deserved to have his own passion even if it was painful.

"But, maybe? . . ."

"No, Brian. No."

I tightened my arms around him and he sobbed quietly until he fell asleep. I covered him with a blanket and kissed his damp forehead. We were both changed.

Chapter 23

✍

Driving home after the show, I decided that if I sold baskets I was going to get myself a truck. I propped my arm in the opened window and the wind felt good. Grandpa let me use his truck anytime. But I wanted my own.

Brian and I had coffee and bagels over the *Press Herald* review of the museum show. "Blue Willoughby, a new young basketmaker from Maine, presented some unusual pieces. While all the baskets were expertly crafted, only Ms. Willoughby's were truly inspired." There I was on the front page of the arts section jabbing my fork into the salmon in aspic. I was going to make it. I was going to sell my baskets, and I was going to buy a truck.

I left the highway at Augusta and the traffic slowed. The strip was lined on both sides with fast places. Fast food, fast dry cleaners, fast banking, fast foto developing. I crept along, playing my clutch and brake back and forth. The guy in the car next to me was singing a song with the radio. I think he had the same station as I did. Peter, Paul and Mary. "Puff the Magic Dragon." I watched him and sang along in my head. He saw me and stopped. Looked out his window away from me. Ahead of me a mother slapped at two children in the backseat who were fighting. Low strip-mall buildings stretched ahead on both sides. "Stan's Drive In Video." "Wong's Instant Chinese." "Instabank." "FastPrint-Now." "Supervalu Drugs." "FotoMat—Film printed while U wait." I felt for the bag on the seat beside me. I carried the film with me everywhere, not sure what to do with it. They wouldn't care here. They didn't know me. I would tell them it was a rush and they wouldn't take time to look at them. I put my blinker on and started to squeeze right. The singer glanced at me, and then turned away. Exiting into the parking lot was not really a commitment. I pulled into a space opposite the FotoMat kiosk which sat all by itself in the middle of the lot.

The young kid in the booth pulled a cigarette out of his pocket and lit it. It hung out of his mouth, smoke rising into his hair. There he sat. The smoke meandered around the booth and made its way out. The film sat in my hand. I could always develop it and then put the pictures away. I didn't have to look at them. To keep them. I could throw them away in this shopping mall. Maybe the pictures wouldn't even come out. Maybe they were overexposed. Maybe he was just out of range of the camera. The guy in the booth flicked his cigarette out onto the pavement.

"I'd like this developed right away." My voice sounded strong. He didn't seem to notice anything. "I'll wait right here."

"Twenty minutes." He held his hand out for the film. I dropped it into his palm.

"I'll wait right here." As soon as I spoke, I realized I'd repeated myself. He didn't seem to notice. I wanted to tell him to be careful with the film. He turned his back to me and began to work. I couldn't see what he was doing. His body just stood there and his arms moved. We didn't speak. I walked around the kiosk and then walked around the opposite way. Finally he rapped on the window and pointed his cigarette toward the package in his hand.

"That'll be twelve seventy-five." He held the package up to me. One hand held the pictures, the other hand wiggled, waiting for the money.

"Oh, right." I dug in my bag for my wallet. I placed a ten and a five on his hand. His fingers stopped wiggling as he took the bills. He handed me the change.

"Some weird pics. Takes all kinds, I guess. Jesus." He sat down and looked straight ahead. The smoke seemed to go right into his eyes. He didn't notice.

I put the pictures into my bag and hurried back to the truck. I expected to hear him shout at me to stop. That I was under arrest. That I couldn't possess pictures like that. As I started the truck I glanced over to the booth. He hadn't moved.

I rolled the window up and pulled out of the parking lot. I drove down the rest of the strip. Endless Chinese restaurants and auto-parts stores. No more fast photo developers. The strip turned into farm country, and I drove without stopping, without turning on the radio, without putting my elbow out the window. I suddenly wished Brian were with me in the truck.

I knew where I was heading. The baby was fine with Grandpa for another little while. I turned down the dirt road and slowed down. I opened the window. Sheep were grazing in the lower pasture. I counted seven of them. She wasn't in the garden. Maybe the barn. I pulled up to the house and sat a moment. The raspberry bushes moved, and I saw her coming toward me with the filled boxes balanced on her arms.

"Let me help you." I walked toward her as slowly as I could. She knelt and placed the boxes carefully on the ground.

"Leonora, they loved me. They loved my baskets." I thought about the pictures in the car and wondered if I could ever look at them. If I could ever show them to her. She wiped off her hands on her shorts and held out her arms to me. Someday, I could show her the pictures.

We sank down into the grass beside the raspberries. Leonora flexed her bare feet and stuck a box of berries between us. "Tell me all about everything. We'll eat berries and talk about the show." I pulled up a handful of them. It was so extravagant, eating handfuls of raspberries and sitting in the sun with Leonora. "I got the paper this morning. The picture, with Brian, great, and the comments."

"I'm going to make it. They loved the baskets." We spoke between mouthfuls of berries. "I want you to meet Brian. We talked. It's hard for him. Us. Everything. He loves me."

Leonora's breath was close to me, her skin was stained with raspberry juice. She wiped her face with her shirt. She looked like a child. I reached out to her shirt and eased it over her head. She closed her eyes and stretched out on the grass. Her small breasts almost disappeared. I put berries on her chest and pressed them into her with my hands. I straddled her and eased myself down on her, my face in the berries, and began to lick. The juice ran over her chest and down onto the ground. She smiled but didn't open her eyes.

My tongue followed the berries where they dripped. Her hands grappled at my tee shirt and I helped her pull it off. I dumped the last of the berries on her chest. I moved on her until the berries were crushed, then pulled away enough to lick some more. "I missed you." My mouth covered her breast, and she moved under me as I sucked on it.

I didn't show her the pictures that day. I didn't even look at them myself. On the way home I pulled over in a rest area. I took the package out of my bag. It was thick, as if all the pictures were there, as if they had all turned out. I didn't want to look at them here, alone, in this place. I put them back into my bag and pulled out onto the road.

They were all there on the porch: Grandpa, Marten, and Mrs. Francis. Grandpa had the newspaper and held it out for me to see before I had even parked the truck. Marten knew me. He knew who I was as soon as I shut the truck door. Suddenly, my breasts spilled over with milk. My tee shirt had two wet blotches in the front.

Grandpa stood up and held him out as I ran to him. I kissed Grandpa as Marten grabbed my hair and pulled me toward him. "Here, someone missed you," Grandpa said. He looked tired, like it was all too much for him, and I wanted to tell him all about the show and Brian. But my breasts were spurting by now.

"You better feed that baby. Here. Sit by me." Mrs. Francis patted the seat next to her on the porch swing and I sat down. Getting my nipple into Marten's mouth was difficult since the milk was spraying into his face. As soon as he began to suck, I giggled. The raspberry juice. He seemed to think his milk was especially good that day.

CHAPTER 24

The baby slept in my bed that night. He nursed for a long time when I first got home and didn't want to be put down anywhere. He howled and held tight to my neck when I attempted to lower him into his crib. "Alright, little one. You'll sleep with Mama." Hiawatha and Ugli and Marten and I all snuggled under the covers. I lay on my side as he nursed, first one breast, then the other, and then back again. I watched as he sucked, his lips surrounding my nipple. His feet kicked softly at my belly. My hand rested on his head. We fell asleep.

We slept all night until the early dawn. Roosters would be crowing at Leonora's. Jimmy Neptune down the road from Grandpa's used to have a rooster, but the raccoons got him one night. I missed the crowing. Marten was nursing again. His head nodded with each suck, covered finally with black hair, like mine, like Grandpa's. He was born with light brown fluff. But the hair was growing in black. Straight and black. Indian hair. He would grow into his name.

His feet kicked as I changed his diaper. He watched every move I made. Moved with me. His hand reached for Ugli, and he laughed. I buried my face in his belly. It was so smooth. And it smelled of milk.

Grandpa wasn't in the kitchen when we went in for break-fast. He was always up early. At least by five-thirty. I knocked on his bedroom door. "Grandpa." I pushed the door open and he was awake. Sitting up.

"Good morning, Miss Brown. I'm a little late this morning. I'll be down soon. We'll go to Leonora's house for eggs today."

He looked so small there in his bed, the same bed he'd shared with Grandma. "I'll make some scrambled eggs," I said.

The eggs sat in the frying pan. I turned off the heat under them and added some basil from the garden. Sunday mornings were special for Grandpa and me. We made a big breakfast and talked about family, the old ways, Daddy, Grandma, prob-lems in the tribe, and now, baskets. The nasturtiums were blooming, so I put a bunch in Grandma's old brown teapot. I waited for him to come to the kitchen. Marten fell asleep in his little bed by the kitchen table. I smelled one of the nasturtiums from the teapot. Daddy grew masses of them in an old ash pit full of gravel. He said that they would only bloom in poor soil. If the soil was too rich, the plants said, "Oh, the soil is too rich. We don't need to have babies." So they wouldn't bloom.

The flowers seemed glued on to the pale green brittle stem. Way at the back of the flower was a secret place. A long trum-pet. Daddy had said everything that was important fell down into it and stayed until the flower died. Everything else washed away with the rains.

We waited a long time for Grandpa. The eggs stiffened and turned cold. I ate the nasturtium. Chewed the whole thing, swallowed it, bit by bit. It seemed odd to eat a flower even after all this time. The secret place was hot, peppery, strong tasting. My tongue burned. The pale green stem was cool, juicy, and soothed the burning. Grandpa entered the kitchen and slumped into his chair. His shirt was untucked and the buttons mismatched.

"Something is wrong," he said. You never had to guess with Grandpa. "I feel so tired. Each breath is hard work." He looked at me, waited to see what I would say.

"Grandpa. Grandpa, the eggs are cold."

"I'm not hungry. I think it's my time. Soon."

"Grandpa, let me fry some more eggs. I have six more left from Leonora's. Here, I'll put these in fried rice for tomorrow. It's no trouble." I took the platter to the refrigerator. Leonora's eggs were on the door, and I removed four of them. "I can heat up the coffee," I said returning to the table to get the pot. "Marten's still sleeping so we can have breakfast in peace. We need to leave at nine-thirty." I cracked the eggs into the frying pan.

"Blue. Come and sit. Please. Turn off the stove."

I stood looking at the eggs. It was easier to look at the eggs than to listen. I turned off the burner and stood, with the spatula in my hand, watching them continue to cook. Not now. I didn't want to hear about it right now. We were going to visit Leonora. All of us. I just wanted him to eat his eggs. But I knew he wasn't going to.

"The eggs aren't important. Come. Sit down. I know you don't want to talk about this."

My back faced him, but I know what he looked like. He was fine yesterday. Strong. Healthy. Tired, but he was an old man. He needed to rest, to eat good food. Maybe too much candy. "Grandpa." I turned, still holding the spatula. "Too much candy corn. I think if you ate more lettuce and carrots. We have them in the garden." I was pleading. I knew he hated that sound in my voice.

His eyes held their gaze. He focused both eyes on my one real eye. "Come." His voice was gentle and strong. Stronger than he looked. "We need to talk. I am an old man." He was so patient. He allowed me to fiddle and babble and do whatever I needed to do to get ready to talk. He knew I would come when I was ready. But he coaxed me just enough. "Come." The last was a quiet plea. I listened for Marten. There was no sound. Perhaps in a minute. "Please." He held out his hand for me.

"Let me fix your shirt and then we'll talk." I rebuttoned the shirt as slowly as I could. I ran my hands over his thick black-and-gray hair as if I had permission. As if he allowed me to do that now that he was weak. But I looked into his eyes. They were deep brown. Clear. His body was wearing out, but he was strong. Inside he was so very strong. Yet I patted his head as I lowered myself into my chair.

"You know, our bodies are only on loan. Mine is old and not working well anymore. I think it is time. I have had a good life. My son. Except for my son." He stopped for a moment and shook his head. I couldn't say anything. Not yet. "I have a little money saved up. And the house. I will be ready to go. Not right now. But soon." He looked at me as if for permission. I wanted to ask where he hurt. What was wrong. "The old ones call it heart sickness. I read about it. We will go to the doctor's and see if I am right. And now we get ready to go to Leonora's."

He had called the reservation clinic and made an appointment for the next day with Dr. Socabasin. He had been Grandpa's doctor for years, delivered Daddy, saw Grandma out, stitched up my foot when I stepped on a broken bottle one summer. The only doctor Grandpa would go to, I was sure of that. Marten and I sat on a stool off to the side, and I told myself that I wouldn't interfere unless Grandpa asked me to. "Nicholas, you and I go way back. We are both People of the Dawn. Your heart is going. Enlarged."

"I know."

"That's causing the exhaustion and the congestion in your lungs. It's not going to get better, but there are things medicine can do to help. Make you feel less sick. Help you deal with the congestion."

Grandpa looked small sitting on the examination table. The johnny shirt was tied in back and his bare legs stuck out from underneath. His ankles were swollen, and I hadn't remembered his feet being so wide. Dr. Socabasin sat in the swivel chair and looked up as he spoke.

"I'm going to give you a diuretic. It will help with the swelling. It may make you feel great for a while. You could live for years with this heart. Depends on how fast it deteriorates."

"I will take the medicine. But I am getting ready to go. I have had a good life." He looked at me for the first time. I nodded to him.

On the way home in the truck we talked about practical things. He would no longer be able to cut the ash for my baskets, but he could gather sweetgrass. He could watch for feathers and beach glass and shells and galls. "Do you remember the day I let you go first? To track the buck? This is a day like that. I am letting you be the well one, the strong one. To try to do otherwise would be foolish."

"I wish I could be as wise as you."

"Not wise. Just honest. Things are not as other people tell you they are. Look and see how things really are. I can't help you with that. That is for you alone."

I wondered for a moment how a man as honest and kind

and gentle as Grandpa could father a man like Daddy. How did it happen that your children didn't always respond?

"When I was young, we went to the Catholic church—St. Mary's," Grandpa said. "I remember looking at Jesus and his mother, Mary, at their kind faces, and thinking that if they were watching me, I would always be happy and safe. Then I learned what the church did to our people."

"Daddy never took us to church."

"I used to think how wonderful it would be to be in heaven with them. I'm not sure I thought of what I would do there. Sit around and sing and groom my wings, I guess. Funny what you think of when you're a child." Grandpa shook a few pieces of candy corn out of his shirt pocket. He bit the bottoms first, then layer by layer. Marten woke up, and Grandpa put his hand on the car seat and bounced him while I drove Grandpa home from the clinic. He brought Grandpa's thick finger into his mouth and sucked on it until we pulled into the driveway.

Grandpa was a little better after he took the diuretic. We couldn't ever be very far from a toilet or a tree after that. He spent his days walking on the beaches, gathering things he thought I might use in the baskets. He found a sheep's skull, bleached white by the sea and sun, perfectly intact. Mussel and sea urchin shells filled boxes in the shed out back. Sea glass overflowed from a bowl on the kitchen table.

He went with the women and gathered sweetgrass. He could do women's work, and they loved him for it. It wasn't hard work, and he worked slowly. He always napped in the afternoon before supper. I cooked soup every night, even in the heat. He said he wasn't hungry, that food didn't taste the way it used to. But he would always eat a little soup.

I bought ash already pounded into strips from one of the men on the reservation. The shed out back served as my studio. Marten loved to lie in his little bed and watch the shadows the trees made while I worked on the baskets. My hands were red and rough, almost like Mrs. Francis'. I closed my eyes, allowing my hands to form the shape of the new basket in the air. I followed the basket inside and out, with all the embellishments hanging off, leaning inward, separating compartments. Sometimes it took a whole day to visualize one basket. The making was easy. After years of weaving traditional baskets my hands moved automatically, and I thought of whatever I needed to feel passion to make the basket. Sometimes I imagined my ancestors, Glue-skub and his helper, Marten, my ancient People of the Dawn, before the whites came, when they created their clamshell mounds in the summer and moved with the game in the winter. Sometimes I thought of Daddy hanging from the rope in the living room, sometimes Mama in the woods with Simon. Sometimes I thought of that first time with Leonora.

Every basket had a feather. I used seagull feathers and osprey feathers. Grandpa found a dead hummingbird in the garden, its feathers iridescent. I wove it into a clam-sized basket with sweetgrass and bits of seaweed. Leonora gave me some chicken feathers after we slaughtered her broilers. Blood from the axe's work remained on one of the feathers. I called that one "Basket of dead souls."

Mama said she liked that one best of all, but she didn't understand why I called it that. Chickens didn't have souls, she said. "And the price. I can't believe you are getting that much for a basket," she said on one of her infrequent visits. "I mean they're nice and all, but, God, that's a fortune. I'd like to carry them at my gallery, but we only take art, you know, wall pieces." If my baskets weren't good enough for her, what about those last pictures my father took?

CHAPTER 25

I knew I was going to lose Grandpa. Every day he woke up a little later. Grandpa, who was always up before the sun, before the rooster down the road. Every afternoon he went for a walk to gather feathers and stones for my baskets, but the walks became shorter. Instead of gulls' and ducks' and ospreys' feathers from the shore, he began to bring pine cones and robins' feathers, from birds killed by Mrs. Francis' cat. The women approached the door and left some of their sweetgrass in paper bags. If they saw me in the kitchen, they would come in for tea.

I worked in my studio every day with Marten. He played in his bouncing chair or slept on the mattress while my hands traced the baskets in the air. I listened for Grandpa to go out, to come home, to fall down. It became more difficult to work, to think of the finished baskets. Autumn was coming and the shed where I worked was cold in the mornings. Sometimes my hands were stiff. There was no heat, and soon I would have to move inside.

I waited at the table for the idea of a basket to form. My

hands traced circles on the worn pine. My fingers pulled at the elastics around my wrist. The mail came wrapped in elastic bands and I collected them on my wrist. I used them for fiddling or reminding myself of appointments or tying my braids. With my index finger, I parted my hair and began to braid. One of Grandpa's robin feathers moved across the table in the breeze coming from the open shed door, and I stuck it in my hair. Passamaquoddy hair. Some of the other young women on the reservation were growing their hair and wearing it in braids. They looked up to me because of my hair. The rest of me looked like Mama—fair, slight, waspy.

My hands lay palm down on the table. Red and rough, calluses along the length of my index fingers, but delicate, slim, not Passamaquoddy hands, not like Grandpa's or Daddy's. Marten would have them, the Passamaquoddy hands, I was sure of it.

Leonora had invited us for supper. Grandpa loved her little farm. He said he and Grandma had talked about having a small farm. Just goats and chickens and maybe a pig. I picked up the new basket, the one I made for Leonora. I planned to give it to her at supper. A small basket, it was woven from lily pad stems and at the bottom was a lily pad with a dried frog, poised to take a leap. Grandpa had found it at the shore, one foot stuck to a small piece of pink granite, the other in a frozen arabesque. Grandpa said frogs freeze sometimes in the winter and then dry in the sun.

I eased the basket into a cardboard box lined with tissue paper. Marten whimpered from his mattress. I thought of that frog I cut into that day with Brian and wondered if Marten would be like that, able to cut into a live thing just to see what makes it work. His pudgy hands reached for me and before he had a chance to yell, I shoved my breast into his mouth. Soon enough he would hold a cup and drink by himself.

"Come on, little one, let's get ready to go to the farm. Remember the goats? And the kittens?" He looked up at me with milk dripping out the side of the smiling mouth.

Grandpa was just getting up from his nap when we went in to get ready. He walked across the floor, like he was in a slow-motion movie. "Almost ready, Blue, I'm a little pokey, that's all."

I grasped his hand to steady him. His fingers were shorter than mine and thick with scratches and scars all over them. "Take your time." The back of his hand was hairless and dry like old leather left out in the sun. I kissed it and left him to dress Marten for the trip to Leonora's.

She was waiting in the dooryard for us, holding Francine. The old cat's tail flicked back and forth as we parked the truck. Leonora put Francine down and approached Grandpa's door. "I have something for you in the house," she sang as she might to a child with a birthday. She helped him with his seat belt. She held his hand as she kissed me on the cheek and gave Marten a hug. "We're having chicken and potatoes and watermelon from the garden."

"Can I do something?" I wanted to touch her, and she knew it. I squeezed her free hand. That would do for a while.

The table was covered with a white embroidered cloth made by Leonora's mother as a young bride in Austria. Leonora's parents were both dead, and she had three much older brothers living in New York. One of them was coming with his family for Christmas. The white flowers blanketed the white cloth, leaving only the impression of flowers, zillions of white stitches like blossoms fallen in June. Leonora's mother had given it to her as she died, a piece of her spirit passed on. Orange and red leaves were scattered on the white, and lit candles floated in a clear glass bowl. At each place was a little dish of candy corn. Grandpa's dish was big and full of candy.

Grandpa took his seat, his teeth already poised on the bottom of a candy corn. "Here," I said, thrusting Marten into Leonora's arms. "I'll get his seat, and I have something for you."

I balanced the baby seat from the truck bed and the box with the tissue paper from the front seat in my arms. I wanted her to like it. She would tell me if she didn't. That was the scariest thing of all.

I let the baby seat slide to the floor and took Marten from her. I waited with the box in my free hand. Leonora waited for me to give it to her. Grandpa waited to watch. "I don't know why I made this one for you. It just came. Just happened." Leonora held out her hands to make the giving easier for me. "It's only a basket. I made it for you."

"It's never only a basket if you made it." I saw Grandpa poised with half a candy, watching. Leonora lifted the basket out of the tissue paper and looked inside. "Oh, God, it's a frog." She turned to me and smiled. "It's a real frog," she said in amazement. She looked into it again for a long time and put it on the tablecloth. "Look, it's trying to leap out, but it's dead. Some morning I will come down and it will be gone. Out of the basket, out of the house. Thank you. Kind of like 'Ode on a Grecian Urn' only it's a basket." She held my face and kissed me lightly on the cheek. "I will keep it always. Now how about some rhubarb wine. Grandpa? Don't say no. I know you love it." She poured his glass without waiting for his reply.

"I love your little farm," Grandpa said during a lull in the conversation. "Maybe someday Blue and Marten will live here with you. Someday when I am not here on this earth anymore."

"I can see you are getting ready to go. Do you think it will be soon?" Leonora waited for his answer as if waiting to hear whether he'd go to the county fair next week.

"Yes. You're very kind to ask. You recognize that I am dying and that it is good. I am an old man. I have had a good life. Now I am ready to go, and we can talk about that. Thank you."

"I'm going to talk to Blue about coming here to live with me after you die, Grandpa. Your house would be lonely for her, and Marten needs another person around. I hope she agrees. She'll still be close to the reservation."

It seemed that I was not there, that they were talking together, alone. I stopped eating and sat motionless, not wanting to intrude. The two of them continued to eat their chicken as they talked about his imminent death.

"Blue will have a hard time when I die. She's just lost her father. And her mother is busy with her own things. Blue will miss me. You will need to help."

"Could you pass the potatoes," she said to Grandpa. "I love Blue, and I want to help her through this."

I was afraid to move. Afraid they had forgotten I was there and might be embarrassed. I had a fantasy about saying, Yoohoo, I'm here, remember me, Blue, the one you're talking about.

"It won't be long. My body is worn-out. But it has served me well, this body. I want to be buried at the reservation and the ashes of my belongings put into one of Blue's baskets and sent off to sea from the shore. Can you make sure that's done?"

When a Passamaquoddy dies, their personal belongings are given away to those who want them. The items no one claims are burned so that nothing of the deceased is thrown away.

"Yes, I will make your basket." The sound of my voice shocked them as they turned to face me. "Grandpa, I will make your basket, a very special basket for the remnants of your life."

"I'm sorry, Blue, I almost forgot you were there," said Leonora. Grandpa said nothing. He knew I needed to hear their conversation.

"It will be hard for me. But I recognize that you need to talk about it." I was crying a little, but that was fine. "I will miss you, Grandpa." Tears were coming faster now, and my chin trembled.

"Here, have some more chicken," Leonora said as she passed me a leg.

CHAPTER 26

Supper at Leonora's tired Grandpa. On the way home we discussed what I would do when he died, but it was difficult to talk and cry and drive all at the same time. The next morning he announced he was going to gather some feathers and stones from the beach. He wanted to go alone and asked me not to call the women. I didn't let him see me cry as he left with his walking stick.

Marten was having his nap, and I lay down on the couch in my studio. "Berry," I called softly. I wanted to hold her. I wanted her to hold me, but I knew she couldn't do anything. "Berry, can you please come." I was crying again. "Berry, Berry, Berry. I wish I knew you. I wish you'd lived." She was there, lying on the rug next to the couch. I never realized how beautiful she was, two brown eyes staring straight ahead, Black Indian hair in long braids. "Berry." No response. I imagined she tried to look my way. "Berry, Grandpa's dying. Did you hear me? Grandpa. He's going to die." She turned toward me and a barely perceptible tear fell onto the rug. "Oh, Berry, I wish you'd lived. I could ask you things, like what to do with Daddy's pictures." I knew if I moved toward her, she would disappear, so I lay still. "If only someone could have helped you. You would look just like me, and we could love each other." We lay for a long time, just being close, until she faded away and I fell asleep.

After supper, Grandpa brought in the things he gathered at the shore. He spread basket makings out on the table-cloth. Nothing terribly significant or astounding. An old fish skeleton, bits of colored sea glass, some dried rockweed with a mussel shell attached, a piece of a hand-knit bait bag, smooth stones from the beach, a seagull feather, and a big bunch of sea lavender.

"When the basket is finished, I will be ready." He watched me for a reaction. "And that is not permission for you to dally." Tears formed in my eyes, and I knew that they would be there for a long time. "Not many people are fortunate enough to know when they will die. I am very lucky. I have time to say good-bye to you, my dearest Miss Brown. And for that I am a very lucky man."

I started on his basket the next morning. Grandpa watched Marten in the house, so I could be alone in my work. I strewed the materials over the old pine table and closed my eyes. My hands began to move. It had to be cozy and safe. It had to be beautiful. It had to have passion. Its strength would be in its tightness, its ability to carry the ashes far out into the sea. I didn't know how much room the ashes would take. How could his belongings be reduced to a quart of ash? When Grandpa died he would be gone. I was making the basket for me. He knew that.

The basket was round. I had originally thought it would be shaped like a boat, but a round shape was safer. I wove sweet-grass together with the fish skeleton around the bottom. I hung pouches full of beach stones and bits of pounded ash inside the basket. Next I drilled small holes in the pieces of colored sea glass and hung them around the rim to catch the sun. Rockweed and mussel shell lined the bottom of the basket. The weaving was very tight so it would float and hold the ashes. My fingers bled as I wove, not used to pulling on the sweetgrass so hard. It took me most of the morning to make the basket, and when it was finished I held it up in front of me. It needed something on the outside to make it go with the wind, something to catch the down east breeze, to take it out far away from shore until the ocean took it down.

The feather was there, in the box where I had left it. I drew a line down the center of the feather, the passion feather, and severed one side from the other with the X-acto knife. We should each have half because it was our feather. The two sides lay there close to each other on the table. Dirty and old but intact.

Carefully I wove the feather onto the outside of the basket so that it ran from top to bottom on one side. I blew on it, and pieces of the feather moved. It would work, move the basket out with the waves, out to where I couldn't see it, before it went down. I cut a small piece of my hair and placed it in the bottom with the rockweed. I wouldn't tell him about that.

Like Penelope at her loom, I knew that when the basket was finished, it would be time. I sat for a long time wishing I didn't have to go into the house, but I knew that Marten would be needing me. If Grandpa could be ready, then so could I.

Grandpa was holding Marten. "Come in, let me see it," he said as I walked toward him with the basket in front of me like an offering. His free hand touched the feather. He handed me his white handkerchief. "It is time. It will be soon. I am proud and happy to think of going to sea in this basket. It is a long journey. My soul will be here, with my things, searching for your grandma." I couldn't respond. He didn't tell me not to cry. "I have a small leather bag with some earth from Mount

Katahdin inside. I'm too ill to go there, to the father mountain, but could you put some earth in the basket?"

The next morning I stayed in bed until I heard him in the bathroom. I made pancakes for breakfast and gave Marten a little bit. He spit it out. Grandpa couldn't urinate. Tried and tried. Nothing. Thought he might have another cup of coffee. And maybe some of the candy corn Leonora gave him. He reached into the dish on the table for a handful.

"Grandpa, you're going to get sick if you eat too many of those things."

"I'm going to have one more handful."

"Oh, Grandpa." It seemed like old times. Laughing over breakfast.

When Marten went for his nap, Grandpa asked me to read to him. We often read to each other, especially since he'd become sick, novels, poetry. I settled in the chair next to his bed. His pillows were plumped behind him and he sat up because it was more comfortable. We were halfway through *The Hobbit*. Grandpa kept interrupting, asking about Bilbo, or what I thought would happen, or how it would end. "Grandpa, be quiet and let me read, put your head back and relax."

Grandpa put out his hand on the bed and moved his thick fingers. I took it and continued to read. My speed picked up and I realized I was reading faster and faster. He squeezed my hand and I squeezed back. I wanted to stop and say something, but I couldn't. I just read faster and faster, to finish the book in time. I looked at his face. It was red, very red, and as he squeezed my hand again, the skin on his face lifted up off the bones for a moment. I stopped reading, breathless. "Grandpa, are you alright?"

He opened his eyes and looked into mine. "Yes."

"I'll stay here and hold your hand." I felt his loneliness. And my own. Each of us on a private journey, joined together but so terribly alone. His eyes rolled back and he exhaled. He looked at me again. Questioning. Wondering.

No tears came like I expected. The redness on his face disappeared and the skin relaxed around his mouth as he exhaled again. He squeezed my hand once more and what had been Grandpa, departed. I sensed his flesh change, become without life. And I held his hand as it happened.

I felt a little like an intruder. His death was personal. His body pushed out a few more bits of air, as if to cleanse itself of anything unnecessary. His eyes rolled back into his head so that the pupils faced inward. With my free hand, I shut them. I knew he was gone, but I sat for a long time, holding. As the flesh became cool, a bruise appeared on his sunken cheek. His lips pulled back a little from his teeth and he ceased to look like my Grandpa. I wanted to make sure he was really gone before I let go. I had promised to stay until the end.

That is how Leonora found me. Sitting, with *The Hobbit* open in my lap, holding Grandpa's hand. She pulled up another chair and sat with me. They say that when an animal dies, you should leave its mate or parent or pal with the body until the animal turns away on its own accord. We remained until he was truly gone. His body was like wet clay, and it was time to do the business of death. I cried then, and she held me until I was finished.

When Dr. Socabasin came to the house, he was kind. "Nicholas was a good friend," he said. "I loved him like a brother." He signed the death certificate and gave us a license to transport the body. "I'll be back soon. Give you time to prepare him." Grandpa's friends would carry him to the grave. He had made me promise no funeral people. Only friends.

"I want to help you with this. He asked me to help you," said Leonora.

"Yes."

My old Grandpa and the body in his bed had little in common. He would come again when the basket went out to sea. His thoughts would be in the basket. But the old body had served him well, and I wanted to respect it. Treat it with softness and love. We were very careful not to stand at the foot of the bed, where the soul begins the journey out through the soles of the feet. We pulled the pillows out from behind him and lowered him onto the mattress. Leonora pulled back the covers and exposed his swollen feet. Undressing the body was awkward. The flesh was heavy, heavier than in life, and it was a struggle. Leonora brought a bowl of warm water and soap and a bottle of lavender oil to the bedside. I began with his face. She held the water for me to dip the cloth into. As I wiped his eyes and mouth the skin seemed to relax under the cloth. All the wise words that came out of that mouth. I moved the cloth around his ears and neck and down his chest, which seemed sunken and misshapen. I hesitated for a moment at his navel, thinking about his mother being attached there and about how we were all attached to someone else. I had never seen his genitals before. They were nearly hairless, flaccid. The passion that was in them with Grandma, gone. Some urine leaked out as I washed and I thought of all the rest of it being inside him somewhere, a whole day's worth. His legs were almost hairless as well, thin, until I got to the ankles which were swollen from the heart condition. His feet were the hardest for me. They had carried him for so many years, on trails in the woods, along the beach, on that last walk to get the pieces of the basket. They would carry him as his soul went out his feet. Carry him on the journey to Grandma.

Leonora helped me turn him and we washed his back. Then she rubbed the oil gently onto his body. The smell of the dead was replaced with lavender, and I was so grateful to her.

I found his flannel shirt in the closet, and we put it on the body. His pants were more difficult. Leonora remade the bed and straightened up the room. On the table next to his bed, I lit some sweetgrass in the smudge bowl and sprinkled some sage on top to help it burn. Leonora placed *The Hobbit* next to the bowl and called Mrs. Francis. They all arrived carrying food. Some of the old men wanted to see the body, but the others stayed in the kitchen, eating, talking about old times, playing with Marten.

Mama came the first night because I called her. She didn't bring Simon. As we entered the bedroom, the Passamaquoddies parted to allow Nicholas' daughter-in-law to approach the body. She placed her hand on the dead forehead. "Nicholas, mee-ta-ouks, mee-ta-ouks." No questions. No answers. Respect. She respected him and knew the people's word for him. Father, mee-ta-ouks. She hadn't really changed, but I saw through a small hole in her persona, a bit of spirit that I could love.

"Oh, Leonora, you're Blue's new farm friend. You have goats and pigs. How wonderful," Mama said over a bowl of stew. "I'm so pleased she has met you." Now was not the time to explain the relationship, but soon, maybe soon.

I couldn't reach Brian in time for him to come up, so I wrote him a long letter. Brian would be sad.

The tribal elders arranged a ceremony for Grandpa at the community center. Grandpa said no church, but the local priest, Father O'Reilly, came to the house. Leonora took him gently by the arm and thanked him for his visit but said that Grandpa would not be having a church mass and burial. He said he would like to come to the ceremony, and he stayed for some venison stew.

Three nights I kept the smudge pot burning as they came. Two women who gathered sweetgrass with Grandpa came every night and chanted at his bedside for hours. They never seemed to tire. The chants were mournful but full of hope. I could hear some Catholic influence, but mostly it was old Passamaquoddy, in the language, in the spirit, over and over.

After everyone left in the evening I sat with him. His pile of possessions had dwindled. Everyone wanted something of Grandpa's. Clothes, books, pipes, even his coffee cup. No one touched his moccasins. They knew I would want them for Marten. That last night only a few books, his ash-pounding maul, which I would save for Marten, some clothes, old letters and pictures remained. I felt like an intruder, looking in his drawers, his wallet, his letter case. His license, his checkbooks, and old business letters I put into the pile for burning. Did I want to keep his socks or give them to Mr. Francis, or should they be burned? I thought of the day we washed his feet and how swollen they were. The socks would have been too small then. Gift packages of aftershave lotion I gave him as a child sat on his bureau, unopened. Why did I give him that? Strange what children give. I went through the pile and pulled out anything that I thought Marten might want and kept some books for myself. I had all the bits of sea glass and feathers and shells that he had collected. I would make a basket for myself out of those.

Leonora and I burned his remaining belongings the next morning before the tribal ceremony. Only a few handfuls of ashes were left to put into the basket. I gathered them up and put them in a bowl for later. Six of the tribal elders came to the house and took Grandpa's body down to the Indian Beach meeting hall. Stephen Francis, his best friend, had made a box for him. Plain wood, no latch, just long enough for Grandpa. Leonora brought a sheepskin from the farm to lay over his body. I allowed the elders to put the body in the box by themselves. Then Leonora and I tucked the sheepskin around him. "Goodbye, Grandpa," I said, as we closed the lid.

The priest came to the tribal ceremony in his suit jacket, no tie, no collar, and I liked him for that. The hall was full of Native People from all over the state of Maine, many in their one ill-fitting suit or good dress, a few in Wabanaki clothing with porcupine-quill-worked designs and beads embroidered in traditional patterns. Jimmy Neptune replenished the smudge pots with sweetgrass and sage as their smoke diminished. Dr. Socabasin wore his moccasins.

The chanting continued around the casket at the meeting hall until the drums began their rhythmic beating at the hands of a young woman wrapped in a robe of rabbit skins. Everyone loved Grandpa, and many spoke about his life.

"Nicholas was a good husband and father."

"We went to school together. He understood the Native way."

"Nicholas's line is strong. Look at his granddaughter, Blue, and the way she makes the baskets. She even speaks some of the language."

The chanting, the drums, the speaking of the others, smell of the smudge smoke, mesmerized me, put me in another century with my ancestors who were me, my being, what I was to become. I saw my great-great-grandmother, sent home by Charles from Massachusetts, my great-grandmother, full-Passamaquoddy, bending over her ash strips, my grandmother, loving Grandpa, her arms encircling him, my mother, saying a word in the language. My grief came without embarrassment, understood by my tribe, supported by people I loved.

After the celebration and burial, Leonora took Marten back to the farm and everyone left me alone. The bowl of ashes looked small in the middle of my pine table cleared of basket-making debris. I was glad that so many of his friends wanted his belongings.

The funeral basket with the passion feather was on

Grandpa's bedside table when he died, waiting for him to fill it. I walked forward into the room toward the table with the basket in front of me like an offering, like I had presented it to Grandpa just a few days before, and placed it next to the bowl. The basket was wet from the soaking. I wanted to make sure that it didn't leak, and the soaking would swell the grass and seaweed to keep out the seawater until it had gone far out to sea. The tide was almost ready to turn, and I wanted to be ready when the water started to go out.

The candy corn was there, in my pocket, in a paper bag. He had tried to finish them all but didn't have quite enough time. I poured them into the basket. Then I tilted the bowl toward the basket and the ashes spilled out on top of the candy corn, filling in the holes made by the seaweed and mussel shells.

"Grandpa, bon voyage."

There was enough room for more things in the basket. I ran to get the smudge bowl next to his bed and remembered the little leather bag with the soil from Mount Katahdin. On top I scattered a few beach stones and covered everything with some more rockweed. The passion feather looked cleaner and fresher, as if having a purpose had renewed it. It was ready now. I picked up the basket. "Thank you for knowing that I needed to do this." I spoke aloud to the dead.

The walk to the shore was long. The blueberry fields that sprawled down to the sea displayed crimsons, scarlets, vermilions, tangerines, magentas, patches of each color splattered around haphazardly but with purpose as if applied by Glueskub for Grandpa's journey. I knew the people watched from behind their curtains. No one was in the street. They let me do this all alone, and I was grateful.

I took my shoes off when I reached the beach. The basket was heavy for its size, and my arms were tired from carrying it. My bad leg ached and I favored it a little. At the waterline, I followed the edge of the sea away from town and toward the point. Boulders of pink granite replaced the small smooth stones, and my pace became easier. The tide turned as I walked. The water was very cold, but the cold numbed the pain from walking barefoot on the sharp rocks.

At the point, I walked over the rockweed and mussel beds, to where the water was up to my waist, and I lowered the basket. I let go for a moment and it floated away from my hands. I wasn't quite ready and pulled it back toward me. The tide was strong, and I knew the basket would go far. It tugged at my hands, so I went out a little farther. When the water was almost to my shoulders, my hands opened up and released the basket to the sea. It turned around and around, the wind catching the feather, spinning it. It floated low in the water and soon I could see only the tip of the white feather when a wave carried it up high enough.

"Wul-lee-wun-e-g-wool-lay-you-yan," I called to the basket. "Grandpa, thank you for being good to me."

I stood in the freezing water until I could no longer see even the tip of the white feather. Our life together was over, but I would never forget him.

Blue and Berry in the hospital.
The only picture. Mattie doesn't know about this.
August 17, 1979

CHAPTER 27

❧

Leonora helped me move. We left behind most of the furniture in the house. Mrs. Francis' son and his new wife were happy to buy the kitchen table and chairs, beds, bureaus, couches. The only big piece I needed was the pine table from the shop.

Grandpa's room was hard. We cleaned around the bed and pulled the furniture out to vacuum. Done in an hour. Strange feeling, that it was gone, the closets empty. We sat on the bed, taking a tea break. She was very close to me. I could smell her hair and put my head on her shoulder.

"This is hard," she said.

"Yes."

"Oh, his moccasins. For Marten?"

I nodded solemnly, but then the thought of Marten in Grandpa's moccasins made me laugh out loud.

One small box remained. "Fleischmann's Gin," it said on the outside. One box of Grandpa's things for me to keep. I was surprised there was so little.

"Let's do your room while Marten's still sleeping, and then we can load the truck."

We dragged liquor boxes into my room. Marten didn't have much except for his crib and some clothes and diapers. My room at Daddy's house had more of my clothes and books. We would deal with that later.

"Oh, pictures," she said, holding the envelope in her hand. "Can I see?"

Her eyebrows remained in the question expression a moment too long. The "Oh sure" from me never came. She held her eyebrows as long as she could.

"Oh." Her hand slowly went back to the drawer with the pictures. "I'm sorry," she said.

"We need to talk about the pictures. I need to tell you something." I wished I had told her right after Daddy died. Not now, while we were packing. "The pictures are of Daddy, when he died. I had them developed and never looked at them. I couldn't. But I need to. Later."

I hoped she would interrupt me. "When I found him, the camera was flashing, set for every sixty seconds, flashing and flashing, no film left, but still clicking and flashing." I looked at the package of pictures. "Shit." I bit my lower lip. "Shit," I said louder. I kicked a Drambuie box to the other side of the room. "My grandfather in a box and my father in an envelope. Shit."

"Blue, we can look at them together if you want. They're your pictures. You can do whatever you want with them."

"I thought about throwing them away, but I can't. What if there was something on them that was important?"

"Do you want me to look at them first?"

"Don't know. Someone needs to, right? I mean, they can't just sit in the drawer. Tonight? After Marten's in bed. You and me. Just you and me looking at the pictures. Right?"

"Sure."

It took us the rest of the day to go to the dump, move the baby's things, and put everything away in Leonora's house—our house. The old photograph from Grandpa's kitchen wall hung over our kitchen table. Our room was big enough for all three of us. The crib was in the corner near the window, so Marten could see out to the barnyard. When he was old enough, he would have his own room. Leonora fixed supper while I put things away. Ugli and Hiawatha sat on my bureau next to a bottle of aftershave. Imagine Grandpa saving it all those years. And he had hardly any facial hair.

"Marten." He turned in the crib to look at me. "Look at the goats." His eyes followed the line of my finger as I pointed outside the window. "We're going to like it here." I picked him up and carried him down to the kitchen, full of mincemeat spices from the pot on the stove.

After supper we did the dishes and I put Marten to bed. I gave him Ugli to hold and he settled right down. I took the envelope of pictures out of the bureau drawer. It seemed so thick, thicker than before. Thirty-six exposures it said on the package. Perhaps Leonora should look at them first. Then she could tell me what was on them.

On my way downstairs to Leonora, I stopped for a moment in the hallway holding the package, like a recalcitrant child readying myself for punishment. But I knew that I could burn them, not look, just throw them in the fire. I glanced at the woodstove. She saw. "No," I said. "We are going to open the package together." I sat at the kitchen table and patted the chair next to me.

The pictures were black-and-white. I knew they would be. Daddy usually worked in black-and-white. But Leonora was surprised.

"What is it?" The stack of photos lay on the table between

us. The one on the top was dark, underexposed. The outline of a window frame sliced through the middle. "I can't tell what that is." I put it face up by the pile, exposing the next one, as if I were playing gin rummy.

The same window frame, this time a little lighter. Something white to the left of the frame. Something white and round. "Oh my God, that's an ass. Somebody's white ass," she said. "Look." She pointed. I knew then whose it was, and I knew who was under it.

The next picture was perfectly exposed. There she was, under Simon, partially obscured by the window frame. Her legs were wrapped around him and her bare feet stuck up from the round white ass. Mama. "God, that's your mother. Your mother and that artist guy."

"Daddy must have taken it through a window. Jesus." I hoped the whole roll was this. Looking through the window at Mama and Simon doing it. The next few pictures were similar, but each one grew clearer, and closer, as he used the zoom. On the last one I could see Mama's tongue in his ear. Her eyes were closed.

"Jesus, he must have known they were having sex, even then. Poor Daddy." I somehow knew that was the last picture of that series. "Tea?" I asked her.

"No."

"OK, just checking." I smiled at her.

Daddy, standing there in jeans and an embroidered shirt. A picture of a picture, the outline of the kitchen table at home around the outer edge. I had seen the picture before, but something was different. I picked it up and looked at the next one. Same thing, slightly different pose. He was looking to his right but his arm was cut off. Then I remembered. Wedding pictures. One hung in the house on the dining-room wall, framed. But no Mama. I looked closer. She was cut out. Very carefully done. The next one was of me as a baby, on the hospital bed, Daddy to one side. I had seen this one before, too. "Jesus, he's cut her out." I looked up at Leonora. "He's cut her out."

"You can hardly tell," she said. "Looks like he is there with you alone."

"Look here's another one." First day at school. Daddy holding my hand. I know Mama had been holding the other one. One of Aunt Maria and Grandpa and Daddy and me. Thanksgiving. The turkey is in the middle of the table. I know Mama had cooked it. She was there in her chair. But no more. Gone. Cut out very neatly. One of Darrel and me with Daddy on one side. Mama, gone. "And another." I flipped over the one of Darrel.

There it was. Daddy, smiling at the camera. Wearing the clothes I found him in. I slapped my hand down on the stack.

"This is it." I knew I sounded panicked.

"Do you want to wait a minute? Maybe now is the time for tea."

"No, just give me a minute. Jesus, how could he do this?"

"It's the only way he could cope, Blue. He wasn't strong like you."

"I know, but Jesus." I blew air out through my lips. It took a long time.

He was getting ready. Climbing on the stool. Working on the knot. Testing it to see if it would hold. It was very slow, going through the pictures. I felt vomit in my throat. I swallowed bitter bile and waited. He stood looking directly into the camera, smiling. Like he was at a party, or graduating from college, or posing. He seemed to know when the camera would click and the light flash. He was always ready, posing. Was this for

Mama? Or me? It occurred to me that maybe he wasn't dead. Maybe I had seen the pictures and thought it was real. I could feel Leonora's breath on me. Warm. When I was finished I would hold her. Would ask her to hold me. The next picture was the rope around his neck. There were several of these. Perhaps he reconsidered for a moment. He smiled for each one. I wondered if he smiled in between the flashes.

"Do you want me to look?" she said.

"No."

I leaned back as far as I could in the chair, as if to separate myself from him. The next one was blurred. Very blurred. There were four more. Each one less and less blurred. I could make out a figure on the last one. No bulging facial features, no wet spot on his pants, just a vague figure. A ghost. Hanging from the living room ceiling. My Daddy. Jesus.

"I did it. I looked at them."

We went through the pictures again, much quicker this time. No one else needed to see these. I put them in their envelope with the negatives and walked over to the woodstove. *How dramatic,* I thought. Well, it was dramatic. I opened the door and placed them on the burning coals. They sizzled a bit before they flashed into flame. I shut the door.

She made love to me that night. I lay inert while she undressed me. "Just lie quietly," she murmured. I closed my eyes and felt that I didn't need to do anything. How wonderful to lie and receive. "I'm going to kiss your face." She kissed my face and ran her tongue down my neck. She raised my arms and buried her face in my underarm. She gently turned me over and kissed me on my back, the spot at my waist, touched me as if I were a favored doll. "Don't move."

"No," I said. "No, I won't."

She lay on my back, naked, covering me. Her hands felt for my breasts, around me, down, past my belly, down to my legs.

She rolled me over and ran her tongue along my ankle scars, following them up my leg. "Hush," she said.

I was quiet. She opened my legs carefully, as if she didn't want to break me. I let my knees fall to the sides. "God, you are exquisite." Her fingers made their way up my thighs and lingered there. Her mouth followed. "Don't move."

"No."

"I love you."

"Yes."

The next morning Marten woke us at 5:00 A.M. I brought him into bed. "Oh, you're a hungry boy." He sucked noisily. "I've got to go to the house today. Got to see the pictures. He must have put them back in the album after he mutilated them. Didn't notice any around the house."

"I'll go with you."

"No, you have a deadline on that book. And what about the pies for Thanksgiving? Mince and pumpkin, remember? I'll be fine. Marten will be with me." We lay there waiting for daylight as Marten nursed. I switched him to the other side and we lay together, all of us, without making any sound.

I hadn't been in Daddy's house for a few weeks. It was going on the market right after the holidays, and we would have to clean it out. I lit the kindling under the birch logs in the wood-stove and put Marten in his seat. The shelf of photo albums looked the same. All lined up straight, according to number. All engraved, "The Willoughby Family." I ran my finger along the dates. Backwards from the album numbered "twenty-seven—Marten." All the way down to number "one—Wedding." I opened that one. The first picture. Daddy and Mama, I knew that's what had been there. But no Mama. I flipped the page. Daddy with Mama cut out. And the next one. Very neatly with a knife. I flipped through the rest of the book. Daddy next to a cutout, the wedding cake, Grandpa, Aunt Marcia, Brian's parents when they were young.

The next album was dated and labeled "Beautiful Baby Blue." I had seen these so many times. I turned the page. There I was, alone, lying on the hospital bed. I had been so tiny, smaller than Marten was. Undershirt and diaper. That's all. My legs just little sticks. I turned to the next page. The picture of Daddy and me with Mama cut out. I stared at it. There was something tucked in behind it. Another picture. I could see part of it through the hole that had been Mama. I found the slit in the plastic and pulled it out. There were two babies. Both with diapers and undershirts. They were the same size. There was nothing else similar. The one on the right was me. Same undershirt, same little features, dark hair. The other. I shook my head as if to clear something. A head and legs and arms. No face. Just holes. No beautiful face or Indian hair just like mine. No blank expression. No expression. No face. The head was open. I saw past the skull into something else. I leaned forward to try to see better. But better was worse, no face, open head, limbs that resembled arms and legs only because they were in the right place. I wondered how or why they put the clothes on it. I looked back to the other baby. Me. Me and my twin. I lived with her in our mother's womb for nine months. And nineteen years in my mind. Berry. My darling beautiful Berry. I looked at the picture. I turned it over as if something else might be on the back. Names or something. "Blue and Berry in the hospital," the caption said. "The only picture. Mattie doesn't know about this. August 17, 1979." Daddy had said there were no pictures. God, no wonder. Why did he keep this? I walked back and forth in the room, holding the picture in front of me. Shit. Back and forth, back and forth. I called Leonora.

Blue, Mattie, and me making gingerbread cookies.
Taken with my new timer, Thanksgiving 1982
Blue is rolling the dough all by herself.

CHAPTER 28

I need to deal with something here. Will you take Marten?"
I said when Leonora arrived. "Just take him home, and I will be
back as soon as I can." I wanted so much to do this on my
own. "I have a lot to tell you, but first I need to take care of
something. I need to do it alone. I'll be back to help with
Thanksgiving."

"Blue, you look like you've been crying. What's wrong?"

"Can you take Marten?"

"Sure, but, what's going on? Are you going to be alright?"
She picked up Marten, who was already in his jacket and hat.

"Please. I'm going to tell you about it as soon as I get back.
It's about the pictures, and it's going to be OK." That was all I
could get out. I wasn't ready to tell her about Berry. I couldn't
do it yet. Her expression told me she was looking at a pathetic
sight. She put her hand up to my face and traced a line down
my cheek following the tears.

"I love you. Remember, I said that before," she said. "Call if
you want me to come. I'm not very far away." I wanted to fall

into her, her arms around me. I put my hand on my pocket. The picture was still there. I could feel it. "God, I hate leaving you in this house—so empty and depressing. Are you going to stay all night?"

I nodded.

"Do you have candles and everything?" She saw the look on my face. "OK, I know, you are a big girl now."

She kissed me on the cheek. "I know this is something you have to deal with yourself. Call if you need me." I kissed Marten and watched as she turned and carried him out. She looked back once, just to see if I was still there.

I lit a few candles and put wood in the stove. The electricity was turned off after Daddy died, and we were just waiting until the legalities were cleared up to put the house on the market. Mama thought about living in it. "But I would think about your poor misguided Daddy," she had said. "Simon and I think we might build somewhere."

I wished I had a cigarette. I didn't smoke. Now seemed the time cigarettes fulfilled their destiny. Sitting down, lighting up, pulling out the picture, looking at it. I could deal with it then. Easier. Daddy was gone, and Grandpa, and Mama was never really there, and now Berry. I made tea that I found in the cupboard and sat down at the table. No cigarette. No wine. I looked around the kitchen, not sure what to expect. The candles made shadows on the walls, and I looked at the place where he did it. I waved my fingers back and forth in front of the flame and the shadows danced around. I felt very alone.

I carried a candle upstairs with me and pushed open the door to my old room. Nothing personal left. Just the bed and a bureau and an old wicker rocking chair. I put the candle on the bureau. The sheets and blankets were still on the bed. A little musty. I pulled off my shirt and jeans and dropped them on the floor. I climbed into the covers and lay on my back for quite a while with the candle going and looked at the picture of my sister and me. In the candlelight the figures in the picture seemed to move. I wondered why he never told me about the picture. I wondered if Mama knew about it. Why did he take it? Why didn't he destroy it? Mama must remember her like that, see her in dreams, in images as she drives down the road. I stuck the picture under the pillow and leaned over to blow out the candle, then changed my mind and left it burning.

I pulled the covers over my head and suddenly wished that I had brought Ugli with me. "Berry," I called softly. I knew she wasn't real. I could just go home to the farm, leave this bed, this house, this town. "Berry, we need to deal with this." She would come. I was sure of that. I felt like I was breathing in my old breath. I pulled the cover down a bit to let in some fresh air. "Berry." My voice sounded more insistent. She was there, the baby, the hideous baby from the picture. So much smaller than the old Berry. She just lay there near my chest. For a moment, I thought I would jump out of the bed, go away from this place. "Berry." The fleshy part where the head should be, moved a little. "I'm so sorry." I let the tears come freely now. "I'm so sorry I never knew you. I'm sorry you never had a chance." The flesh lolled to the side and was quiet. Gone was the perfect face with two eyes, the flawless skin. "I never really had a sister, did I?" I spoke softly and slowly. My calmness surprised me. I wanted to reach out and touch it, but it didn't need comforting. It couldn't understand anything. No brain and no face. And it had died long ago. I slowly pulled the covers down, knowing that it would disappear.

I wept softly for a long time until my limbs wouldn't move, until I felt empty. The picture was still under the pillow. I could feel it. I pulled it out and looked at it one last time. I leaned over to the candle and caught the corner of the picture in the flame. The flame traveled from that corner to the opposite one. The ash fell off onto the top of the bureau and I dropped the remaining piece just as the flame hit it. It was ash by the time it hit the base of the candlestick. I got out of bed, dressed, and carried the candle ahead of me down the stairs. I blew it out and tapped the ashes from the candlestick into an envelope and put it in my pocket.

"Leonora," I said into the phone. "Sorry it's so late. I'm coming home."

"I'll put on the tea."

Tea with Leonora. It seemed so far away. So hard to find. The door sounded loud behind me. Final. I closed the door of the truck gently, so that it wouldn't make noise. No one was here, but the front door had made so much noise. I pulled out of the driveway and onto the road.

To tell or not to tell Mama? She knew all along or she didn't know all along? That he took her picture. Berry's. And that it was in the photo album all this time. Right behind the picture of me. Christ, she was just a blob. I wondered if they were sure that it was a "she." Did it even have sex organs? But they must have had some reason to call it a girl, and it sure wasn't nice legs and long curls.

Not much traffic this time of night. The late-nighters were already gone, and the fishermen weren't quite up yet. I opened the window all the way. The air was cold. Mama must have seen it, probably held the thing. She was embarrassed, ashamed to have birthed a mistake. That was it. She was lucky I came along at the same time. At least she had someone to mother. My Berry was gone. She never really existed. Before I found the picture she could have been. Now, after the picture,

I knew she couldn't. Never. No possibility. She had been my best friend. My sister, my twin. Now she was nothing but an illusion.

"Fuck you, Daddy." He knew I would find it. What did he want me to think? He saved it for a reason. Then he fucking hung himself. Set it up for me to find. Jesus. What a family. I turned the radio on. Fiddled with the dial. Needed a diversion. Oldies. Sixties. I tried to sing along, but the crying wouldn't stop. I closed the window and turned up the radio.

"Hello, you're on the air."

"I have a problem." It was a woman's voice, shaky and weak. "My sister and I had a row and now we're not speaking. I hate to be the one to give in and call, but it is my sister. What do you think?"

"What's more important to you? Your sister or your pride? You're the only one who can answer that . . ."

I turned the dial. Jazz. Lionel Hampton. Vibes. I opened the window again. She wasn't going to call me, that was for damn sure. She couldn't even suck for God's sake. She didn't even have a mouth. And I sure as hell couldn't call her.

I had a hard time seeing the road in front of me. I couldn't call her again. That thing would come. No more beautiful Berry with the two brown eyes. I swerved back into my lane. My tongue licked salty tears off my lip. I was almost home, and the horizon foreshadowed dawn.

Leonora was waiting up for me, sitting at the table, teapot in front of her. Two mugs, honey, four gingerbread women with frosting all over them. "I was so worried," she said, patting the table across from her. "My mother always made gingerbread cookies when I was upset about something. She said it was an Austrian custom, but I think that was just her way of fixing the problem. You better have one." I held her head close to my chest and kissed her hair.

"Gingerbread cookies. Gingerbread women."

She poured my tea as I sat down and took a cookie from the plate. "Marten crawled. All the way across the room. He kept stopping and looking back. Like he was surprised."

"He crawled? My little Marten, crawled. Soon he will need moccasins. He crawled, and I wasn't here. He'll crawl again tomorrow. I have something I need to do, and I want you and Marten to go with me, to be part of it. You won't believe what I found." I bit the head off the cookie. "As soon as it's light enough. OK? I have a few things to do first."

"Sure. I'll put the turkey in. It's all stuffed."

Blue Willoughby with her latest basket.
Beautiful, but strong, for potatoes.
Ellsworth Gazette, November 1997

C H A P T E R   2 9

Mrs. Francis said it was my best basket. Passamaquoddy. Round. Perfect. Made from the sweetgrass Grandpa had gathered when he became too sick to pound the ash into strips. So tight that the water would take a long time to fill it up. The tide would be going out in an hour. I glanced at Marten in his crib. Still sleeping. I sat on the bed and took the top off the basket. It was small, too small for ashes from all one's belongings, just right for ashes from a photograph. I placed the envelope containing the ashes in the basket along with a lock of hair I snipped from my head. Black Indian hair. Like Grandpa's. I sprinkled it over the envelope and put the cover on. The piece of the feather was still in the old pencil box that Brian gave me. That half of the aged turkey feather. That would help it go out to sea. Out with Grandpa. I wove it to the side of the basket with some sweetgrass.

Marten always woke up with a smile. "Dada," he said, looking up at me.

"Mama. Mama." I held out my arms. "Happy Thanksgiving little one. Come on, we're all going to the shore."

I gathered Marten and the basket in my arms and went downstairs. Leonora was waiting for us. "Here, let me help you."

"No, I need to carry everything myself. I need to. Really."

She held the door for me. The feathers from the turkey she had slaughtered the day before lay scattered around the chopping block. "I'll drive, but where to? And what's in there?"

"Berry. The real Berry."

I explained it to her on the way over to the reservation beach. Everything. The photo, the Berry who came to me in the night in times of trouble, whenever I called her, with two eyes, the Berry who was a piece of flesh, no eyes, no mouth.

Marten sat between us in his car seat. "Dada." He looked at me. So proud. "Dada."

"Mama," I said. "Mama." He grabbed my hair and pulled. His fingers were thick. Strong hands.

Leonora cradled him while I set the basket in the water. It was cold this time of year. Thanksgiving. I didn't wade in all the way like I did with Grandpa's basket. The waves lapped at my rubber boots, each time receding a little bit. The basket would go out with the tide, gentle for November. The breeze caught the feather and spun it around and out with the ebbing wave. It dropped lower in the water, slowly, but perceptibly.

"It's over," I said out loud. Just saying it made me feel stronger. Leonora moved closer to my back, no talking, just moving closer to me. We watched from the rocks as the little basket bobbed up and down in the waves. It went far enough out so that it would not surface when the tide was low. Fifty feet at least, before it sank. No one would see it there. Too far out. Too far down. "It's over," I said again. "She's gone. Let's go home."

"Are you sure you've had enough time? I'm not in a rush."

"No. I'm ready."

I turned toward her and Marten. She took my hand, and we walked toward the truck. I drove this time. Leonora played with Marten. Grandpa would understand about the feather. The two most important parts of my growing-up life were gone. They shared the feather. But there were other things now. Other people to love.

A buck sprang out from the woods, full antlers. Probably chasing his doe. It scared me. My depth perception made it seem like he was only inches from the car. I braked hard as he cantered across the road in front of us. Otuhk. He was probably dead by now. "Look, Marten, a deer." The buck stopped by the edge of the woods, his nose up, sniffing. "He's looking for his mate." Marten pounded his wooden ring on Leonora's hand.

"Look." Leonora pointed for him. He grabbed her finger.

I pulled the truck over to the side of the road. "I want to stop here. Let's go for a walk in the woods. Come on."

I hefted Marten to my back as we walked through the fir forest. "If you want to see the ones who live here, you must walk like a shadow," I said to them. I led the way, Leonora followed behind, carrying a potato basket over her arm. She stepped on a few twigs and I could hear her breathing. Marten snuggled in the backpack, quiet, motionless. On my good side I saw the pawed spot, under the old spruce, earth and debris scattered around. I held my arm out to the side. Leonora stopped. I turned to her with my finger up to my lips. Up ahead, in the clearing stood a doe, tail held up and off to the side. No sign of the buck. We watched until we were sore from holding still, until my leg shook.

"Dada."

The doe sprang, suddenly alerted to danger. Her tail flicked white behind the cedars, and I could feel her pounding under my feet, through the ground. She would find the buck.

"Marten, did you see the deer," Leonora said.

"Mamama."

"Did you hear that? He said my name. Marty, you said 'Mama.'" I put my hand over my shoulder to touch him. He grabbed my finger.

"Dada," he said.

On the way out of the woods, we stopped while I picked branches and roots to put in the basket. We passed a clump of hackmatack trees, their yellowed needles beginning to drop. I stopped and pulled off some pieces of bark. "Pkqum-mosis," I said to them. "Pkqum-mosis." Grandpa and I picked this for tea. "When you have a cold you drink a cup of pqomus tea." Just before we got to the road, we entered a small clearing with sweet fern and blueberry plants. Most of the leaves had fallen off the blueberries, but a few struggled to hang on. My fingers pulled off a few and tucked them into the basket, under the bark, so they wouldn't blow away. "I picked this for Mrs. Francis. She makes tea from the blueberry leaves for her arthritis. Says it clears her right up. 'Zauht.' That's easy. 'Zauht.' It means blueberry. One word. Not two words like in English."

Tears came then. "Why did she name us those names? Why not Susan and Joanne, something that didn't go together? That would have made it easier," I said between the sobs. "Christ, 'Blue' and 'Berry.' What was she thinking? She saw what Berry was. Why name her at all?" I looked at Leonora as if she would have some answer to the questions. I knew she would have nothing to say. We sat in the clearing, the potato basket between us, while I cried for what never was, for what never had been, for what I remembered. It would take some time. Berry had been my friend for years, all my life, she couldn't disappear with a basket sent out to sea, but that was a start. I would miss her. Leonora cried a little, too. Marten slept.

"Brian will be here by now. We'd better go," she said.

Brian's car was in the yard when we pulled in. He said he would come early and help with dinner. Mama and Simon were coming with Aunt Maria around one. We had invited Mr. and Mrs. Francis, too. The idea that I had made a big mistake occurred to me. I wasn't sure how much Mrs. Francis knew about my relationship with Leonora, but she loved me, and I felt she would work through it. Now Mama was a different story. She'd probably think it was groovy and tell all her friends but hate the idea inside of her. No more babies to talk about. Leonora and I discussed Simon. I know things had been difficult with Daddy, but Mama lied about Simon. Said they weren't lovers. Still, I would try. Do my best. She was my mother, and for that brief moment in Grandpa's house after he died, I had seen something from deep insider her, something loving and real that I couldn't now ignore.

Brian was standing in the middle of the feathers holding one up to the sun when he saw me. I left Leonora with Marten. "Briiaaaaann." I ran to him.

"Hey, Blue." He hoisted me up. A few months since I'd seen him and he'd changed. Filled out, older, stronger. "Let me look at you." He held me at arm's length like he always did. I smiled and looked up at him. "Are you happy? God, you look great. Can't wait to see Marten." He brought my face close to him. He smelled like Brian. "And the lover, what's her name?" he whispered. "Quite a looker."

I pushed him back, caught him off guard. "You know her name." We both laughed, like we used to when we were kids. We walked hand in hand over to the others by the truck. I knew Leonora would be nervous. She knew about Brian, how he loved me, wanted me. I had told her about that night in the hotel.

"I have a surprise for you," he said.

"Let me guess. Ummmm, flowers, candy?"

"She's in the house. Taking a pee. She's nervous, too. Madelyn her name is. She knows about us. Baked a pie in the dorm just to bring up here. It doesn't look very appetizing, but pretend."

I squeezed his hand. It was going to work. Everything. Leonora put Marten down on the grass, and he started to crawl toward Brian and me. I held my arms out to him. "Come on, Marty, you can do it. Look, Brian, Marty's crawling."

Leonora extended her hand. They shook. "Let me take a look at you," as he held her at arm's length.

He probably said that to all the women in his life. I looked to the front door. The girlfriend was standing there, holding her pie. Trying to smile. A kind of crooked little smile.

"Leonora, right? I'm Brian," I heard him say.

"I know," she said.

Marty finally cried himself to sleep and I put him in his basket on the floor by the woodstove. The sage aroma from the turkey filled the kitchen. Madelyn peeled potatoes with Leonora. We had some time before the others arrived.

I took Brian's arm and guided him into the other room. "Let those guys do all the work. Let's you and me catch up."

"The Willoughby Family, Book IV" lay on the coffee table in front of the couch. I had shown them to Leonora the night before. "Thought you'd get a kick out of them." We sat down side by side, Brian with a funny smile on his face. And Brian always knew which side to sit on. I never had to tell him.

"Well, what do you think?"

"What do you think?"

"I think we should look at the pictures," he said, with a wink.

I kissed his cheek, trying to avoid his thick glasses, and moved closer to him. We looked at page after page, first day of school, coming home from pond picnics, my tenth birthday party.

He flipped the page. There's me. On my bike. The day we went to the frog pond. I can tell because I had mud all over my boots. I was twelve. "Remember this?" I said.

He remembered.